Consigned to Death

Consigned to Death

Jane K. Cleland

ROBERT HALE · LONDON

First published in Great Britain 2007

ISBN 978-0-7090-8306-1

Robert Hale Limited
Clerkenwell House
Clerkenwell Green
London EC1R 0HT

2 4 6 8 10 9 7 5 3 1

This is for Joe

Typeset in 10/12pt Dante
Printed and bound by
Biddles Limited, King's Lynn

acknowledgments

The author is grateful for the information and assistance provided by Dayle Hinman, criminal profiler, and Hans van den Nieuwendijk, fingerprint expert. Thanks also to Mary Ann Eckels, Susan A. Schwartz, Deborah Miller, and Katie Scheding. Special thanks to Ben Sevier, my editor, for his astute observations, and Denise Marcil, my agent, for her wise counsel.

author's note

This is a work of fiction. All of the characters and events are imaginary. While there is a seacoast region in New Hampshire, there is no town called Rocky Point, and many other geographic liberties have been taken.

chapter one

'Eric!' I shouted from under the table.

'Yo!' he answered cheerfully, close by.

'Didn't I tell you to use linseed oil on this one?'

'I did.'

I pushed myself out from under and stood up, brushing the grit from my hands on to my jeans. 'Not on the back of the legs, you didn't.'

'I thought I did,' he said, beginning to hedge.

I'd been working hard and I was tired. Fighting an inclination to snap, I reminded myself that Eric was only nineteen, basically untrained but willing to learn, reliable, mostly honest, and pleasant to be around – overall, a much-better-than-average employee. I smiled a little, hoping to blunt the force of my next comments.

'I just looked at it, Eric. You missed the backside of all four legs. Everyone considering bidding on this table will know its quality. And if they're willing and able to pay the price I expect it to fetch, they will damn sure get down on their hands and knees and examine it closely.'

He began to look embarrassed. The Mission-style table dated from the early twentieth century and featured select quarter-sawn oak finished in a warm brown. When properly oiled, the finish became lush and supple. It was a beautiful piece.

'The problem with poor-quality work,' I continued, 'is that it creates a negative image for the firm, implying that we're lazy or sloppy. People may even think we're sleazy. For instance, potential buyers might figure that we slapped some oil on the table as a quick fix, to disguise its previous ill-treatment. Does that make sense?'

'Yeah,' he said, grinning sheepishly. 'Sorry. I was in a hurry.'

'Don't be. I pay you by the hour – you don't need to be in a hurry with a job like this.'

'Got it.'

I nodded and smiled again, sincerely this time. 'Don't get me wrong. Being in a hurry is a good thing most of the time – you know me, I hate slow.'

'Don't I know it,' he responded, grinning back.

'Josie!' Gretchen called, her voice echoing in the cavernous warehouse. 'Josie? Where are you?'

'Here, in the Wilson corner!' I answered, projecting my voice, referring to a roped-off area near the back where the Wilson estate's goods were being catalogued and readied for Friday's auction preview.

'There's a police officer to see you.'

'What?' I called back to her, startled.

'A police chief,' she answered, as if that helped to clarify the situation.

Leaving Eric at the table, I walked quickly toward the front, my unpolished engineer boots click-clacking on the concrete. I spotted a tall, broad-shouldered man, somewhere near forty, with dark, pockmarked skin and graying hair, waiting by the door that led from the warehouse to the entryway. He wasn't smiling. My heart began to thud. The last time a cop had asked to see me, it had damn near ruined my life.

Gretchen, my assistant, stood beside him, her copper-colored hair falling in cascades below her shoulders. Her green eyes were big with news, and her flawless ivory skin showed a slight flush.

'Hi,' I said to the man as I approached. 'I'm Josie Prescott.'

'I'm Chief Alverez. Is there somewhere we can talk?'

'Sure,' I answered, my internal trouble spotter whirring into high alert. 'What's going on?'

'I'm the chief of Rocky Point,' he told me, flipping open a worn leather case, showing me his badge. Rocky Point, a city of about hundred thousand, included almost three miles of New Hampshire's eighteen-mile coastline about ten miles south of Portsmouth.

'Chief of police?' I queried. 'What's up?'

'I have a few questions about a case.... Maybe it would be better if we talked in private.'

'Sure ... Gretchen,' I said, turning to her, 'you can go back to work.'

She left, and I moved away from the door toward some used, oversized crates stacked like bricks in a corner of the warehouse near the office door. 'Is this all right?'

'Sure.'

From where I stood, I could see the entire warehouse, stocked with furnishings of various types, periods, and quality. To unknowing eyes it probably looked chaotic, but I knew better; it was a production line in perfect working order. Items came in for sorting; the good stuff got primped and primed and sent to auction, usually in-house; the junk, with a good piece or two thrown in to entice the faithful, was left in 'as-is' condition for our weekly tag sale. Right now the warehouse was about half-full, and half-full was good. We were busy, and growing.

'Okay,' I said. 'We're private. What's going on?'

'I understand you knew Nathaniel Grant.' It sounded more like an accusation than a question.

' "*Knew*" him?' I responded.

'Did you?'

' "*Did*" I? Are you saying … Is he … What are you saying?'

'You haven't heard the news?'

'What news?'

'Where have you been this morning?'

In a nanosecond, I went from confused and slightly impatient to angry and rebellious. Tired of playing cat-and-mouse, I got mad, almost like a switch had been thrown. I stood still and stayed silent, eyeing him, waiting for information.

'Answer my question, please,' he said quietly after a pause, his calm contrasting with my agitation. 'Where were you this morning?'

Words my father used to speak heading into a difficult business meeting came to mind: *the best defense is a good offense.* 'Not another word will I say,' I stated, 'until you answer *my* question about what's going on.'

Alverez took a step closer to me. He was probably a foot taller than I was, which made him six one or better, and I suspected that he was using his height and bulk to try to intimidate me. It was working. I felt my palms become moist. I was shaking, but not enough, I hoped, for him to notice.

'Nathaniel Grant was murdered this morning,' Alverez said.

I stared at him. 'Mr Grant was murdered?' I asked.

'Yes,' he answered, watching me.

Tears came to my eyes. I swallowed and brushed them away. 'Oh, my God! Poor Mr Grant!' I exclaimed. 'What happened?'

'I'm hoping you can help me sort that out.'

I turned away, tears spilling down my cheeks. I couldn't speak.

'Seems like you knew him pretty well,' Alverez said.

I shook my head, swallowed again, and used the back of my hand to dry my cheeks. I'd always felt things deeply, but I used to be good at controlling my emotional displays. I could hear my father saying, *Feel all you want, Josie, but show nothing. In business, the more you show, the more you lose.*

When I'd worked at Frisco's, the big auction house in New York City, before I'd been the prosecutor's star witness at my boss's price-fixing trial, I'd shown nothing. It wasn't the trial that got to me, although it was grueling; it was my co-workers' reaction to my involvement that stunned me speechless. Once my participation was known, colleagues whom I'd previously trusted wouldn't give me the time of day. I was shunned, and within weeks, I was forced out of the company. And then, a month later, my father died, and it was as if the world tilted, leaving me utterly off balance.

I was closer to being on even footing now, but I wasn't there yet. To say that I found it harder to contain my feelings didn't even begin to describe my lack of emotional control. It was as if my nerve endings were a little nearer to the surface.

I shook my head a bit to chase the memory away. I took a deep breath and looked up at Alverez, trying for a smile. 'I'm being stupid, I know,' I said. 'I didn't know Mr Grant, not really. I only met him a couple of weeks ago. And look at me.' I swept away more tears. 'It's just such a shock. And he was such a sweetheart.'

'Tell me about him,' Alverez said, leaning against the concrete wall.

I paused, thinking of what to say. 'He looked like Santa Claus, except that he was short and sort of shriveled. But he had the beard and the belly and he was jolly as all get out.'

'How did you come to meet him?'

'He wanted to sell a lot of furniture and art.'

'Out of the blue?'

I swallowed again, fighting back sudden emotion. 'Not really. His wife died, you know, about three months ago. The house is huge. Well, I suppose you know that. It was too much for him, I guess.'

'So,' Alverez said softly, 'where were you this morning?'

'Is that when ... I mean ... when was he killed?'

'The medical examiner is still working on it.'

I nodded. 'I just can't believe it. Mr Grant! I'm sorry ... Okay ... Let me think.' I sighed and paused. 'Okay. I got in around eight and was here working,' I said, gesturing with a sweep of my hand that I meant inside the warehouse, 'until around eleven-ten or eleven-fifteen. Then I drove out to Mr Grant's house. I got there around eleven-thirty. We had an appointment, but he wasn't there.'

'How do you know he wasn't there?'

'I knocked and rang the bell. I went around back and knocked on the kitchen door. I even peeked in windows, but I didn't see anything.'

'What did you do then?'

'I thought Mr Grant had mistaken the day. He's pretty old.'

Alverez nodded. 'So then what?'

I shrugged. 'I sat in my car awhile. At quarter to twelve I rang the bell again, in case he hadn't heard it the first time. Then I left a message on his answering machine and came back here.' I wiped away another tear. 'I was planning on calling him again later today because I wasn't sure he knew how to use his answering machine.' I smiled a little. 'He was such a nice man. What happened?'

'We don't know yet. Do you?'

'Me? I don't know anything.'

'Sure you do. You knew him and you were there this morning. What would be best is if you came with me to the station.'

'Why?' I asked, startled, and immediately wary.

'To answer some more questions.'

'I can't. I have too much work.'

'I'm afraid I'm going to have to insist. It's important. And I could really use your help.'

I looked at him, wondering what I should do. The Wilson estate needed careful sorting, and there were only two days until the auction preview. Sasha, an art-historian-turned-appraiser who worked for me, could handle that, I supposed. I'd remind Eric to be diligent. Or maybe not. I'd made my point earlier. Gretchen would hold the fort as she always did.

'I guess,' I said. 'I'd better call my lawyer.'

'Why don't you have him meet you at the station house,' he suggested.

'I'll let him decide.'

'Who's your lawyer?'

I worked with lawyers in my business all the time, but I'd never needed one personally before. I swallowed, trying to focus. Who should I call?

Max Bixby came to mind. He was one of the first people I'd met when I'd moved to Portsmouth. I remembered his friendly welcome at a Chamber of Commerce breakfast, and he'd been pleasant and accessible ever since. 'I'm going to call Max Bixby,' I said.

'He's a good man.'

I turned away, heading for the office to talk to Gretchen. Before I reached the door, I stopped and turned back to him. He hadn't moved. His eyes were dark and knowing.

'May I ask you something?'

'Sure. Whether I answer, well, that depends.'

I nodded. Tears came again, unexpected and unwanted. I turned away and wiped them away.

'How was he killed?' I asked quietly.

He shook his head. 'That's under investigation.'

I shut my eyes and shook my head. 'Was he in the house?'

'Yes.'

'Alone?'

'Yes.'

'This morning?'

'Probably.'

I shivered. Murdered and left alone to die in his own home.

After trying his office, I reached Max at home. I could hear a child crying in the background and a woman's raised voice.

'I'm sorry to disturb you at home,' I said.

'It's okay, Josie. I'm glad to have an excuse to remove myself from the situation,' he said with a laugh. 'What started as a nice family lunch has disintegrated into a temper tantrum.'

'Well, I hate calling you there, but I think I'm in trouble, Max,' I said, getting to the point.

'Tell me,' he ordered, and I told him the whole story.

'It's good you called,' he said when I'd finished. 'I'll meet you at the station house in a half hour. Wait for me in the parking lot.'

I found Alverez where I'd left him, standing by the crates, scanning the room. I told him what Max said, and he nodded.

'Half hour's fine,' he said. 'I'll see you there.'

I watched as he walked away, leaving me feeling alone, confused, and frightened.

Max and I stood on the edge of the sand dunes watching the ocean as we spoke. I know that it's popular not to like lawyers, but it's impossible not to like Max. He's paternal without being patronizing, direct but always respectful, and old-fashioned without being stodgy. He's probably about forty-five, but you think he's older from the way he dresses and conducts himself. He wears tweed jackets and bow ties, and he's almost courtly in manner.

'If I tell you not to answer any question, don't. Stop talking when I tell you. If you're unsure about an answer talk to me in a whisper first,' he instructed me. 'If you know the answer and I haven't stopped you, answer only what is asked. Don't give any extra information. The shorter your answer, the better. One-word answers are good.'

'What if I can't give just a one-word answer? What if he asks for my impressions of something?'

'Assuming I don't stop you, try to answer it in one short sentence. Don't expound.'

I nodded my understanding and agreement. The ocean was rough today. The bottle green water was dotted with whitecaps, and the waves were bigger than usual. It was mostly overcast. A storm was brewing.

Max told me his fee and I was glad that I had enough in savings so it wouldn't pinch to pay it. We crossed the street and entered the station house. The Rocky Point police station was new, built in the last year or two and designed to look like a beach house with a peaked roof and shingles left to weather to a silvery tone just like most of the houses along the shore.

Alverez pushed through the swinging wooden gate to greet us, then held it open for us to pass through.

'Thanks for coming. How you doing, Max?' he asked.

'Fine, thanks,' Max said. 'How've you been? I haven't seen you since last summer's clam bake.'

'That was a good time, wasn't it?' Alverez asked. 'Cathy,' he called, 'we'll be in the back.'

A big blonde hurried out from somewhere on the left. 'Did you see my notes?' she asked. 'You had calls.' She scooped up old-fashioned pink While You Were Out message sheets from a Formica-topped desk and handed them to him, spotted us, and looked at Alverez, a question in her eyes.

'This is Josie Prescott,' Alverez said to her. 'And her lawyer, Max Bixby. We'll be in room two, Cathy.' To me he added, 'Would you like some coffee or an iced tea or anything?'

'No, thanks,' I said.

'You?' he asked Max.

'I'm fine, thanks.'

He led us down a short hall to a cheerless room with a floor-to-ceiling wire-mesh cage partitioned in a corner. 'That's creepy,' I said, nodding toward it.

'Yeah. But necessary sometimes for our unruly guests.'

'I guess,' I said.

'Have a seat. I won't be long.'

I sat so the holding cell was in back of me, out of sight. The chair was hard and uncomfortable. Max sat across from me and pulled a yellow legal pad from his briefcase. I leaned forward, resting my eyes on the heels of my hands, my elbows perched on the scarred wooden table.

Max didn't speak, but I could hear him turning pages on his pad. Unexpectedly, the door latch clicked home with a sharp snap. I looked up, startled by the sound, feeling as trapped as if I'd been locked in the cage behind me.

Without a watch, which I never wore since it always seemed to get in the way when I was working, I had no way of knowing how long Max and I sat. It seemed a very long time, but I felt a sense of unreality, so maybe it wasn't long at all.

'Sorry to keep you waiting,' Alverez said when he came back, businesslike, carrying a collection of papers. 'I have the medical examiner's preliminary report. Before I tell you about it, though, let me get the recorder set up.'

'Recorder?' I asked.

'Tape recorder. So I don't have to take notes.'

I looked at Max and he nodded.

'That's fine. I'm assuming we can have a copy of the tape?' Max asked.

'Sure,' Alverez said.

I watched as Alverez positioned the small unit on the table and pushed a button. A red light appeared and I heard a whirring sound. Alverez gave our names, the date, and time.

'I appreciate your coming in to help,' Alverez said. 'Just a formality, but I'm going to ask you to sign a form indicating that you've been advised of your rights.' Alverez slid a piece of paper across the table to Max and read me my Miranda rights. It felt hard to breathe. I forced myself to listen, and when he asked me if I understood, I answered that I did. Max nodded that it was okay for me to sign the paper. *Never sign something you haven't read*, my dad had taught me. I read it and signed my name.

'Okay,' Alverez said. 'So. The medical examiner. The preliminary report is in.'

'What did he say?' Max asked.

'She. Dr Young said death occurred this morning.'

'When?'

'Between nine and noon, as best she can figure it.'

'Oh, my God!' I exclaimed. 'I had a horrible thought before that it was while I was on the porch that he was dying, and now you're saying it's true!' Tears came again, but this time I let them fall.

Max patted my arm gently, and whispered, 'Don't speak.'

'I had an officer check things out,' Alverez said, looking at me, changing the subject. 'We found your appointment in Mr Grant's diary.

It lay open to today's date on the kitchen table. Apparently, he hadn't forgotten that you were to meet him.'

I shook my head. 'Poor Mr Grant.'

'And your message was still on the machine – apparently unplayed.'

'How did death occur?' Max asked.

'What about it, Josie? Do you know?'

'What?' I asked, horrified as the implications of his question sunk in. He thought I knew something about Mr Grant's murder.

'Do you know how Mr Grant died?' he asked again.

'No. Of course not.'

'Well?' Max prompted, tapping his pen on the table. 'Fill us in.'

'Mr Grant was stabbed.'

'Oh, God,' I exclaimed, and began to cry again. 'How awful.' I used the sides of my hands and pushed gently under my eyes. The tears gradually stopped.

Struck by a sudden thought, I turned to Max and in a soft voice asked, 'I just thought of something. How did they know he'd been killed?'

Max nodded and repeated the question.

Alverez leaned back in his chair, balancing for a moment on the back two legs, keeping his eyes on mine. 'His daughter called from Massachusetts and asked us to check on him.'

'She did?' I asked, looking from Alverez to Max and back again. 'I don't understand. Why?'

'She got a call from his lawyer, Epps his name is. Mr Epps was concerned that someone was trying to strong-arm Mr Grant into selling his treasures for a song. The daughter, hearing this, was, of course, concerned, and immediately started calling him, but she couldn't rouse him. Her messages were on the answering machine, too. She called a neighbor, but the neighbor wasn't home. She called both her dad and the neighbor a few more times with no luck. So finally she called us.'

'Someone trying to strong-arm Mr Grant! That's terrible! Who would do such a thing? Did the lawyer give a name?'

'Yeah, he did. He told Grant's daughter that it was a shark named Josie Prescott.'

chapter two

I stared, speechless. What Alverez said simply didn't register. I watched as he waited for me to react. But I couldn't. I felt frozen. I couldn't think.

A shark. Epps had called me a shark. I shook my head, my confidence shattered. So much for my hopeful future, I thought, and fought back tears. I should have known not to trust in hope.

In the dark days after the price-fixing scandal hit the news, after I wore the wire that recorded my boss conspiring with his chief competitor to hold commissions steady, I'd learned that hope could be a mirage. Day after day, I'd maintained optimism as I joined thousands of other New Yorkers in expressing shock that such a well-respected executive as the CEO of Frisco's would participate in such a dastardly crime. I cringed as I remembered going to work the day after the news broke, expecting to be treated as a hero for blowing the lid off the conspiracy. I'd been naïve enough to expect my peers to admire me, and even after it became clear that they did not, I persevered in trying to win their acclaim. I'd developed a keen ability to deny facts that, to others who were less emotionally involved, were patently obvious. I'd learned the bitter lesson that, no matter what winning football coaches and inspirational motivational speakers claim, desire isn't enough. My former colleagues turned their backs on me then, and here, today, I was being called a shark. A shark!

I took a breath, reminding myself of the promise I'd made as I drove my loaded rental van past Frisco's en route to my new home in New Hampshire – never again would I allow despair to lead to wishful thinking. Paralysis lifted, replaced by righteous rage.

'A shark?' I snapped, outraged.

Max told me to be quiet.

'That's what Epps said.'

'Britt Epps?' I asked, ignoring Max's admonition.

'Yes.'

'The son of a bitch.'

'Josie,' Max repeated. 'Be quiet.'

'You know him?' Alverez asked me.

'Josie,' Max said quietly, 'Don't speak.'

'I want to answer, Max. Yes, I know him. I thought we were friends. Well, sort of friends. Business friends. I like Britt Epps! Or I thought I did.' I couldn't believe it. 'I can't believe it!' I said aloud. 'A shark? He called me a shark?'

'Yeah,' Alverez said.

I heard compassion in his voice as he spoke that one word, and it made me uncomfortable. I hated the thought that my situation led him to feel sorry for me.

'How well do you know him?' Alverez asked.

I flipped a hand up. 'I don't know. I've met him here and there at fund-raisers and Chamber of Commerce breakfasts, things like that. I've been trying to get in to see him to pitch my company. I'm new in town, well, a couple of years, now, but that's still considered new around here. So I'm trying to meet people. Anyway, most of my business comes from referrals from lawyers and he's one of the most respected in town. So naturally I've been trying to get an appointment. He's always been polite and friendly. I thought we'd never connected because of scheduling snafus. I can't believe he called me a shark. I just can't believe it.'

'Why not? With a house full of valuable items up for sale, wouldn't you expect sleazeball dealers to come out from under rocks? Wouldn't it make sense for relatives of older people who decide to sell off their possessions to worry on their behalf?'

'Yes, everything you say is true – but I'm not one of those sleazeball dealers and Epps knows it! I have a stellar reputation – one I've worked hard to develop – and anyone who knows me knows I'm not a shark!'

'I'll be asking him more about it,' Alverez said. 'Did a lawyer introduce you to Grant?'

'No.' I shifted in the chair, the horizontal slats hurting my back.

'How did you hook up with him?'

Max touched my arm, and whispered, 'Is there anything I should know about this? Any personal relationships involved? Anything unusual?'

'No. Utterly aboveboard,' I answered in an undertone.

He nodded, indicating that I could answer.

'Mr Grant called me.'

'How did he get your name?' he asked.

'How do you *think* he got your name?' Max interjected, stressing the word 'think.'

'Fair enough,' Alverez said, sounding relaxed, as if he had all the time in the world.

'He got my name from the NHAAS brochure,' I answered.

'What's that?'

'The New Hampshire Antiquarian Appraisal Society. It's an industry association. I'm a member. I'm local. As far as I know I was the only person Mr Grant called.'

'Luck?' he asked. 'Was it random?'

'I don't know.' I shrugged. 'It's not unusual for someone to select the appraiser based only on proximity.'

He nodded. 'So he called and you made an appointment?'

'You bet I did.'

'And what happened next?'

'And as soon as I got there, I recognized that I'd walked into a great opportunity. Did you see his stuff?'

'Yeah, but not to notice. Why, was it special?'

'Extraordinary. I wouldn't even know how to start to describe it. He had an eighteenth-century American oak game table with a chessboard built in – it's magnificent – inlaid in mahogany and rosewood. He had three Jules Tavernier paintings, all garden scenes. He had a Paul Revere silver tea service. Hell, he had a set of Louis XV chairs in perfect condition – including the original fabric. No joke.'

'How much are we talking here?'

'Unclear. Some of the items, nothing like them has been to auction in a generation. Some items are probably unique and priceless.'

Alverez whistled. 'And he had locks you could pick with a credit card.'

'Yeah,' I agreed. 'Amazing.'

'What was his reaction to your appraisal?'

'I didn't do a formal appraisal. Nothing in writing, and I didn't go piece by piece or anything. I just saw enough to know I wanted the lot.'

'And his reaction to your reaction?'

'Believe it or not, he didn't seem much interested in the things themselves. I got excited by the chess table, for example. He said his wife had bought it in Boston more than fifty years ago. But he didn't want to talk about the table. He wanted to talk about his wife. How he'd met her during the war. World War Two. It was a real love story.' I shook my head. 'He refused to go to auction. He said that it would just drag the process out.'

'That doesn't sound smart.'

'No, but it's not unusual. Some people, after a spouse dies ...' I paused. 'I just can't believe this. Mr Grant was a nice old man. Epps knows I'm not a shark. None of this makes sense.' I felt shell-shocked, somewhere between incredulous and hurt. I teared up again.

'So if he didn't want to go to auction, what did he want?'

'He wanted me to buy everything outright.'

'How much?'

'I don't know. I couldn't afford to just give him cash. He was okay with consigning the goods to me. I promised everything would be sold within a month.'

'A month. Isn't that pretty quick?'

'Unbelievable,' I agreed. 'I would have had to bring in outside experts and begin advertising right away.'

'What was his hurry?'

'I don't know. He mentioned that his family was coming for a visit. Maybe he wanted it over and done with before they arrived.'

'Because they'd be upset?'

I shrugged. 'He didn't say.'

'But you thought his selling out was unusual?'

'I wouldn't say it was unusual, exactly. It wasn't ordinary, that's for sure. But on some level, every sale is unique. I mean, there is no such thing as a "normal" sale.'

'What might have motivated him to sell out?'

'I have no way of knowing.'

'Fair enough. Speculate for me.'

I glanced at Max. 'Just so long as you acknowledge that Josie is talking theoretically,' he said. 'She's made it clear that she has no specific knowledge of Mr Grant's motivation. Agreed?'

'Understood,' Alverez acknowledged.

Max nodded at me, indicating that I could answer. I paused for a moment to gather my thoughts. 'There are lots of reasons why people sell their possessions, and I'm sure there are more that I'm not thinking of.'

'Like?' Alverez prodded.

'Like routine estate planning. Or they want or need cash for some particular purpose, like college tuition or an around-the-world trip. Maybe they're hoping to avoid a family feud somewhere down the line. Or they've tired of the items and want new or different things. Or they want a fresh start, like maybe after a divorce. Or, and this might apply to Mr Grant, there's some kind of grief reaction – you know, they want to get rid of objects that remind them of someone who's died, in Mr Grant's case, his wife.' I shrugged. 'Whatever was motivating him, he didn't act troubled in any way.'

'What do you mean?'

'He didn't seem desperate for cash or anything, or like he was regretting having to sell out. He was chatty and pleasant every time I saw him.'

Alverez nodded. 'Did you ask any questions to try and figure it out?'

'No. I never do. I mean, I need to know enough about what's going on to gauge whether I should act happy or more serious, you know? But I never pry.'

'Can you guess? I know you don't know,' he added, glancing at Max. 'But I'm wondering if you took away a general impression. What do you think? Which of those reasons applied to Mr Grant?'

'I wish I could help you, but I can't. I just don't know. I never know. That's not my job. I took him at his word, just like I do everyone. He wanted to sell out. I wanted to put together the deal. That's it.'

Alverez tapped his pencil on the edge of the table and leaned back in his chair, thinking it through. 'Okay, then. So, all told, how often were you there?'

'Three times. Once to meet him and discuss what he wanted, once to catalogue and videotape the contents, and once to make the offer. Today's meeting was to finalize the deal. On the phone, he said he was ready to go.'

We heard the recorder click off, and Alverez turned the tape over and pushed the Record button.

'What did you two talk about while you were there?' he asked.

'What do you mean?'

'Well, you said he was chatty, did he show you pictures of his grandchildren, talk about what he planned to do with the money, what?'

'Nothing like that. He always asked me how I was feeling, and usually he asked about my business. We chatted about the weather and inflation and nothing in particular.' I paused to think for another moment. 'Once I got started, he left me alone to do my cataloguing.'

'How come you went there alone? Wouldn't it have been quicker to bring in help for the cataloguing?'

'Would it ever! Jeez. But I'm a businesswoman. And I didn't have a signed deal yet. It can be anxiety-producing to have strangers going through your possessions. So I went alone.'

'In the times you talked with Mr Grant, did he mention anyone else? You know, that he'd be having dinner with a friend, that he'd stopped by a coffee shop, or maybe bought a newspaper at the corner store, anything like that?'

I thought for a minute. 'No. No one in particular. But we talked some about how capable he was. I mean, he brought it up. The first time I was there, he made a point of telling me that I shouldn't think he was decrepit – that's the word he used, decrepit – just because he was old. That he could still drive and he still balanced his checkbook to the penny. We laughed about that because I told him I couldn't.' I smiled a little. 'He offered to work for me and be my bookkeeper. He winked and said he had a good head for numbers. Talking to him, I believed it. The questions he asked about my business showed without a doubt that all of his marbles were intact.'

Alverez nodded and paused. He looked at me and I looked back. He looked liked an outdoors man, rugged and fit. He also looked reliable and honest, but I reminded myself that looks can be deceiving, and that sometimes people use their good looks, youthful appearance, or innocent demeanor for devious ends.

'How you doing?' he asked.

'I'm okay.'

'Ready for that coffee?'

I asked him the time and was surprised that it wasn't yet three. I'd thought it was later. 'How about a martini?' I countered.

'No can do, ma'am.'

'Figures,' I said. 'Still, it's been a martini kind of day.'

'Yeah,' he agreed. 'So, change of subject. Have you ever been fingerprinted?'

I reacted as if Alverez had ripped a Band-aid off without warning, and I closed my eyes to shield my dismay.

Yes, I answered him silently, *I've been fingerprinted*. It had happened on a Tuesday and I was thrilled. Frisco's policy held that all new hires had to go through a comprehensive security check, and I'd passed. But I didn't want to tell him that. I didn't want to talk about my past at all. I didn't want to reveal how much I'd loved my job, nor explain how hurt I'd been when I'd been forced to leave. I considered lying, rationalizing that a lie isn't a lie if the information solicited is irrelevant. Yet I knew that in all probability, Alverez would expect that an art and antique auction house as prestigious as Frisco's would fingerprint new staff. Plus, nothing said I had to talk about any other aspect of my years at Frisco's except the fingerprinting. Certainly there was no need to reveal my involvement in the price-fixing thing. What was it Max had said? Not to volunteer information. Got it.

Suddenly, words my father spoke echoed in my head: *Stop, breathe, think. Stop, breathe, think.* It was a refrain he used to chastise me when I heedlessly rushed to action. Those words calmed me now and allowed me to regrasp control.

I opened my eyes and took a deep breath. Alverez's face revealed nothing. His eyes stayed steady on mine.

Max cleared his throat and leaned toward me. 'Are you okay?' he asked.

I smiled as best I could, took a deep breath, and said, 'You bet.' To Alverez, I added, 'Sorry. I just couldn't believe my ears.'

'Is that a yes? Have you been fingerprinted in the past?' Alverez asked.

'What a question!' I replied, feigning indignation.

'No offense intended. There are lots of reasons people get fingerprinted. Security clearance, that sort of thing.'

Appearing slightly mollified, I shrugged. 'Yeah,' I admitted. 'I was fingerprinted once. For a job.'

'Then you'll be familiar with the procedure,' he said.

'You want to take my fingerprints?' I asked.

'Yeah, we need to.'

'Why?' Max interjected.

'Because Josie was in the house looking at the contents carefully, touching everything, and we need to know which prints are hers.'

'We'll consider it.'

'Come on, Max,' Alverez said. 'Don't drag it out. You know I can get a court order.'

Max looked at him for a moment, leaned over to me, and whispered, 'Did you touch anything we don't want them to know about?'

'No,' I answered softly, shaking my head in disbelief. 'Max, I didn't do anything wrong!'

He patted my arm again. 'She'll be glad to let you take fingerprints.'

'Let's get it over with,' Alverez said, standing up.

'Then can I go?' I asked.

'Yeah, but we should plan on talking some more tomorrow.'

'Why?' I asked.

'Tomorrow I'll know more about what's going on. Will you be around?'

'Yeah, I'll be working. I have an auction preview on Friday and our regular tag sale's on Saturday.' I stood up and stretched.

'How about we touch base around noon?' he asked Max.

'Sure,' he said.

'What will happen then?' I asked, anxious for more information, dreading his answer all the same.

Alverez led the way to the main room as I spoke.

'By then I'll know if I need to ask you some more questions,' he said.

Cathy was filling a coffee mug with water from a standing dispenser as we passed through the main room to a smaller area on the right. I watched her drink a little and return to her desk, ignoring us, as Alverez methodically took my fingerprints. Max stood nearby, watching the process, solemn and silent.

After I'd cleaned up, Alverez led us to the exit. He opened the front door and the rush of fresh chilly air felt good. I looked at him.

'Here,' he said to us. 'Take my card. If you think of anything, call me.'

I slipped the card in my purse. Max put out his hand. 'I'll take one, too,' he said to Alverez. Turning to me, he added, 'If you think of anything, *don't* call him. Call me.'

Heading back to Portsmouth because I had nowhere else to go, I gave myself a mental shake. I felt lonely and afraid, and that would never do. *Get over it*, I told myself, and decided to go get a martini and drink to Mr Grant, a decent man who'd died too soon. I called Gretchen and told her where I was going and why.

'Don't worry,' she said, 'Eric, Sasha, and I have everything under control.'

'Thanks, Gretchen. But there's so much to do.'

'Sasha's finished cataloguing the Wilson goods. She's in the office doing some research.'

I could picture Sasha twirling her hair, biting her lip, concentrating as she read something on the computer. She'd earned a Ph.D. in art history, and research was her favorite part of the job.

'I might come back to work, I'm not sure.'

'No need,' she said, her instinct as a caretaker overtaking her business sense.

As I headed back to town I again began to cry. At first I thought I was crying about Mr Grant, but then I realized his death was only a small part of it. Of course I was sorry that such a kind man had died, but after all, I hadn't really known him, so my grief was about something else – probably, my father.

Even though nearly four years had passed since my father's death, I still felt raw. I missed him every day. He'd been my best friend and only family. I was thirteen when my mother died of cancer, but that loss had been nothing like as hard as the sudden loss of my father. When my mother died, I'd been able to say good-bye.

I rolled down the window and the rush of bitter air helped chase away the blues. I smiled, remembering the exhilaration I'd felt when I landed the Frisco job right out of college, a dream come true. I told my father that as excited as I was, I hated the thought of leaving him behind in Boston, and joked that he ought to move to New York, too.

'Ah, Josie,' he said, 'why would you even think about that? You're moving to New York, not Mars.'

And so I went. Luckily, since my new career required that I navigate the complex and unfamiliar terrain of the antique business, he came to visit often, offering wisdom and support. In fact, for the next decade, he came almost monthly. We were a team, my dad and I.

Until his death left a black hole in my heart and a vacuum in my life. Even Rick, the man I was dating at the time, couldn't help fill the void, and our relationship had faded to nothing within weeks of my father's death.

I shook my head, recognizing how far I'd come. I could barely even remember what Rick looked like. And mostly, I could think of my father without tears. To a greater extent than I realized, it seemed, I'd moved on, yet that accomplishment was tinged with regret. Every step that brought me closer to ending mourning seemed to take me further away from my father.

'Oh, Dad,' I whispered aloud, holding tightly to the steering wheel. 'Goddamn it. Talk to me. Tell me what to do.'

And after a moment or two, I concluded that my tears weren't shed for either Mr Grant or my father. I was crying for myself because I felt scared and powerless, like a wood chip floating down a river, pummeled by rocks and a current that couldn't be controlled.

I was sitting at the Blue Dolphin bar trying to decide if I wanted to nibble or eat. Jimmy, the bartender, a chubby-cheeked, freckle-faced redhead, had offered another bowl of mixed nuts, but I was thinking that I wanted something more substantial. I took a bitter-sharp sip of my martini. I liked the way it felt to hold and drink out of a martini glass.

'I'll take the shrimp cocktail,' I said. 'Thanks, Jimmy.'

An old George Benson tune was playing softly. Three groups of people were concentrated near the bow windows that overlooked the Piscataqua River and Portsmouth Harbor. Their conversations were indistinct. The candles positioned along the bar turned my glass into a prism. I half watched as colors shifted when I moved the glass, but mostly I thought about the murder.

'Are you Josie Prescott?' someone asked, breaking into my reverie.

I turned on my barstool. A short, pudgy young man, who looked barely old enough to vote, stood beside me.

'Yes,' I answered. 'I'm Josie.'

'Wes Smith,' he said, offering his hand.

I shook it, feeling puzzled.

'From the *Seacoast Star*,' he said. He fished a card out of his pocket and handed it to me.

'Really?' I asked, looking at it. According to the card, he was a reporter.

'Why are you surprised?' he asked.

'I've never actually spoken to a reporter before.'

'May I join you?'

I shrugged. 'Sure,' I said.

'Thanks,' he said, smiling, and sat on the stool next to mine.

'How ya doing, Wes?' Jimmy asked as he approached. 'What can I get ya?'

'Bring me a cup of coffee, okay?'

'You got it.'

'Quite a situation – the Grant murder, I mean,' Wes remarked.

'Yeah,' I said.

'So I have a couple of questions for you.'

'For me?'

'Yeah. Since you're involved.'

'What? I'm not involved.' The fear that had been dulled by martinis returned.

'That's not what I hear,' he said.

'What are you talking about?'

'Weren't you interrogated for hours at the Rocky Point police station?'

'I wouldn't call it interrogated. I'd call it interviewed. But that's neither here nor there. How do you know anything about it? How do you know me?'

'Confidential sources,' he said as if he enjoyed saying the phrase. 'And I looked you up on your company's Web site. The photo of you is a good likeness. You were easy to spot.'

'How did you know to find me here?'

'I spoke to someone at your office and she told me you'd be here.'

That would be Gretchen. I wondered how I felt about her telling an unknown man that he could find me in a bar in the middle of the afternoon, and I decided I didn't care. I smiled a little. I could hear my mother warning me how a girl gets a reputation. *Maybe true*, I said to myself, but I guessed it was a rep I didn't mind getting. A long-ago memory came to me from a college spring break vacation to Mardi Gras. My at-the-time boyfriend bought me a T-shirt that read Good Girls Go to Heaven. Bad Girls Go to New Orleans. I'd worn it so often I'd nearly worn it out.

'Why did you want to find me?' I asked, bringing myself back to the here and now as Jimmy delivered the shrimp. I squeezed a lemon wedge elegantly covered with cheesecloth and dipped a shrimp into the spicy cocktail sauce. It was good.

He looked around. No one sat on either side of us. Still, he lowered his voice.

'What did Chief Alverez ask you about?' he asked.

'I don't think I should answer that.'

'How come?'

I smirked at him, a give-me-a-break look.

'Seriously,' he prodded.

As I took another shrimp, I said, 'I don't know much about police work, but I know enough to know that Chief Alverez wouldn't want me to discuss specifics about an ongoing investigation with a reporter.'

'Our paper is going to print a story including the fact that you were interrogated for hours today, and may be a suspect in the murder. Don't you want the article to include your point of view?'

'You're going to write that I'm a suspect?'

'That you *may be* a suspect.'

'That's irresponsible and outrageous! I'm *not* a suspect.'

'How do you know?'

I stared at him, speechless. I reached for my glass and finished the last of my second martini. Martinis tasted better, I'd discovered over the years, the more you drink them. I didn't answer. Instead, I ate a shrimp slowly, thinking about what I should do or say.

'Why do you think I'm a suspect?' I asked, relieved that I sounded calm and in control.

'Answer a question with a question, huh?' Wes said with a smile. 'Okay. I'll play. Apparently you were the first person questioned. You were *interviewed*,' he said, stressing the word 'interviewed' as if to mock my earlier usage, 'in an interrogation room, and you were there for more than two hours.' He shrugged. 'If it walks like a duck and quacks like a duck ...'

As I listened, I realized he was right and that I was in deeper trouble than I'd realized.

I didn't say another word to Wes, not even that I wouldn't comment. Instead I stood up and signaled Jimmy that I wanted my check. While I waited, I ate another shrimp. Wes said something, but I wasn't listening. When the check arrived, I paid it, and without a backwards glance, I left.

In my car, I turned on my cell phone to call Max. Rooting through my purse to find my address book, I came across Chief Alverez's card. I perched it on my thigh, found the address book, and called Max's office. A cheerful voice told me that he wasn't there. I tried his home number, but got a machine and hung up before the beep. His cell phone went to voice mail and I left a message. I looked at Alverez's card. It listed his cell phone number, and on impulse, I dialed it.

He answered on the second ring with a curt, 'Alverez.'

'It's Josie Prescott.'

'Well, hello,' he said.

His tone had changed. I thought I heard warmth instead of curtness, and I felt some relief. Maybe my instincts weren't out of whack. Maybe it would be safe to talk openly to him.

'I have a question.'

'Shoot.'

'Wes Smith from the *Star* tried to interview me.'

'He did, did he? What did you tell him?'

'Nothing. But he said that the newspaper is going to print a story tomorrow referring to me as maybe a suspect. That's my question. Am I?'

I could hear him breathing. 'Where are you?' he asked.

I remembered Wes remarking that I was answering a question with a question. I'd done it to avoid answering the one he'd asked. I shivered, fear chilling me.

'Why?' I asked.

'This sounds like a situation we should talk about.'

'I have a call in to Max,' I responded.

'Makes sense,' he answered, and I felt a wave of terror wash over me. Now I knew: I was, in fact, a suspect. I heard the click of call waiting, told Alverez I had to go, and switched over to the other call. It was Max. I told him about Wes and Alverez.

'Where are you?' Max asked.

'In my car. In Portsmouth.'

'Stay there. I'll call you right back.'

I waited and watched the world go by. I saw a couple walk by arm in arm, shoulders touching, laughing. Two women stopped for a moment, deep in conversation, then continued down the street. A man walking a boxer struggled to control the dog's impatience to run ahead. An old woman with a limp made slow progress along Ceres Street. The phone rang.

'It's me, Josie,' Max said. 'First, don't call Alverez. Call me. Agreed?'

'Okay,' I said, feeling like a fool.

'Second, Alverez was very professional. He refused to call you a suspect, which is good news, but in reality, it doesn't much matter because even if you're not a suspect per se, you're certainly a person of interest. I made an appointment for us to meet with him at noon tomorrow. I'll pick you up at your office at eleven-thirty and we can talk en route.'

I agreed to the plan, went home, got the Bombay Sapphire out of the freezer, and made myself another martini.

Cathy looked up when we entered promptly at noon the next day, but didn't speak. Chief Alverez was standing at a file cabinet near the back, and when he saw us, he closed the drawer.

'How you doing?' he asked me, after greeting Max.

He led us into the same room we'd been in yesterday, and I selected the same chair.

Alverez turned to Max, and said, 'We have some new information.'

'What's that?' Max asked.

'Fingerprints.'

Max and I waited for Alverez to explain. Still speaking to Max, he added, 'As we expected, Josie's fingerprints were everywhere. We learned she's pretty darn thorough. We found her prints under furniture, on the back of picture frames, and inside drawers.'

'Makes sense,' Max commented. 'She's a professional appraiser.'

'Yeah,' Alverez agreed. 'But we also found her prints someplace they shouldn't be.'

'Oh, yeah?' Max asked. 'Where's that?'

'On the knife that was used to kill Nathaniel Grant.'

chapter three

Max gripped my shoulder. 'Josie,' he said, keeping his eyes on Alverez, 'don't say a word.'

'But I can explain,' I protested.

'Say nothing.'

He looked determined and grim, and I shivered. I nodded slightly, signaling that I'd do as he asked.

Max squeezed my shoulder again. I couldn't tell whether he was offering support or thanking me for doing as he instructed. He turned back toward Alverez, picked up his pen, and queried, 'Fingerprints on the knife?' His voice was calm, his tone pleasant.

I kept my eyes lowered and sat, silent and still.

'Yeah,' Alverez said, nodding. 'That's right.'

'Where?'

'On the handle.'

'Distinct? Complete?'

Alverez glanced at his notes. 'According to the tech guys, there wasn't enough ridge detail for an ID from most of the prints. But there was one clear index print from Josie's right hand. A sixteen-point match.'

'What does that mean?' I asked.

'It means your print is on the knife. For sure.'

Max patted my arm to calm me. 'It sounds as if the knife had been wiped, but not thoroughly.'

'Apparently,' Alverez agreed.

'Okay, then. Would you excuse us for a minute? I want to talk to my client privately.'

'Sure,' Alverez said. His chair made a loud scraping noise as he pushed back. The door closed behind him with the same disconcerting click I'd heard yesterday. Max cleared his throat and flipped to a fresh page on his yellow-lined pad.

'Okay, Josie,' Max said, his pen at the ready. 'Explain why your finger-prints are on the knife.'

I looked down at my lap, unable to think in sentences. Now that I had permission to speak, all that came to mind were words of outraged protest. I wanted to shout and rail and pound the table.

'*Now*, Josie. We don't have a lot of time.'

His admonition helped me focus. 'Do I need to whisper?' I asked, remembering Max's instruction that I was to whisper when I wanted to talk to him privately.

'No,' he said. 'When we're alone like this, you're free to talk natu-rally.'

'Okay.' I paused to think. 'It was Thursday of last week,' I said, 'the second time I was there. We'd settled on our next appointment and I was saying good-bye when Mr Grant asked me to have some tea.' I shrugged and flipped a hand. 'So I did. We went into the kitchen. I thought it was very sweet of him. I cut the cake.' I shuddered. 'That must have been the knife that was used to … that must have been the knife.'

'How was it that you cut the cake?' Max asked, keeping me focused.

'What do you mean?'

'Well,' Max asked, tapping his pen on the pad, 'did you take the knife from him? Did he hand it to you?'

'I took it from the knife block on the counter.'

'Why would you do that? I mean, you don't just walk into someone's kitchen and grab a knife.'

'No, no,' I exclaimed. 'It wasn't like that at all. I didn't grab the knife. When we got to the kitchen, Mr Grant had everything ready.'

'In what way?' Max asked.

'Well, he'd set out cups and saucers, teaspoons, some little plates, and a Bundt cake. He'd brewed real tea and the pot was sitting on the table along with a sugar bowl.'

'Okay. Then what happened?'

'He started opening drawers and pawing around, looking, he said, for the cake knife. Finally, he said he couldn't find it. He wasn't upset or anything. I remember we spoke about how odd it is that things disap-pear on their own. I told him about my father. How when I was growing up and something was misplaced – you know what I mean – when the can opener that lived in the top drawer was found, after an exhaustive search, in the bottom drawer, well, my father used to blame it on Oscar, the poltergeist. Mr Grant laughed and said that made perfect sense and explained a lot of things.'

Max nodded. 'Then what?'

'Then I said it didn't matter that he couldn't find the cake knife, that any knife would do. But he wanted to use the right knife. He said his wife was a stickler about things like that, using the right fork for the pickles and the right spoon for the jelly. But finally he gave up. He asked me to take a knife from the block on the counter. I took one randomly. We laughed about it because the knife I selected was huge! It had, I don't know, maybe an eight-inch blade.' I looked away for a moment, remembering Mr Grant's jolly laugh.

'Mr Grant made a joke,' I said softly, 'saying that he'd paid full price for the Bundt cake, so it had better not be stale and need a knife that big to cut it.'

Max shook his head sympathetically. 'And after you had tea?'

'After we were done,' I said, taking a deep breath, 'I helped him put the dishes in the dishwasher and I took a sponge and wiped down the table. Then I washed the knife by hand.' I thought back, remembering standing at the oversized sink and enjoying the ocean view. 'I watched the waves awhile as I dried the knife, not well, apparently, and put it back in the slot in the block.'

I began to tear up again. Using my middle fingers, I pushed the skin under my eyes until the tears stopped. I sniffed and wiped them away with the backs of my wrists. Max patted my shoulder while he made some notes.

'Okay,' he said. 'I don't want to mislead you, Josie. Chief Alverez obviously considers you a viable suspect.'

'But, I swear—'

Max raised a hand to stop me. 'Look at it from his point of view. You were there. The knife was there. And your fingerprints are on it. As near as I can tell, his focus now will be to figure out a motive. He's wondering why you might have killed Mr Grant. You know, how it might benefit you to have him dead. Until he can answer that question, probably he won't charge you with murder.'

I felt light-headed. Sitting in a police station listening to a matter-of-fact description of my vulnerability felt surrealistic. Someone was thinking of charging me with murder. I shook my head in disbelief.

'But if he can answer the motive question in a way that satisfies him,' Max continued, 'well, we need to be prepared in case he does charge you.'

'It's inconceivable,' I said.

'Expect the best, Josie, but prepare for the worst.'

My father used to say that, and hearing Max speak those words momentarily reassured me, but that comfortable delusion disintegrated into bone-deep sadness immediately followed by waves of overwhelming dread. Panic suddenly threatened to overtake reason. I gripped the table and blinked away tears of frustration and anger. I couldn't risk thinking of my dad. Not in my current situation. Forcing myself to breathe calmly, I pushed thoughts of him aside, and swallowed. When I could speak again, I asked, 'So, now what?'

'Now we try to be smarter than Alverez and get the answer first. You tell me. How do you benefit with Mr Grant dead?'

I shook my head. 'I don't. Think about it – with Mr Grant dead, I've lost a huge deal. A career-making deal.'

'Unless the deal was already lost. Unless when you went there yesterday morning, Mr Grant let you in and told you he'd changed his mind for some reason. And you lost your temper.'

I stared, speechless. I opened my mouth to protest, but no words came. What he said made sense, and it terrified me into silence.

'Well?' Max prodded.

'I don't know what to say,' I answered, my voice cracking. 'It's logical, but it didn't happen.'

'Can you prove it?'

'Of course not. How can I prove something *didn't* happen? We were due to sign the letter of agreement yesterday. I told you what happened when I got there.'

'I understand. But it's going to be a problem.' He tapped his pen a few times on the table, staring into the middle distance, his eyes narrowed in concentration. 'Probably Alverez is looking into it right now. If he can find evidence that you lost the account, he's got a motive.'

'What should I do?' I asked quietly.

'Tell the truth. Just like you've been doing. Keep repeating that you didn't do it. Alverez is a good man, Josie. He's not looking to railroad you.'

I nodded.

'Any questions?'

'No,' I answered.

'Let's call Alverez in,' Max said. 'Remember ... tell the truth. And the shorter your answers, the better. Explain the whole thing, including how you came to take the knife.'

I felt dazed and only half listened as Alverez asked if it would be all right to tape my explanation about the knife for the record, and Max agreed. I watched as Alverez plugged in the tape recorder and wiggled the cord, tugging gently, making certain it was secure. It was as if I were watching a movie. It seemed to have nothing to do with me. Alverez pointed to the machine.

'Are you ready?' he asked me.

I looked at Max and he gestured that I could begin. Alverez spoke the date and time, gave our names, and told me to begin. As I spoke, I kept my eyes on Alverez, alert for clues to his thinking. He nodded encouragingly, and smiled a little when I spoke about Oscar, the poltergeist. I felt relieved, convinced that he believed me, and that therefore I was well on my way to clearing my name.

'So let me be sure I understand,' Alverez said when I'd finished. 'You had a cup of tea and, directed by Mr Grant, you put the cups, saucers, and plates in the dishwasher. Is that right?'

'Yes,' I answered. 'That's right.'

'Why didn't you put the knife in the dishwasher, too?'

His handsome face gave away nothing. He either flat-out thought I was lying or he was trying to trap me. Fear morphed into anger. 'You don't put good knives in the dishwasher,' I answered sharply. 'You wash them by hand.'

'Did Mr Grant tell you that?' Alverez asked, unmoved by my tone.

'No,' I countered. 'He didn't need to. Everyone knows that.'

Alverez paused to think. I heard the soft whirr of the tape recorder and a heavy thud from outside as a truck lumbered by.

Finally, Max asked, 'Is there anything else? Can we go now?'

Alverez stopped the recorder. 'How about if we plan on meeting again in the morning?' he asked Max.

I touched Max's elbow before he could respond, and whispered, 'No. I have to get ready for my regular Saturday tag sale and the Wilson auction preview starts tomorrow.'

'What hours will you be working?'

'I'll start setting up the tag sale around seven. The auction preview starts at ten and runs until nine in the evening. Both the auction and the tag sale are on Saturday.'

'That makes for a couple of long days, doesn't it?'

'Yeah,' I agreed. Calling them long days was an understatement. I'd be running full tilt from dawn until late evening both days.

'Keep your cell phone on and with you at all times. Even when you sleep. Agreed?' he asked, his urgency palpable even in a whisper.

'Okay,' I said.

'No excuses? I'm about to promise our availability. Don't make a liar out of me. Okay?'

'I promise. My cell phone will be with me always.' I gripped the edge of the table, sort of angry, but mostly intent and ready to respond.

'Tomorrow won't work for us,' Max said to Alverez, and explained my situation. 'I'll keep my cell phone on, and Josie and I have arranged it so I can reach her on an as-needed basis. I think you have my number, but just in case, here.' He reached into his jacket pocket for a business card and slid it across the table.

Alverez picked up the card, but looked at me. I met his eyes, trying to look nonthreatening. I couldn't read him at all. I realized that he might be weighing whether he should arrest me on the spot or let me go, thinking that maybe if he gave me enough rope I'd hang myself. Nonetheless, I was relieved when he turned to Max, and said, 'Okay.' To me, he asked, 'You won't be leaving the area, right?'

'No,' I replied, swallowing. 'I'll be here.'

Alverez nodded and stood up. 'All right, then.'

Cathy wasn't in sight as we passed through the central room, but two young men in uniform were. They stared at me as I walked by. I was glad to escape to the parking lot, but didn't feel free until Max had driven us away and the police station was out of sight.

I watched the ocean as we drove. The tide was high, so I could see waves roll in through breaks in the dunes. 'Max ...' I said.

'Yeah?'

'I've had a thought....'

'What's that?'

'Maybe I'm not the only antique dealer that Grant contacted after all. I thought I was, but maybe the motive you suggested – losing the Grant deal – is true, but applies to someone else, not me.'

'That's interesting,' Max agreed. 'How much money are we talking about, anyway? For whoever got the deal.'

'Who knows? Mr Grant wanted to sell items that would have fetched at least hundreds of thousands of dollars at auction. Maybe more than a million. To a dealer that represented tens or hundreds of thousands of dollars in commissions. Plus a worldwide reputation as a power player.'

'Sounds like motive enough to kill.'

'Yeah,' I acknowledged. 'Well, I wonder if mine were the only finger-prints they found.'

'On the knife?'

'Yes, on the knife. Or anywhere. Under the furniture, I mean. Think about it ... if they found prints from another antique dealer, auctioneer, or appraiser in places where only a professional would look, well, that implies that I wasn't the only person with something to lose. Wouldn't that person have a strong motive to have killed Mr Grant if he thought that I was about to close the deal?'

'Makes sense, Josie. Besides fingerprints, there's another way of tracking a competitor down. Phone records. To see if Mr Grant had contacted anyone else. If he called another dealer, or if another dealer called him.'

'That's a great idea!' I exclaimed enthusiastically. 'Maybe we could ask Chief Alverez to look at the records for us.'

'The timing's wrong. I'll make a note of both ideas, but I think we should hold off.'

'Why?' I asked.

'Well,' Max said and glanced at me. 'In both cases, the fingerprints and the phone logs, what if the answer is no?'

'No' hadn't occurred to me because I knew I was innocent. And if I was innocent, someone else was guilty. 'Good point,' I acknowledged. 'But should I just sit here and not defend myself?'

'From a strategic perspective, yes, you shouldn't defend yourself, because you haven't been charged with anything. If and when you are, we'll hire private detectives to investigate. I don't want to imply that our relationship with Alverez is adversarial, but it's always a mistake to volunteer information. Remember what I told you? Short answers.'

'Thank you, Max,' I said. Having thought of a line of investigation that Max considered worth noting boosted my spirits a little. It was one thing to theoretically expect the best and prepare for the worst. It was another thing altogether to simply sit back and wait for Alverez to make his judgment about my guilt or innocence. Maybe Max was right and it wasn't time to act, but still, I was getting prepared for the worst. I'd be ready to act if I needed to do so. All my adult life, I'd found that the only reliable antidote to feelings of powerlessness was action.

We drove in silence for several minutes. As we passed the Grant house, shielded from sight by dense boxwood hedges, I said, 'I wonder who gets the contract now.'

'The decision will be made, presumably, by whoever inherits. Whether to sell at all, and if so, to whom.'

'How can we find out who that is?' I asked Max.

'That's one question we can follow up on right away. I'll ask Epps.'

I lifted and lowered my shoulders a few times, trying to relax my muscles a bit. It had been as if I'd been locked in a cold, dark, window-less room, and now I felt a surge of relief, as if the door had only been latched after all, and outside it was sunny and warm. Max and I, we had a plan. It was the first bit of hope I'd felt since Alverez had walked into my warehouse two days earlier, and it felt damn good.

But I remained wary. While it felt damn good to have a plan of action, I had no illusions. *Hope*, I repeated to myself, *but also prepare for disappointment.*

I got back to the warehouse just before two. Gretchen was talking on the phone with the receiver wedged between her shoulder and ear, her head tilted, and her red hair spilling over the unit, falling nearly to her waist. She looked uncomfortable, but she sounded as relaxed and pleasant as ever. I stood and waited while she finished.

'Yes, the preview is still on,' she said. 'No, absolutely no change. Uh-huh. Right. Registered bidders only. Right. Yes, sir. The auction is on Saturday, starting at two.'

Listening to Gretchen's cheery words reminded me of the first time I met her. It was a Thursday, the day after I'd closed on the warehouse. When I drove up at eight in the morning, she was waiting at my front door wearing a navy blue suit, white blouse, and heels, clutching a *Seacoast Star* opened to the classifieds with my ad circled in pink highlighter. Observing her as I walked from my car and noting her outfit, I'd hoped she was a prospective client. She gave me a dazzling smile, and said, 'Hi, are you Josie Prescott? I'm here for the job. I wanted to be first. Am I first?'

I hired her forty-five minutes later, an oddly impulsive act for a systematic, research-oriented sort like me. Especially since she was reticent to the point of mysterious about her background. She volunteered that she moved to Portsmouth from a small town upstate, but when I asked which one, she rolled her eyes, and said, 'Oh please, I escaped, let's leave it at that.' And gave me another blinding smile.

Awed at her dictation and typing skills as much as her light-hearted, engaging charm, and her can-do attitude toward customer service, I speculated on whether she was too good to be true. I told her that I would certainly want to invite her back for a second interview while thinking that I needed to check her references. 'I'll look forward to seeing you next week,' I started to say.

She stopped me cold when her smile faded away. Her eyes became mournful, and she reached across the desk and touched my arm. 'Hire me. I'll help your company grow. Really. I will. I'm honest and hardworking. You won't be sorry. Offer me the job now. Please.'

'Why? What's your hurry?'

'I've just moved. I need a job and this is the one I want.'

I paused, thinking. She seemed perfect. 'Why did you move, Gretchen? Is there something I should know?' I asked quietly, watching her for any sign of deception.

She shook her head. 'No, nothing. It's just that I need a fresh start.'

'Why here? I'm an antique appraiser. Not the best place for a fresh start.'

'Why not? Why isn't it a good place for a fresh start? You're starting a new business. It's a perfect place for a fresh start.'

Warning myself that I'd probably regret it, I offered her the job and she accepted it. Two years later, I knew that hiring her was one of the best decisions I'd ever made. And I still didn't know where she'd lived before she'd arrived on my doorstep.

She hung up the phone.

I said, 'Hey, kiddo. How are you doing?'

'I'm fine. How about you? Are you okay?' she asked me.

'A little the worse for wear, but okay. How are things here?'

Gretchen smiled a little. 'Busy. In a good way. Sasha's done with the catalogue and wants you to review it so we can get it copied and bound.' She reached to a corner of her desk and handed me a thick document held together with a black clamp. 'We have more than a hundred people registered for the preview and the phone keeps ringing with inquiries.'

'More than a hundred?' I asked, slightly awed. 'That's almost double the number we had last time. Wow. The Wilson stuff is good, but it's not that good.'

Gretchen nodded and looked away. 'I think there may be a curiosity factor at work here.'

'What do you mean?'

'Well, several reporters are among the registered bidders. I'm guessing it's about the, you know, the Grant situation.'

I froze for a moment, then brushed hair out of my eyes. I nodded. 'Yeah, probably that's it. Have any reporters called to talk to you?'

'Yes. I keep saying "No comment," and eventually they go away.'

'Good,' I responded. 'Keep it up.' After a pause I added, 'Thanks, Gretchen.'

She waved her hand dismissively. 'It's nothing,' she said. 'Change of subject. We lost two regular part-timers for Saturday. The tag sale. Mae and Gary.'

'Why?'

'The flu.'

'Oh, boy. If it's not one thing, it's another.'

'I've already called Peter at Temp Pros.'

'Thanks, Gretchen. I don't know what I'd do without you.'

She looked embarrassed. 'It's nothing,' she said. 'So. What's the latest news?'

'Well,' I said, trying for light and frothy, 'let me put it this way ... it's pretty clear that I was in the wrong place at the wrong time.'

She nodded with a sympathetic grimace, but before she could comment, the phone rang.

'Where are Eric and Sasha now?' I asked as she reached for the unit.

'Helping with the auction setup. Along with the temp guys. They've been at it since about noon.'

'Good. I'll go there now. Anything else I should know?'

She shook her head as she picked up the phone and answered with her usual upbeat 'Prescott's. May I help you?'

It was another inquiry about attending the auction. Under normal circumstances, I'd be thrilled at such a stellar response. But the circumstances were anything but normal. Instead of pride and pleasure, I felt edgy discomfort. Some of the people coming to the auction preview tomorrow would be there not to buy but to judge me, and maybe even to intrude. I could picture ambitious young television reporters, with their earnest crews wielding spotlights, pushing microphones in my face. It made me feel anxious, vulnerable, and cranky.

I walked across my warehouse to an area on the left, passing the sliding dividers that, with a push of a button, would segregate the far corner from the rest of the space. When the partitions were in place, it became an elegant, spacious room, not a concrete cavern. The design and layout were my own, and I thought it was a clever way to transform an over-sized industrial space into an attractive and utilitarian venue on an as-needed basis. Clever, but expensive.

I stepped on to the maroon industrial carpeting that covered the concrete floor and served to subdue the sounds that echoed through the rest of the warehouse. I made my way to the low platform at the front, skirted in black polyester. A podium faced the seating area. The outside concrete walls, to my right and ahead of me, were whitewashed. Acres of burgundy brocade hung from big black wrought-iron rings dangling from two-inch pipes I'd had painted black and that stretched from the stage to the far back wall and along the back wall from the far corner to the divider. Tomorrow, we'd slide the dividing walls into place, converting this section of the warehouse into an antique haven, suitably decorated and appropriately quiet. Everything looked fine, except that we'd need to add more seats.

I spotted Sasha directing Eric and three temporary helpers as they positioned the Wilson goods into numbered, roped-off areas against what would be, once the dividers were in place tomorrow, the inside wall of the room. Looking at it now, the placement seemed arbitrary, a fifteen-foot-deep channel filled with antiques, positioned some fifty feet in from the outside wall.

'Over here.' Sasha directed two of the men, pointing to a space labeled 12. They carried a heavy, Russian-made, nineteenth-century cedar hope chest fitted with brass hardware into the area. Sasha consulted a three-ring binder containing, I knew, a copy of the Wilson listing, confirming that the hope chest's placement in area 12 matched its catalogue entry as lot 12.

Waving hello, she closed the binder and joined me in an empty aisle as Eric ensured that the chest was plumb to the line where the wall would be. 'We're making good progress,' she said.

'I can see you are,' I said with a smile.

Eric took a lighthouse quilt from the chest, a remarkable work dating from the eighteenth century, probably crafted by a local teenager, and draped it over a black metal free-standing rod. Sasha went over and smoothed it out so the bits and pieces of cotton resolved themselves into a landscape of accurate perspective and awe-inspiring detail. Tiny seagulls, created from peanut-sized white and gray scraps of cloth and sewn with nearly invisible stitches, seemed to flutter across the pale blue sky. It made a dramatic backdrop for the hope chest.

My mother would have loved it. She admired excellence in craftsmanship in all things. I learned business from my father, but I gauged quality with my mother's eyes. Well could I remember the hours we spent at museums.

I could picture us as we stood together in the Peabody Museum in Cambridge, gazing, speechless, at the glass flower collection. At the Isabella Stewart Gardner Museum in Boston, we whispered about the odd, eclectic mixture of treasures on display. And when I was eleven, we traveled to New York to visit museums. We spent the first two days at the Metropolitan Museum of Art, where I stared, awed and thrilled, at one after another masterpiece.

I recall pointing, excited, to the cat in George Caleb Bingham's 1845 painting *Fur Traders Descending the Missouri*; remarking on the vivid yellows and reds on the earliest-known Nepalese painting on cloth, dating from around 1100; and wondering how a statue created almost five thousand years ago could still exist. Every moment was filled with wonder, but it was on the third day that my life was changed forever.

With a wintry wind blowing from the east, we kept our heads down and hurried along the Midtown streets until we reached the Museum of Modern Art.

'Oh, Josie,' my mother had said, staring through moist eyes at Picasso's *Les Demoiselles d'Avignon*, 'wouldn't it be wonderful to spend your life surrounded by such magnificence?'

'Yes,' I answered, and then and there, I silently vowed that I would find a way to work with items of great beauty.

Looking again at the quilt, I felt a spurt of pride. *If only my mother could see me now*, I thought, and smiled.

'Hey, Josie,' Eric called, and walked toward me. 'Doesn't it look great?'

'More than great,' I said. 'You guys are incredible! How much more do you have to do?'

'Four more lots,' Eric said, dragging his arm along his forehead, catching dripping sweat. 'Not bad.'

'Not bad at all. Good job, guys.' I added the instruction about the chairs, gave Eric a thumbs-up, promised Sasha I'd sign off on the catalogue ASAP, and left.

As I approached the spiral staircase that led to my private office, an area once used to monitor manufacturing processes, Gretchen paged me.

'What's going on?' I asked as I walked into her office.

'Max Bixby wants you on line two,' she said.

I picked up the phone, and said, 'This is Josie.'

'What's your fax number?' Max asked without even saying hello.

I told him, adding, 'What's the big deal? Gretchen could have told you the number.'

'Epps faxed something over to me and I want you to see it right away. For your eyes only.'

'Okay,' I responded, attentive and worried. I heard the fax machine kick on. 'Do you want me to call you back after I've looked at it?' I asked.

'No,' Max said. 'I'll hold.'

The phone rang in back of me and Gretchen answered it as usual. It was another inquiry, but I barely registered the interchange. I stood silent and intent, watching the fax machine drop a one-page document into the receiving tray.

I was holding a copy of a letter, dated Friday of last week, the day after I'd shared Bundt cake with Mr Grant. It was signed by Britt Epps, written on his law firm's letterhead, and my heart skipped more than a beat as I read the text introducing Barney Troudeaux to Nathaniel Grant.

'I've read it,' I said.

'Do you know Barney Troudeaux?' Max asked.

'Yes,' I answered. 'Of course.'

'He's an antique dealer based in Exeter, right?'

'Right.'

'What do you know about him?'

I forced myself to ignore my personal feelings about good ol' Barney and his bitch-queen wife. Instead I reported the truth as perceived by the vast majority in the industry. 'Barney is very well respected. I mean, he's the head of the NHAAS.'

'That's that industry association you mentioned?' Max asked.

'Right,' I said, and shrugged. 'It's pretty prestigious.'

'So Epps recommending him wouldn't be out of line?'

'Hell, no. It would be an obvious choice. Not a good one, necessarily, but certainly it would be low risk.'

'What do you mean?'

'Well, between you, me, and the gate post, Barney is lazy. His research is cursory, so he misses a lot of opportunities to maximize his clients' profits.'

'So he's reputable but incompetent?' Max asked.

'I wouldn't say he's incompetent. He's knowledgeable and a terrific negotiator. The problem is he's lazy. He delegates research to other people, usually his wife, who knows nothing but acts as if she knows everything, and he never checks or corrects her work.'

'How do you know?'

'Because on two separate occasions I've bought items he's sold, not because they were sort of a bargain and I knew I could mark them up and make a decent profit but because they were inaccurately described in his catalogues, and I got killer deals. I sure wouldn't want to be a client of his, but I doubt you'd find a client who'd say so, or even one who discovered the truth. He's great with people. His clients love him. But from where I sit, it's as if he doesn't care as much about the value of the items he's entrusted with as he does about getting the deal.'

'Why would Epps recommend him?'

I made a noise involuntarily, a small snort of contempt. 'Because he's low risk. Don't you see? He's the prez of a major industry association. He's personable. Forgive my cynicism, but from a lawyer like Epps's point of view, it doesn't matter how good a job an appraiser does. All that matters is that his client never comes back with a complaint. But I got to ask you, Max, what does all of this have to do with the price of eggs in China?'

JANE K. CLELAND

'Well,' he said after a pause, 'here's the thing, Josie. Epps told me that Grant asked him to recommend a reliable dealer. This letter shows that Troudeaux's the dealer he selected. It might imply that, in fact, you'd lost the deal – or that you were about to.'

'In other words, you're saying that, on paper at least, Alverez might think I had a motive for killing Mr Grant.'

'Yeah, but actually, I think it may be even worse than that. Epps told me that the letter was just a matter of form, that he'd given Mr Grant Troudeaux's name on the phone when he first called and asked.'

'What?' I exclaimed, shocked.

'He said Mr Grant was very appreciative for the referral.'

'When was this?'

'According to Epps, it was two weeks ago.'

I did a quick mental calculation. That was just about when Mr Grant and I began to talk. I felt sick. I closed my eyes and leaned against the desk.

'I can't believe it,' I murmured. 'I just can't believe it.'

'Why? Wouldn't it be good business for Mr Grant to have consulted more than one appraiser?'

'You're right, of course,' I answered. 'I just had no idea, and from the way he acted, it seems so unlikely.' I sat up and opened my eyes, startled by a thought. 'Wait!' I said. 'That means I'm not the only suspect.'

'Except that you were at Grant's the morning he was killed. And Epps said that he was certain that Barney had pretty much locked in the deal.'

'How can he be so sure?' I asked, sounding calmer than I felt.

'Well,' Max said, and hesitated for a moment. 'Troudeaux told Epps how excited he was about the Renoir, and said that Mr Grant had agreed to sell it to him privately.'

'The Renoir?'

'I have the title here somewhere....' I heard the rustle of papers being shifted. 'Here it is. It's called *Three Girls and a Cat*. Epps explained that Troudeaux wanted to buy it for his wife for her birthday.'

The world seemed to reel, and I held on to the desk. Gretchen finished her call, and I heard her get up and open a file drawer. I forced myself to ignore her presence and focus instead on Max.

'Max,' I said.

'What?'

'Mr Grant didn't have a Renoir.'

After a long pause, Max said, 'Maybe he'd already sold it to Troudeaux.'

42

'Or maybe Barney's lying.'

'Maybe,' Max acknowledged.

'Oh, jeez,' I said, startled by a new thought. 'I think I might have the answer.'

'What?'

'If there was a Renoir it had to have been hidden somewhere because I never saw it.'

'Okay, that makes sense.'

'So, what we need to do is find the hiding place.'

'Maybe he had a safe,' Max suggested.

'Not a conventional one. I would have spotted it.'

'We could explain our thinking to Alverez and ask him to search the house.'

'We don't need to,' I said confidently. 'I know how to find out.'

'How?'

'The video. Don't you remember, Max? I videotaped every inch of that place!'

chapter four

As I hung up the phone, Eric came into the office, grime streaked on his face and T-shirt, looking tired clear through. Forcing a smile, I said in as light a tone as I could muster, 'Man, if I didn't know better, I'd guess you've been working.'

'Yeah,' he agreed, grinning, 'just a little. Anything else right now?'

'Are all of the lots in place and approved by Sasha?'

'Yup. I let the temp guys go.'

I nodded. 'Good job.' Turning to my assistant, I asked, 'Gretchen? Anything for Eric?'

She shook her head. 'No. We're set, I think.'

'You heard the woman. You're free to go.'

Eric left with a wave, saying he'd be in by eight the next morning. I watched from the window as he made his way across the parking lot to his old truck and signaled his turn from the lot even though there was no one behind him or on the road in either direction. I smiled. A man who follows rules, even in private. I bet he was heading home to Dover, a small town about twelve miles northwest of the warehouse. I'd driven past his house once, an old Victorian in depressing disrepair. He lived there with his widowed mother and two much-loved dogs, a black Lab named Jet and a German shorthaired pointer named Ruby. I spoke to his mom once when she'd called to remind him to pick up some potatoes on his way home. She'd sounded uninterested in speaking to her son's boss, irritable, and tired.

I picked up the catalogue pages Gretchen had set aside for me. 'You should leave soon, too,' I told her. 'Tomorrow's going to be a killer day.'

'In a little while,' she said. 'I want to finish updating the roster for the Wilson preview and I have some calls to return about tag-sale stuff.'

'Okay. I'll be in my office,' I said, and left her transferring names from her handwritten notes on to a spreadsheet.

Before going to my office, I crossed the span to the auction-site corner, shivering a bit as I made my way across the cold concrete floor. It was always dim inside the huge space, even with fluorescent overhead lighting, and somehow the darkness made it seem colder than it really was. Eerie shadows shifted as I walked. I was glad to reach the smaller, more homey-looking zone, and I flipped the light switches illuminating hanging chandeliers and wall sconces. Between the soft, incandescent lighting and the thick burgundy carpet, the smaller space was a world apart from the warehouse proper, more welcoming than utilitarian. Plus, it felt warmer.

I walked the aisles looking carefully at each roped area. The lot numbers were in place. All items were positioned well, dust free, and labeled with small typed cards. Scanning the center area, I noted that Eric had added rows of chairs and lined them up properly. A sign reading Prescott's hung from the podium. Skirted registration tables stood near the side door through which the registered bidders would pass tomorrow. I felt pride and accomplishment as I stood alone near the stage. We were ready. I turned off the lights as I left and headed for the spiral stairs that led to my office.

I had a television/VCR combo set up in a bamboo armoire in a corner, and looking at it made me want to skip proofing Sasha's typed catalogue pages. I was eager to get to the Grant tape, but duty called. With a sigh, I forced myself to read carefully and stay alert for typos, inconsistent formatting, and information gaps.

Just before six, as I finished proofing the catalogue, Sasha poked her head into my office, and said, 'Gretchen asked me to tell you that she left for the day.'

'Okay.'

'How are you doing?' she asked.

I felt an unaccountable urge to confide in her. I had no one to talk to and it would be a relief to bounce ideas off someone. With my dad gone, and my friends in New York a world away, I felt alone. Since arriving in New Hampshire, I'd focused on building my business. Fleetingly, I wondered what it would be like to be married, to have an ally waiting at home, eager to share confidences.

Sasha was brilliant, with the instincts of a collector. Confiding in her might be foolhardy, though. Without doubt, she was smart and educated, but she was also a scared mouse of a woman, eager for approval, yet continually braced for censure. Only when discussing art or related subjects was she confident and well-spoken. Otherwise, her anxiety was apparent in everything she did, from the way she twirled her limp brown shoulder-length hair to her inability to meet people's eyes. I couldn't risk trusting her. Challenged by a stronger being, she'd probably fold, trading my confidences for goodwill.

Pushing aside my lonely need, I answered, 'Thanks for asking. Everything's fine.'

Better to lie than reveal a vulnerability. I wondered what my father would think about that decision.

She gestured toward the catalogue pages. 'How does it look?' she asked.

'It looks great,' I said.

'Th-th-thanks,' she whispered, embarrassed. She blushed and looked down, her standard response to praise.

I pointed out the few typos I'd found, and Sasha said, 'I'll make the corrections and go to the quick-copy place.'

'Sounds good,' I told her.

I heard the click-clack of her shoes as she descended the stairs, then nothing. I was alone.

Watching the tape was upsetting. Seeing certain items, like the inlaid chess table that had belonged to Mr Grant's wife, triggered memories of the pleasant conversation we'd shared about its origin. I now perceived his jolly Santa Claus demeanor as a veneer disguising a big bad wolf licking his chops.

Well, I chided myself, maybe that was unfair. Just because his behavior felt like a betrayal didn't make it so. I sighed. Mr Grant had owed me nothing, and I had no complaint. If, as it now seemed, he was just using my appraisal to benchmark value so he could negotiate wisely with Barney, well, that was his prerogative, and in fact, was probably a savvy business move.

I couldn't pretend that I wasn't disappointed, but I could learn from the experience. My naïveté and gullibility had facilitated his research. I still believed he'd liked me. But now I understood that liking me hadn't mattered a whit. *Don't be stupid, Josie*, my father had told me once. *In business, it's all about the business. If someone won't make money doing business with you, they won't do business with you no matter how much they like you.*

It felt good to remind myself of my father's words. Doing so allowed me to view the tape with more objectivity than I otherwise might have been able to bring to the task.

As expected, there was no Renoir in sight, nor was there an empty space on a wall where it might have hung. Either Barney had already purchased it, as Max thought, or someone else had done so. Either

Barney or Epps was lying and there was no Renoir at all, which wouldn't surprise me a bit now that I was less naïve and gullible, or the painting was secreted somewhere.

I paused the tape to consider why Mr Grant might have wanted the painting hidden. He had three sterling-silver tea sets dating from the eighteenth century and two mint-condition seventeenth-century Chinese square porcelain bottles on display, a Regency period dining-room set constructed of perfectly matched rosewood that he used daily, and scores of other priceless and near-priceless items all in plain sight. Why would he hide one painting? Obviously, he didn't keep it hidden just because it was valuable. There had to be another reason.

It was hard to imagine, but maybe the painting had been stolen. Impulsively I turned to my computer and brought up an Internet browser, and then clicked on an Interpol site I'd bookmarked that was devoted to tracking stolen art. I typed in the painting's title and 'Renoir.' Nothing.

I shook my head in frustration. I had no way of knowing if it was true that Mr Grant had ever possessed the painting, nor did I have a clue whether, if he had, discovering his reason for hiding it mattered. I warned myself not to lose sight of my goal. Whether I was being framed for murder or was an accidental victim, I needed to arm myself with knowledge.

I went through the tape again and counted twenty-three paintings. Not one was even close to a Renoir in reputation, importance, or value. None was remarkable even when compared to the other treasures in the house. The only artist whom I recognized was the nineteenth-century illustrator Jules Tavernier. Mr Grant had three of his pastoral scenes oddly framed in contemporary-looking black boxes.

I did a quick Internet search for Tavernier prices. The paintings were lovely, but would be unlikely to fetch more than $7,000 to $8,000 each. A lot of money for a painting by some standards, but nothing compared to the millions a Renoir would bring.

The other twenty paintings were even less special than the Taverniers. Value aside, any of the paintings could hide a wall safe. The Renoir could have been taken out of its frame and rolled, fitting easily in a specially designed hole in the wall.

An hour into the tape, I was listening to my discourse on two Windsor chairs, a seventeenth-century hanging tapestry showcasing birds in a jungle, and an eighteenth-century English partners' desk. I wondered if the painting could be attached to the underside of a chair via a fake cushion or tucked into a safe located behind the tapestry. And while I'd examined the desk at length and had spotted long, thin dove-tail joints that had confirmed its pedigree, I realized I hadn't discovered the hinged cabinet door frequently found at the back of the desks' knee-hole openings.

I paused the tape, and stared at the screen, my mouth opening, my mind racing. A thorough search would easily discover if there was a wall safe or if the painting was hidden in a closet or under a false bottom attached to a chair or table, but I bet I'd found the stash – a hidden cabinet in the partners' desk. We needed to look. And we needed to look now.

'Max!' I exclaimed when I had him on the phone. 'I think I'm on to something.'

'Tell me,' he said. I heard children's laughter in the background.

'I've watched the tape. Old partners' desks had kneeholes. You know, an opening where your knees go. Many of them had cabinets built in at the bottom. Not exactly secret, since the hinges and lock unit were in plain sight, but semisecret, since someone would have to be on his hands and knees to spot it.'

'And Mr Grant's has one of these hidden cabinets?' he asked, excited.

'No. It doesn't seem to. But in reviewing the tape, I noticed that there's space for one. Some of the partners' desks had the cabinet secreted behind a wood panel. It's rare, and I'm betting that Mr Grant's desk is one of those. Max, it would be a perfect place to stash art.'

'Let me understand,' Max said. 'You're saying that even though no cabinet hardware, like hinges, is visible, you still think there's a cabinet there. Is that right?'

'Exactly. I'm saying it might be there. It's worth a look. I have some other ideas of where to look, too.'

'Like where?'

'Like behind the paintings for a wall safe, and under chair cushions – it would be fairly easy to create a false bottom.'

'It sounds possible, Josie. Well done.'

'Thank you. Now what?'

I took a breath, waiting for Max's assessment, eager, yet fearful. My thoughts were inchoate; understanding why Mr Grant had hidden the painting, if he had done so, and what it might mean to me one way or the other, was unclear to me. I waited for Max to speak, certain another shoe would drop.

'Now we consider how knowing about the Renoir would affect your situation.'

'And your conclusion?'

He paused. 'I think we should alert Alverez and see about a search.'

'Are you sure? Should we reveal what we know?'

'Alverez knows about the Renoir and Epps's relationship with Barney Troudeaux already. It seems to me that we have nothing to lose and a lot of goodwill to gain.'

'I understand,' I said, and I did. Like pieces of a jigsaw puzzle latching into place, I saw how our volunteering our idea positioned us as an ally. People with nothing to hide volunteer to help. And since we were revealing nothing new about Barney or Mr Grant's murder, there was no downside.

'I'll call you back,' Max said, and hung up.

Max called me back ten minutes later, the sounds of laughter louder than before.

'Good news,' he said. 'Alverez is intrigued. He agreed to meet us at the back door of the Grant house in half an hour.'

'I'm thrilled!' I exclaimed. 'Finally, we're doing something! Max, this is great.'

'I'll pick you up in fifteen minutes. All right?'

'Are you sure? I hear laughter in the background.'

'Yeah, I'm sure. No problem, Josie. Remember, the same rules apply to our meeting with Alverez as before. Don't volunteer information. Answer questions as simply as you can. Remember that Alverez isn't your lawyer.'

My momentary euphoria faded with his words. 'Got it,' I responded.

I shut down the computer, rewound the videotape, and turned off the lights in my office. As I started down the spiral stairs, my thoughts whirring, filled with anticipation, I heard rustling from somewhere downstairs and realized that Sasha must be back with the finished catalogues.

I was about to call out to her when I spotted a shadow behind the crates, the stack of empty wooden boxes where Alverez had stood when we'd first spoken, and felt my heart skip a beat. Sasha wouldn't be behind the crates. In fact, thinking about it, I realized that she wouldn't be anywhere around at all. At just after eight, it was too soon for her to be back from the quick-copy place.

I tiptoed back up the steps and slid into a corner of the landing, shielded from direct light, but with a clear view of the entire warehouse below. I listened hard but heard nothing. I saw nothing else of note. I stayed still.

Eric, maybe. Eric often shifted crates, organizing things, rearranging packing materials. Not at this hour, though. Not on this day. He'd left hours ago, tired and dirty.

I shook my head, confused. Everyone was gone. I scolded myself that I was making much ado about nothing, that I was tired and stressed, and that actually there was nothing there.

As I was girding myself to step out from behind my hiding place, I heard another rustling sound and stopped cold, allowing myself to trust my instincts. I wasn't imagining things. I'd heard something, a movement, a kind of rubbing, fabric maybe, brushing against wood.

In the high-ceilinged, open warehouse, sound reverberated. I thought the soft noise, a hiss or a scrape, had come from near the crates, but I might have been wrong. I pressed my back into the wall and scanned the room, seeking out something that would account for the noise, that would explain an odd shadow behind the tall stack of crates, but I saw nothing out of the way.

I swallowed. My heart was pounding so hard I was having trouble breathing. To hell with it, I told myself angrily. Probably the noise was the building settling, and I'd imagined the shadow. Silently cursing the anxiety that clung to me like barnacles to a rock, I stepped out from the corner. I was tired of jumping at shadows and fretting about small noises. No one could make me fearful but myself. Straightening my shoulders and lifting my head, I began the descent, circling down the staircase.

I heard a click and froze. The door. Someone had quietly latched the door. Were they going out? Or coming in? I stood and listened. Nothing.

Slowly, my heart racing, I moved forward toward Gretchen's office and the outside world accessible through the front door. I paused at the threshold and peered in every corner. Nothing looked out of order. Making my way to the front, I peeked out the window. There was no moonlight visible through the cloud cover. The perimeter lights that illuminated the parking lot for auction or preview nights weren't on. The rural blackness was complete.

I reached for the doorknob, ready to leave, when all at once, I stopped. Another noise, this one a kind of low rumble, broke the stillness, startling me. I glanced over my shoulder. *It's outside*, I told myself. *You're safe.*

I peeked out again, and suddenly headlights scissored through the dark. A car was heading toward me. I tensed and pulled back from the window, terrified that my gut had been right after all, that there had been an intruder who, for whatever reason, had returned.

chapter five

Forcing myself to look through the window once again, I recognized Max's car, and sighed with relief. Wrenching open the door, I flung it wide, and stepped out into the damp, foggy night.

'Hey, Josie,' Max said, smiling, lowering his window. 'Are you ready?'

'Max …' I took a step and stopped. I didn't know what else to say. I couldn't figure out how to begin. The look of weariness on Max's face alerted me to the fact that asking my lawyer to accompany me on an evening venture threatened to cross the line between capitalizing on his dedication to duty and imposing on his good nature.

'What's wrong?' he asked, his smile fading slowly as he looked at me.

'Someone … I think someone was inside,' I said, sounding calmer than I felt.

He climbed out of his car, and I noted that he was still wearing his bow tie and jacket. 'What?' he asked.

'I heard something. I saw a shadow.'

'My God,' he said, sounding aghast. 'Are you all right?'

'I guess.'

'Are you sure?' he asked, walking toward me.

I looked away under his scrutiny. 'I'm okay, just a little shaken up.'

'Did someone break in?'

'Maybe. No, I guess not. Probably they just came in. The door wasn't locked.'

'When did it happen?'

'Now. Just now.'

'In the warehouse?'

'Yes.'

'Are you sure you're okay?'

'You bet,' I answered, trying to smile. I didn't want to upset him.

'Come on. Let's go see.'

'Okay.'

He led the way, and I followed close behind, switching on lights. We stood together in the center of the warehouse, looking in all directions, listening.

'I thought the noise came from over there,' I said, pointing to the stacks of crates.

'I don't see anything. Do you?'

'No. I must have imagined it,' I said.

'Maybe,' he answered. 'Let's take a look around, to be sure.'

'Okay. Thanks.'

We walked the length of the warehouse, peering down each row, looking through the open shelving and around corners, and climbed the staircase to my office. In the auction area and by the loading dock, Max tugged on the outside doors to ensure they were locked. As we confirmed each section was empty, I switched off the lights. We made our way back to the front door.

'Thanks, Max. I feel better.' I took my coat from the hook by the door. 'Ready?'

He nodded toward the alarm box. 'It wasn't set?'

'No. The last person out for the night sets it.'

He nodded. 'And you were alone in here?'

'Apparently,' I said, trying for a grin.

'Don't joke about it, Josie,' he admonished. 'Someone might have been inside and left before I got here.'

'How? I was here, watching and listening.'

'You said you climbed back up. It's a spiral staircase so sometimes your back would be to the open area.' He shrugged. 'The sound of your own footsteps might have covered theirs, no matter how quiet you tried to be.'

'I guess,' I said, anxiety returning.

'Lock up, okay?'

I nodded and punched the alarm code, saw the green light turn to red, and stepped outside. Max followed, pulled the door shut, and wiggled the knob to be certain it held fast.

He took my coat and draped it over my shoulders for the short walk to the passenger side of his car, cupping my elbow as if to support me, a service I didn't need but a kindness that I appreciated. Old-fashioned courtesy unwomaned me even when my emotions were under control. Now, raw from worry and exhausted from stress, I wasn't on even ground, and his gesture left me feeling irrationally cared for. I thought of an incident, years ago, when my father and I lived in the suburbs of

Boston, before I left for Princeton. My father told me that if a man didn't open the car door for me when he brought me home after a date, I should just tap on the horn and he, my father, would come right out of the house and escort me inside. I smiled at the memory. *Oh, Dad.*

Max reached down and raised the lever so the passenger seat lay all the way back. When I got in and leaned back, I was supine.

'You look exhausted,' Max said as I got settled. 'Just rest on the drive over.'

'I was going to offer to drive,' I said. 'You look tired, too.'

'I'm fine. Go ahead and shut your eyes.'

I started to protest out of a long-standing habit of pretending I was completely self-reliant, but stopped when I realized I was in Max's capable hands. Instead of arguing, I said, 'Okay, Doctor.' After a pause, I added, 'Thank you, Max, for coming out. Tomorrow's going to be a bear. It'll be easier for me to get through the day tomorrow knowing that we've looked for the Renoir tonight.'

'You're welcome. Rest, now.'

I heard nothing but the comforting hum of the engine until there was a small clicking sound. Opening my eyes, I saw Max ease the car on to I-95 south as he entered numbers into his cell phone. He was calling Alverez. I closed my eyes again, but stayed alert.

'Josie thought she heard something in the warehouse. We looked around, but didn't see anything out of the way.' Max said. 'Okay ... uh-huh ... okay, I'll tell her.... We should be there in about ten minutes.'

The car was warm. I felt oddly removed from responsibility, disassociated, as if I were floating on a cloud. I was aware of utter fatigue, Max's words, the even drone of the motor, and nothing else.

'Josie?' he asked quietly, maybe thinking I'd drifted off to sleep.

'Yeah?'

'Chief Alverez is going to have some technicians come over tomorrow and look around the place.'

'There's no need,' I protested.

'Stop being so damn polite.'

I smiled, eyes still shut. 'Okay.'

After a while, I sat up. Our headlights cut through the thickening fog. As we drove toward the ocean, I became increasingly somber. The frightening reality of tonight's events was sinking in. Alverez's saying he would send a technician obviously meant that he thought it was possible that someone had entered my domain.

'Max?' I asked.

'Yeah?'

'Do you have any idea about what's going on?'

'With what?'

'With everything? This whole situation?'

'No. Do you?'

'None. I'm completely mystified. I hate the feeling of not understanding what's going on.'

'Just for the sake of argument, forget about Mr Grant's murder. Assuming the two events are unrelated … can you think of any reason why someone was in your place tonight?' Max asked.

I considered for a moment. Why would someone have entered my building? Had the person known I was there?

'Maybe it's a coincidence,' I said, trying to think of alternatives. 'You know, it could be just a garden-variety attempted robbery.'

'Maybe,' he responded, sounding unconvinced. He cleared his throat. 'Hard to think so. Be a pretty spectacular coincidence.'

'Yeah,' I agreed. 'Especially if we learn that nothing was taken.'

'So what other reason could there be for someone to break in?' Max asked.

'Maybe whoever it was wanted to prevent the sale of some item,' I mused. 'But if that's the case, why not just tell me? It happens fairly often.'

'Really?'

'Sure. Just last week a woman walked into the office and asked me to sell her a sterling-silver tea set that was scheduled for sale at auction. Turns out that it had been her great-grandmother's and had ended up in a cousin's used furniture store, of all places. When the store went out of business, the mortgage holder sent everything to me to be sold, including the tea set.'

'What happened?'

I shrugged. 'I sold it to her.'

'How'd you price it?'

'We negotiated. I gave her the range I expected it to sell for at auction and she made me a lowball offer. I didn't hold her up. We worked it out.'

'Do you think that's possible?'

'I don't have any way of knowing. But I shouldn't think so. I mean, the best stuff I have in-house is from the Wilson estate. There's no family that I'm aware of who might want a certain item. The auction was ordered by Mrs Wilson's executor. She left everything to some charity, I forget which, and obviously they just want the proceeds.'

'Yeah. It doesn't sound likely that's the reason, does it? Okay, then, if it's not a robbery or someone after a specific item, what could it be?'

'I have no idea,' I said, sounding frustrated.

'Take heart. Maybe Alverez will come up with something when he checks it out tomorrow.'

Max signaled and turned left on to Tunney Road. I shook my head, trying to clear my mind of dark thoughts that seemed to grow as time passed. It didn't work. As we pulled up behind Alverez's vehicle, I felt weary, angry, fearful, and alone.

We were in a dirt alley at the rear of the property. Standing beside Max's car, I listened to the ocean, the sound of the waves unhurried and close. High tide on a quiet night. Despite the fog, there'd be no storm.

'Hey,' I greeted Alverez. He looked relaxed in jeans and a blue sweater.

'Hey,' he answered. 'You okay?'

I shrugged. 'A little spooked.'

He nodded. 'I'll meet you at the warehouse first thing in the morning and we'll take a look at things.'

I nodded. 'Thanks.'

We pushed through a white picket gate framed into the hedge, and entered the grounds. I looked at the weathered clapboard house and counted four chimneys. Off to the right I saw parts of the wraparound porch. Alverez led the way down the winding, cracked concrete path lined on either side by thick, six-foot-tall lilac bushes not yet in bud. In May, the white and lilac blooms would hang low and heavy on the gnarled branches, giving off the aroma of old money.

Max and I stood off to the side of the freshly painted red door as Alverez used the silver-white moonlight to sort through a fat ring of keys. He held his selection like a knife and sliced through both yellow police tape that crisscrossed the entryway and an official-looking paper pasted across the doorjamb.

Opening the door, he reached in and flipped a switch. The overhead bulb was of low wattage and cast a shadowy dim light. Stepping into the house, we were in a kind of mud room. I felt a stab of sadness. There was an unpleasant, unlived-in feel to the place as if someone had recently died. Which was true.

I shivered.

With Alverez in front, we walked into an old-fashioned pantry, and through a swinging door into the kitchen. I followed him, and Max brought up the rear. As we tramped past the oversized sink, I noted the knife block. There was an empty slot where the knife I'd used to cut the Bundt cake had been.

I looked away.

'It's in the study, right, Josie?' Alverez asked.

'Yeah. Next to the living room.'

We made our way through the vacant house to the wood-panelled room. The shelves were lined with leather-bound books. I hadn't catalogued them individually, but I'd been unable to resist looking at some, including a book on witchcraft annotated by Dr Samuel Johnson.

I passed by a dark green club chair and stood in front of the desk. Just as I recalled, it had a wide kneehole opening, large enough for a big man to sit comfortably. Seeking out the hidden cabinet was tricky. Max and Alverez switched on all of the lamps. There were two on the desk and four on nearby tables. Still, the room was dim.

'Here,' Alverez offered, handing me an oversized flashlight he'd taken from the back of his SUV.

'I think I'm okay,' I said.

Sitting on the floor, peering into corners, I used the mini-flashlight that always hung on my belt when I was working, and aimed the beam into the back crevices.

Finding the latch was easy, once I looked. A small, raised flower, carved out of wood and attached on the left side easily disguised a device used to open the door. My heart started pumping, adrenaline coursed through my veins, and I felt a burst of energy.

'I think I've got it,' I said, my excitement palpable.

Both men leaned over and watched as I worked, although in the shadowy darkness, it was unlikely they could see anything much.

I pulled on the rosette frieze. Nothing. I pushed it. No luck. Finally, I twisted it gently to the left as I repeated the rhyme my father had used to teach me about valves when I was a child. *Righty tighty, lefty loosey.* I felt the back panel nudge forward and slide like a wheeled vehicle on an oiled surface into a perfectly aligned slot. *Okay,* I said to myself, *here we go.*

'Okay,' I said aloud. 'Are you ready?'

'Go,' said Alverez.

I took a deep breath, and used the flashlight to examine the entire inside area. Nothing. Empty. There was nothing there.

Overwrought, I started to cry. I'd been so sure we'd find the Renoir. I gulped and forced myself to quash my emotional meltdown. 'Nothing,' I managed to say, embarrassed by my tears. My voice cracked as I spoke.

'Are you sure?' Alverez asked matter-of-factly.

I looked again. It was utterly empty. *Could there be another hidden nook,*

I wondered? I leaned back on my heels and thought about it. I'd never heard about a nook within a nook. But that didn't mean it couldn't exist. I reached forward and tapped and used my light to examine the panels inside the cabinet. No luck.

Standing, I said, 'It's unlikely there'd be anything like that in the desk.' I swept my hand left and right, indicating I was referring to the entire room. 'Look at this place. A secret area, if there is one, could be anywhere. Behind that panel,' I said, pointing to the back wall. 'Or in a drawer of the desk. Or anywhere. All we know so far is that the Renoir isn't in that cabinet.'

We'd only been inside ten minutes. That's all it took to dash a world of hope.

chapter six

We stood in the foggy night air in the alley beside the Grant house. It was bone-chillingly damp, more like November than March.

'I'll take Josie to her car, so you can head home right away,' Alverez said.

'Are you sure?' Max asked.

'Not a problem,' Alverez answered.

'Don't be discouraged,' Max said to me, looking at me through his rolled-down driver-side window as he got ready to leave.

'I'm okay,' I lied.

'Tomorrow's another day, Josie.'

'I know.' I smiled to show good spirit, and oddly, doing so helped lighten my mood a bit. 'I'm okay. Really.'

'Thanks for seeing to Josie, Ty,' Max called to Alverez as he drove away.

'Ty?' I questioned.

'Yeah,' Alverez answered. 'That's my name.'

I wondered if his name was Tyrone. I glanced at him. He didn't look like a Tyrone. We stood silently until Max's taillights disappeared around a bend. Once the car was out of sight, he turned and I felt his eyes on me, but my attention was focused on the step I'd have to climb in order to gain access to his SUV.

'This is a big step,' I remarked.

'What is?' he asked, thinking, I gathered from his tone, that I was referring to some proposed action, though he wasn't sure which one.

'This one,' I said, nodding toward it. 'To get in to the, what do I call it? A car?'

'You could call it a car. It'd be better to call it a vehicle.'

'The step to get into your *vehicle*,' I said, stressing the word, 'is very high.'

'Nah,' he responded. 'You're just short.'

'I am not. I'm normal sized.'

'How short are you?'

'How short? What a question. I'm not short. I'm five-one.'

He opened the door and I pulled myself up.

When he was seated behind the wheel, he said, 'Feel free to close your eyes if you want.'

'Do I look that beat?'

'Yes.'

'How about you?' I asked.

'How about me what?'

'Are you okay to drive?'

He looked at me sideways. 'What do you mean?'

'I mean, do you need me to stay awake to keep you company?'

'No. I'm fine. What kind of friends do you have, anyway, that you have to stay awake so they'll be okay to drive?'

'I was just being polite,' I answered.

'You don't need to be polite. You should just rest now.'

Exhaustion, when it came, came quickly. I had no memory of drifting off to sleep, and felt groggy when Alverez awakened me by quietly calling my name.

'Wow,' I said. 'I guess I fell asleep.'

'Yeah.'

'Where are we?'

'At your house.'

The rickety house I rented stood to the right. It didn't look like home to me. It looked like the place where I'd slept since moving from New York.

Since I didn't like to come into a dark house, I always left a small lamp lit in my bedroom. I stretched and yawned, and looked up, reassured by the soft golden gleam from my upstairs window.

'Wait ...' I said, sitting up, coming fully awake. 'Where's my car?'

'Right where you left it. I'll come get you in the morning and drive you to work.'

'Oh, no, that's too much to ask. I'm okay. I can drive.'

He smiled a little. 'Except that you were asleep before I hit the highway. I have to go to your place in the morning anyway with a technician to check for prints and see what we can see. I can pick you up en route.'

'Are you sure?'

'Sure I'm sure. I don't live far.'

'Really? Where do you live?'

'Over on Fox Point,' he said, naming a narrow inlet not far away.

'That's close.'

'Yes. So I'll pick you up. When? Seven?'

'Seven is good.'

'Okay, then.'

'Thank you,' I said, but maybe he didn't hear me because he was out of his car, ahem, vehicle, by then, and in a few long strides reached my side.

'Can you hop down? If you want, I'll lift you.'

'I can get down myself,' I told him, half wishing he'd scoop me up. I jumped down with more vigor than I felt, waved good-bye, and walked toward my porch door, the entry I used most frequently.

I wanted to ask him in, but didn't. I told myself not to be stupid. He had no feelings for me, and the feelings I had for him were probably a result of feeling anxious and vulnerable in the presence of a handsome, strong man. *Don't act like a fool*, I chastised myself, reiterating that neither of us had personal feelings for the other. My desire was just a spasm, a pathetic attempt to avoid entering my lonely house alone.

Screw it, I said as I approached the porch, and turned back. He hadn't moved. He stood by the still-open passenger door, the ceiling light illuminating his craggy face and dark hair like a halo.

'Want to come in?' I asked.

'Yes,' he said, and paused. 'But I can't. Not now.'

I nodded.

The next morning, riding in with Alverez, I felt a little awkward, but his conversation focused on the weather and the busy day ahead, and my anxiety dissipated in the face of this matter-of-factness.

When we got there, I said lightly, 'Thanks for the lift.'

'Anytime,' he answered sounding casual or indifferent, I couldn't tell which.

Within a few minutes of arriving, there was so much going on, I was wishing I had magical powers and could be in three places at once.

It wasn't yet eight when I spotted Wes Smith. The *Seacoast Star* reporter who'd cornered me at the Blue Dolphin earlier in the week was trying to interview a temporary worker at the tag-sale site.

'Wes,' I said, smiling as I approached. 'How ya doing?'

'Good,' he said, reaching out to shake my hand.

'Thanks for holding off on writing that article,' I said, thankful that the exposé he'd threatened to write referring to me as 'maybe a suspect' hadn't yet appeared.

He shrugged. 'Still researching, still checking things out.'

'I can see you are. What are you looking into now?'

'I was just asking Yolanda here how your notoriety was affecting business.'

'Notoriety? You flatter me, Wes, you devil. But I gotta ask you to vamoose.'

'Just a couple of questions.'

'Sorry, but we've got to set up.' I turned on my thousand-watt smile, cursing him silently. 'You, my friend, are in the way of business.'

'Are you tossing me out?' he asked, raising his eyebrows, trying to look tough.

My smile firmly in place, I shook my head, and said, 'Sadly, yes. You can leave this way.' I took his elbow and guided him to the wire mesh gate, which had been latched but unlocked since seven-thirty in the morning so staff could get in. I figured that's how he'd entered.

He took it in good spirits, play-shooting me as he left, and said, 'You won this one. Next one's mine.'

I kept smiling but didn't respond, pleased that I had chased him away without offending him. Since I wanted good publicity for my business, I couldn't see how pissing off a reporter would help my cause.

When I got to the auction hall, about nine, I was greeted by a flood of increasingly impatient preview attendees waiting to register and complaints from Gretchen that the laptop wasn't working.

'What's wrong?' I asked.

'It won't let me open the spreadsheet software,' she explained. I restarted the computer, but the problem persisted. 'Is it working on your desktop?'

'Yes,' she answered. 'And I have a backup on CD.'

'Okay, then. We'll deal with it later. It's more important to get people signed in.'

Shutting the laptop down and slipping it under the table, I grabbed a printed copy of the registration list that Gretchen, showing prescient judgment, had produced earlier that morning, and began to help with the process. The doors would open promptly at ten, and it was a courtesy Prescott's was known for that early arrivals got processed before the doors officially opened.

Fourth in line was Martha Troudeaux, the lazy and bitchy researcher who was married to Epps's pet appraiser, Barney. I greeted her politely, but without warmth.

'You're to be congratulated on winning the Wilson estate,' Martha said, sounding patronizing and insincere.

'Thanks, Martha,' I said, finding her name on the list. 'How are you and Barney doing?'

'Good. Barney will be here later. Have you added better lighting to your charming little room?'

Every sentence was an insult, from implying that Barney couldn't be bothered to schedule an early viewing to making my company sound rinky-dink, and she did it with slippery precision. The auction wasn't until tomorrow, so it didn't matter when Barney arrived, but her tone implied that it did. My auction hall wasn't small or poorly lit, but her words suggested otherwise.

Doing what I always did when confronted with difficult situations, I thought of what my father would have done. He once told me that the trick to outwitting sarcastic people was to ignore their tone and deal only with their content. I wondered if that strategy would work with Martha. It was a better tactic than hitting her, which was the only other approach I could think of.

'I hope you'll find it bright enough, Martha. Will you tell me if you don't?' I said, feigning concern. 'And I'm so pleased you find the space charming.' I smiled, a hundred-watter this time, and looked toward the next person in line. 'May I help you?' I asked. Out of the corner of my eye, I observed Martha's lips thinning. I was pleased that she seemed disappointed that she hadn't gotten a rise out of me.

At ten, when we opened the doors and the early birds had been taken care of, I left Gretchen to handle things and thought about what to do next.

I wanted to stay and observe the evil Martha at work, and I wanted to return to the tag sale and make certain that Eric had everything under control. I also wanted to see how Alverez and his team were making out. As I weighed my options, I decided that since observing Martha would only irritate me, and Eric would call for help if he needed it, I would head to the front where Alverez had set up shop.

I found him looking over his notes not far from the stack of crates. A technician wearing khakis, a sweater vest, and latex gloves was leaning over an empty crate, looking for I couldn't imagine what. Earlier, Eric had confirmed that no crates were missing.

'Hey,' I said as I approached. 'Any news?'

'Not yet,' Alverez answered, looking up from his notebook. 'You said the noise came from somewhere near the crates, right?'

'I think so,' I said. 'I'm not sure. Noise reverberates.'

'Yeah. Regardless, it'd be a pretty good place for someone to hide, so we figured we'd start here.'

I went into the front office and checked the voice-mail system, scanned through some mail, bills mostly, and reviewed the list of auction bidders. I hadn't been there more than three or four minutes when the technician called in an excited tone, 'Chief, look at this.'

If Alverez replied, I didn't hear it. I swung out of the chair and was no more than a step behind him as he joined the technician, who stood partially hidden by the stacks of crates, in the far corner of the warehouse.

'There,' the technician said, gesturing toward a crate midway up in the last row. He'd removed the back panel so it stood open to our view. I was able to see a long, white cardboard tube. 'All the other crates were empty,' he added.

'What is it?' Alverez asked.

The technician shrugged. Alverez looked at me. 'Josie? Any ideas?'

I shook my head. 'I've never seen it before.'

'Let's take a look, okay?'

'Sure,' I said, and immediately wondered if I should have agreed to let him look.

Alverez slipped on latex gloves and reached into the crate to extract the tube. I watched as he used a fingertip as a lever on the top plastic cover. It came off easily. He reached inside and pulled, freeing a rolled-up canvas.

The technician moved closer, but I backed away until my shoulders pressed into the concrete wall. Holding the canvas by its edge, Alverez gave it a little shake, and it unfurled smoothly. A vivid and evocative painting of three girls sitting in the sun under a tree playing with a cat was revealed.

'Oh, my God,' I whispered. I stood frozen in disbelief.

The Renoir had been found.

That explained why someone had entered my warehouse. But it raised other questions. Why would someone searching for the multi-million-dollar painting go to the trouble of sneaking into my warehouse and then leave without it? Or, more ominously, had the person entered not to take it away but to leave it behind? Why? I shivered, as much from mounting confusion and fear as from the cold concrete wall behind me.

chapter seven

By the time Max joined me in the Rocky Point police station interrogation room, it was nearly eleven and I'd made a decision. I was going to try to find out for myself what was going on.

'No charges have been filed,' Max said by way of greeting as he pulled out a chair and sat.

'That's good news,' I acknowledged.

'Alverez will be in soon. He's going to ask you questions about the painting. Before he gets here, I need to know the truth. All the truth. Do you have any knowledge of how the painting got into your warehouse?'

'No.'

'Do you have any ideas about why someone would have placed it there?'

'No.'

'Have you ever seen it before, anywhere?'

'No, never.'

'Okay, then.' He stopped, smiled, and reached across the table to pat my hand. 'Josie, you'll be okay. We'll figure this out.'

What a nice guy, I thought. 'Thanks, Max. I sure hope so.' I paused. 'Do you remember how you said we should wait to hire a private detective?'

'Yeah, I remember.'

'Do you think it's time yet?'

'No, not yet. If and when you're charged with something – that would be the time to think about it. But we may not need to even then.'

'You're talking about gathering evidence. I'm talking about figuring out what's going on.'

'I understand your impatience, Josie. But it's a bad idea. It implies that you're worried.'

'So what? What bad outcomes could possibly result if people think

64

I'm worried? Why wouldn't my efforts create the perception that I'm serious about learning the truth?'

Max paused, thinking, I guessed, how best to express concerns that were, to him, self-evident. 'You'll signal fear, and once the world gets a whiff of it, you're done for. You'll look desperate.' He shook his head. 'Let the experts do their work. The police are doing a thorough job.'

I sighed. 'I don't get it, Max. It's as if we, and the police, are a step behind all the time.'

'I know it's hard, Josie, but you need to trust in the system. Everything in its time.'

A gentle rat-a-tat-tat on the door was followed by part of Alverez's face. 'Can I come in?'

'Sure,' Max said, apparently confident that our conversation was over, that he had succeeded in bringing me around to his point of view.

He was wrong. Max might think we needed to stay passive until I was charged with something, but I didn't. I was no longer willing to wait. And I didn't understand why he was. His explanation seemed to me utterly lame. Bad strategy or not, I was going to act.

As Alverez got situated and hooked up his tape recorder, he asked, 'You okay?'

I brushed hair out of my eyes. 'Yeah.'

He nodded and started the recorder, gave the time and place, and read me my rights for the second time. While he recited the words, I looked at him. His face seemed composed of more angles than curves. His eyes were recessed under a forceful brow, his nose was straight, his cheekbones looked sculpted, and his chin was strong and determined looking. Only the pockmarks, scars from long-ago acne, perhaps, were rounded. They weren't deep, and mostly, they were camouflaged by his five o'clock shadow. I bet he was the kind of guy who looked as if he always needed a shave.

When he finished stating the Miranda warning, he slid the written version across the table, and once again, I read it and signed my name, indicating that I understood my rights.

'So tell me what you know about the Renoir,' he said.

'Nothing.'

'You've never seen or heard of it?'

'Only what you know about.'

'Has anyone else talked to you about it?'

'No.'

'So all you know is what I told you?'

'Right. I have never touched it. Period.'

Alverez nodded. 'Any ideas about how it got there?'

I shook my head. 'No clue.'

'Change of subject,' Alverez said. 'Have you had time to look through the warehouse and offices and see if anything is missing?'

'No, I haven't looked everywhere. I haven't had time. I mean, I looked at the auction site, and I'm sure I, or Sasha, who supervised the setup, would have noticed if something was missing. But just looking around won't necessarily help. A lot of my goods are small and grouped in lots.' I shook my head and gave a palms-up gesture, indicating that it was hopeless. 'There's just too much for me to notice it all right now.'

'How do you control inventory?'

'We use a bar-coding inventory-control system. I'll be able to tell you tomorrow if any of the items scheduled to be part of the tag sale are missing.'

'Bar codes?' Alverez asked. 'What are you, Wal-Mart?'

I shook my head a little, and smiled. 'I wish. The software's cheap nowadays, and easy to use.'

'You'll let me know as soon as you verify your inventory. All right?'

'Sure.'

'And take stock of office equipment, computers, and so on.'

'All right.'

'Do you have a safe?'

'Yes.'

'Have you looked?'

'No, not yet.'

'What's in it?'

'Some estate jewelry. I don't sell fine jewelry to the public.'

'None?'

'Some costume pieces. That's it.'

'How come?'

'It's too hard to appraise and too easy to steal.'

'What do you do with the good stuff?'

'I wholesale it to a specialist in New York.'

'How does that work?'

'Aren't you getting a little off on a tangent?' Max asked.

Alverez shrugged. 'Until we know what's going on, it's hard to know what's a tangent and what's a clue.'

'True,' Max said, and waved a hand at me, gesturing that I could answer Alverez's question.

'When I have something special, I call him, and he comes up. Sometimes he calls me and tells me he's going to be in the area.'

'Then he stops by?'

'Right.'

'And?'

'And we go over the pieces and he pays me in cash. Which I declare as income on my tax return.'

'I'm sure you do,' Alverez said, smiling. 'How do you know you can trust him?'

'I've known him for years and years. He's reputable.' I shrugged. 'Also, don't forget that I know where the jewelry I'm selling came from, so I know which pieces are likely to prove valuable. Plus,' I added with a modest half smile, 'while I'm not an expert, I know enough so it wouldn't be all that easy to rook me.'

Alverez nodded. 'When can you let me know if anything is missing from the safe?'

'Later today. When I get back there, I'll look.'

'Another change of subject. What size shoes do you wear?'

'What?' I asked, unsure I'd heard correctly, as Max asked, 'Why?'

Alverez paused, and Max added, 'Come on. You know the drill. Connect it for us.'

Alverez nodded. 'We might have some physical evidence. A partial on a footprint. I want to eliminate Josie as a suspect. So,' he said to me, 'what size?'

'What size are the prints?' Max asked.

Alverez answered without hesitation. 'Women's nine narrow.'

I felt the weight of the world fall off my shoulders. Max leaned toward me and whispered, 'What size do you wear?'

'Five,' I whispered back, smiling.

'This is good news,' he said, and patted my shoulder. 'You can go ahead and answer.'

I sat up and looked at Alverez. 'I wear size five. So I'm in the clear, right?'

'Maybe. Maybe not,' Alverez answered, quelling my hopes. 'It's unclear what we're looking at.'

'What do you mean?' Max asked.

'We know these prints were left by a size-nine narrow shoe. We don't know the size of the foot wearing that shoe.' He shrugged. 'Maybe Josie put her size-five foot into a size-nine shoe.'

I shivered.

'How certain of the size are you?'

Alverez paused, considering, perhaps, how much to reveal. 'We found two partial footprints on the far side of the crates and a lot of others that are just a mishmash and useless. The technicians tell me they extrapolated data to calculate the foot size.'

'Still,' Max insisted, 'it looks like Josie didn't leave those footprints.'

'Probably not, so yes, it looks as if she's out of it, except that we don't yet know what "it" she's maybe out of. And maybe she did leave those footprints. We don't know yet.'

Max started to argue the point, but Alverez stopped him by raising a palm, and said, 'Come on, Max, you know how it goes. As far as I know at this point, those prints could be six months old and unrelated to anything and Josie could still be deep in it.' Turning to me, he asked, 'With further elimination in mind, do you know what size shoes your female employees wear?'

I thought for a moment. 'No, I can't say I do. But nine is a fairly large size, and neither Gretchen nor Sasha is tall.'

'According to the tech guys, that doesn't necessarily correlate. Some big women have small feet and vice versa.'

'Yeah, I guess that makes sense.'

'Do you have a theory as to how someone came to leave footprints?' Max asked.

'Everyone leaves footprints this time of year. It's spring – mud.'

'And it was damp yesterday,' I said, remembering.

'Hard to tell how long they've been there.' Alverez shrugged.

'But you're assuming that it's related?' Max asked.

'We're checking it out,' he answered. To me, he asked, 'Who mops the floor?'

'A cleaning crew. I use an outside firm.'

'Which one?'

'Macon Cleaners.'

He made a note. 'Do you know when they last mopped that section of the warehouse?'

'No, I don't, actually.'

'I'll check,' Alverez said.

'You said you only found partial prints. Are any of them good enough to use as evidence of anything besides shoe size?' Max asked.

'Maybe. We can trace the brand and model of the shoe from the markings and match it exactly through the tread patterns.'

'What kind of shoe is it?' I asked.

Alverez paused again before replying, 'The specifics are pending. But I can tell you it's a running shoe. Do either Gretchen or Sasha wear running shoes?'

'Not that I know of. Sasha wears sensible shoes, tie-ups or loafers, you know the kind. Gretchen wears heels. She's a stylish dresser.'

'And you wear boots.'

'And I wear boots. Heels sometimes. But even when I wear heels, I'm not a stylish dresser.'

Alverez smiled, but didn't speak.

'Any other questions for Josie?' Max asked after a moment.

He tapped his pencil on the notepad. 'No,' he said. 'That's it.'

'Okay, then,' Max said, and pushed back his chair.

'Still no plans to leave town?' he asked me.

'No,' I answered, swallowing. 'I'll be around.'

Standing beside our cars, facing the blue-green ocean, Max surprised me by saying, 'You need to be prepared for a search.'

'What?' I objected, offended.

'They found stolen goods – a Renoir – in your possession. They'll want to find the sneakers that match the tread pattern on the footprints. Pro forma,' Max responded, his calm contrasting with my spurt of indignation.

Ignoring my protest, he asked, 'Do you have anything illegal in your possession? Pornography? A gun? Cocaine? Anything?'

I stopped objecting, and focused. I thought of the gun in my bedside table. My father had taught me to shoot handguns when I was in my early teens, encouraging me to fear the people who misuse weapons, not the weapons themselves. He hadn't been a collector, exactly, but he'd liked guns, and had respected the elegant simplicity of their design. When I was preparing to leave New York, I'd sold all but one of them, keeping only his favorite, a Browning 9-mm. I'd been meaning to get a permit for it since I'd moved, but I hadn't gotten around to it.

'I have a gun. No permit,' I answered.

'That's it?'

'That's it.'

He pulled on his earlobe and turned back to the ocean. 'They'll be searching both your home and your business.'

'What should I do?' I asked.

'It's a funny coincidence. Here you have a gun and I'm thinking about getting one. You know that the legislature is considering allowing people to carry concealed weapons? Well, they are. If they go ahead with it, I'm going to get one for Sally, my wife, to keep in her purse. As you know, I work long hours.'

'Yes, I'm aware of that,' I answered, impressed at his approach, wondering if I was supposed to play a more active role in this charade.

'So, what kind of gun do you have?' he asked.

'A Browning nine-millimeter.'

'Do you like it?'

'Yes. Part of it is that it was my father's. Sentimental attachment, if you will. But it fires straight, and it's comfortable in my hand.'

'Any chance I could borrow it for a look-see?'

'You bet,' I said, not smiling, playing it straight.

'Would you get it now and bring it to my office?'

'Sure.'

I confirmed that I'd drop it off within an hour or so.

'When you report in after checking your safe, call the police station, not Alverez's cell phone, okay?'

'Okay,' I said.

'Don't ask for him. Just leave a message. All right?'

'Sure.'

'And if anything is missing,' Max said, 'call me instead.'

I agreed, and thanked him for everything.

We got in our separate cars and Max waved that I should go first. I drove slowly along the coast. The sun was trying to come out from behind thick clouds, and the ocean glinted gold when it succeeded. Behind me, I saw Max signal and turn off toward the interstate, presumably to return to his office. I stayed on the back roads and got to my house just after one.

It was odd being home during work hours. The sun was brighter here, away from the coast. I ran up the narrow stairs, found the gun, and slipped it into a canvas tote bag. Half an hour later, I watched as Max put the Browning in an envelope, labeled and signed it, sealed it with heavy clear tape, and placed it in his safe.

It was a relief to get back to work. Gretchen was in the office, her red hair glistening in the now-bright sun that slanted through the oversized window near her desk.

After greeting her, I asked, 'Anything going on that I should know about?'

'Nope. Everything's under control.'

'You are so good,' I said, meaning it.

'Thanks, but it's not just me. It's all of us. Any word about the Renoir?'

'Nothing definitive,' I answered. 'I know this is a crazy question, but … what size shoes do you wear?'

'I wear an eight. Why?'

'It's a long story. Another time, okay?'

'Okay,' she said, implying with her tone that she was willing to placate me.

'Where is everyone?' I asked.

'Sasha's at the preview. I just spoke to her and she said it's slowed down some. Eric and the temps are almost done setting up the glass-ware. I think he said art prints would be next.'

I nodded. 'Sounds good. I'm going to run up to my office for a sec, then I'll be around and about. Have you eaten?'

'Yeah. Sasha and I traded off lunch breaks.'

'Order me a pizza, will you? I'm starved.'

'Anything else?'

'Not now. Thanks.'

Upstairs, I dialed the combination of my floor safe and saw that everything was intact. I sat at my desk for a moment to call in to Chief Alverez, as promised. I got Cathy, the big blonde, who noted my message without apparent interest. I could picture her writing on a pink While You Were Out pad.

I opened a bottle of water from the case I kept in my office and leaned back with my eyes closed, my determination to take charge allowing me to relax in spite of the ever-present fear.

'Oh, jeez,' I said, sitting up with a start, realizing that I could begin my independent research right away, 'I never checked.'

As I turned toward my computer, Gretchen called to tell me that the pizza had arrived. Hunger overpowered curiosity, and I headed down-stairs to eat.

Entering the front office, I was so intent on my own thoughts, I was only vaguely aware of Gretchen. It had just occurred to me that previously I'd searched an Interpol site to see if the Renoir had been listed on the official law enforcement site as stolen. But I'd never searched for information about the painting itself. I brought up a browser and entered the painting's title and the artist's name.

'Can I help you with anything?' Gretchen asked.

I considered telling her. Gretchen was plenty loyal, but she was young and social. She told me once, just after she started working for me, that she loved gossip. She laughed when she said it, as if it was a rather charming quality, girlie and cute.

She didn't exaggerate. Gossip was more than a hobby. It was almost an obsession. She spent every lunch hour at her desk, nibbling on a salad, surfing celebrity gossip Web sites, except once a week, when the trashy tabloid newspapers hit the stores.

On that day, she'd dash out to pick up copies and read them, too.

About a year after she started, she pointed to a photograph on the front page of one of the tabloids. A baby, apparently a movie star's newborn, appeared to weigh almost twenty pounds.

'Isn't that awful?' she asked.

I looked at the trick photo. It was awful.

'Yeah,' I agreed. 'How do you think they did it?'

'Oh, you mean the photo? No, no. It's real. The baby's size is a deformity, a rare side effect of a medication his wife took while she was pregnant. Isn't it horrible?'

I looked at her, gauging her level of credulity, and concluded that it was high. She thought the oversized baby was real. If I asked her why no other media mentioned the abnormality, probably she'd whisper that it was a conspiracy funded by the pharmaceutical industry.

I didn't want to get roped in, so I smiled vaguely, and said, 'You never know, do you? I'm off to the Finklesteins'. I should be back by two.' And I left before she could tell me anything else she'd discovered in the gossip columns.

I didn't understand her enthusiasm at all, but knew enough not to judge. My mother had been a closet tabloid reader, lingering at grocery store checkout racks to sneak quick reads. It wasn't something we discussed openly, but my father and I would often exchange knowing looks as we pretended to be occupied in another part of the store to give my mother time to finish a story.

Toward the end, when my mother became bedridden, my father bought a copy of every gossip newspaper, true-confession magazine, and scandal sheet he could get his hands on, and their pictures and stories helped ease my mother's pain.

Still, Gretchen's love of gossip didn't inspire confidence that she knew the value of discretion, so I decided to keep my own counsel. If nothing else, she was young, and discretion generally wasn't a virtue of youth.

'No, I'm fine,' I answered.

'Sure?'

'Thanks. I'm okay.'

'Then I'm going to go see if I can do anything for Eric, all right?'

'Good,' I answered absent-mindedly.

I clicked the Search Now button, and in seconds got eighty-nine hits, mostly art museums, poster shops, and reference sites, like encyclopedias and university art history departments. But one site was unique.

Hardly able to believe my eyes, I clicked on a link to a site claiming to track art stolen by the Nazis before and during World War II.

While I read, I ate two pieces of pizza without tasting either one. According to the Switzerland-based organization whose Web site I was on, *Three Girls and a Cat* was one of seven paintings that had been stripped from the walls of the Brander family home in Salzburg in 1939 in return for a promise of exit visas for the family. According to the meticulously kept Nazi records recovered after the war, the paintings had been stored in a barn pending determination of their final destination. But mysteriously, only one daughter, Helga, then twenty-one, had been granted an exit visa. Apparently, neither the rest of her family, nor the seven paintings, had ever been seen again. Until now.

The phone rang, and I was so intent on what I was reading, I nearly missed the call. 'Prescott's,' I said, 'May I help you?'

'You run tag sales, right?' a stranger asked, wanting driving directions.

Hanging up the phone, I read on. After the war, in 1957, Helga Brander Mason, married and living in London, had petitioned the Austrian government to locate and return the pillaged works. They'd promised to try, but whether they'd done anything more than register her request was anybody's guess. Almost fifty years later, her son, Mortimer Mason, had picked up the search. He was listed as the contact for information regarding the seven missing paintings.

Reeling from my discovery, I stared into space, stunned and disbelieving.

'Things are looking great out there!' Gretchen said as she walked into the office. She looked at me and stopped, tilting her head. 'Are you all right?'

'What?' I asked, distracted, having trouble switching my attention to her.

'Are you okay? You look, I don't know, funny.'

'Yeah. I'm okay,' I answered. I bookmarked the URL and closed the browser. 'How's Eric doing?'

'Fine. He says he doesn't need help.'

I nodded. 'Good.'

'Any calls?' Gretchen asked.

'Just one. A woman wanting directions.'

Gretchen sat at her desk, and soon I heard tapping as she typed something. The phone rang and I heard her answer it.

It was inconceivable to me that Mr Grant had owned a Renoir that had been stolen by the Nazis. Maybe, I thought, the purchase was innocent. Perhaps he hadn't known the painting's sordid history. I shook my head in disbelief. Mr Grant was a sharp businessman, way too savvy to buy a multimillion-dollar painting without first verifying its authenticity. Since he hadn't mentioned the painting when we'd talked about the sale, it was more likely, I thought, that he'd purchased it knowing full well that it was stolen. Or that he'd stolen it himself during or after the war.

I was beyond speechless. I was in shock.

chapter eight

Wiping my hands on one of the small napkins the pizza parlor had included, I thanked Gretchen for ordering the food, and added, 'Hand out the rest to anyone who wants it, okay?'

I knew that I needed to pull myself out of what, increasingly, felt like a quagmire, but I was uncertain how to proceed. I considered calling Mortimer Mason, the alleged lawful owner of the Renoir, but I thought better of that idea almost immediately. Since his painting was safe, and I didn't know what to say to him, or even what questions I should ask, and since I had no clue what I should say in response to whatever he might ask me, I decided to delay making the call. Maybe, instead of calling, I thought with an unexpected thrill of excitement, I'd go to London and knock on his door.

I started toward the tag sale grounds, but stopped as I approached the stacks of crates that were still segregated from the main area of the warehouse by waist-high, crisscrossed lines of yellow police tape. Seeing the tape reminded me that prudence is an important aspect of bravery. Since I didn't know what was going on, it occurred to me that I ought to keep my research private.

I reentered the office, and blocking the monitor from Gretchen's watchful eyes, I deleted the Web site URL I'd just added to my 'favorite' listing. I also deleted all temporary Internet files for good measure. I hoped that the police wouldn't impound the computer, since I suspected that an expert could easily track my Internet movements despite my attempts at subterfuge, but it was the best I could do, and I hoped that it would outwit a less experienced spy.

At the tag sale venue, I surveyed the rows of six-foot tables that stretched for just shy of a hundred and fifty feet. Every ten feet, a shorter table jutted out, forming a sea of U-shaped booths.

The weekly tag sales were my bread and butter, and it pleased me to see that the booths were well stocked. Since most items were relatively inexpensive, profitability depended on volume. I'd modified my father's often-repeated admonition to buy cheap and sell high – I bought cheap and sold just a little higher. Tag sales were close to the bottom of the antiques-business food chain, and it was important to remember that fact when setting prices. About a month ago, I'd witnessed a middle-aged woman showing off a Sandwich glass salt cellar she'd just purchased for $21. She'd whispered to her friend, 'I can't believe the deal I just got! There must have been a mistake in the pricing.' With that one sale, a loyal customer was born.

About halfway down the back row I saw Paula Turner, a regular part-timer, carefully sorting boxes of art prints. Paula, a sophomore at the University of New Hampshire, had worked for me for two years on the tag sales. She was wearing low-cut jeans and a cropped white T-shirt that read There Are No Devils Left in Hell … They're All in Rwanda. She was a serious young woman, earnest and hardworking. She wore no makeup; her ash blond hair hung straight to her shoulders; and she had surprisingly small feet. No way they were size nine narrow.

'Hey, Paula,' I said as I approached the table where she was working.

'Hey, Josie,' she said.

'How's it going?'

'Pretty well.'

'Have you seen Eric around?'

'Yeah,' Paula said. She turned toward the parking lot. 'There he is,' she said, pointing.

Spotting him standing just outside the wire mesh gate, smoking a cigarette, chatting to Wes Smith, I felt a flutter of anxiety. I was beginning to feel stalked.

'See you, Paula,' I said. I turned and walked at what I hoped appeared to be a casual pace.

'Hey, Eric,' I said as I approached. 'Hey, Wes,' I added with a fake smile, 'long time no see. Whatcha doing?'

'Eric and I were just getting acquainted,' he said.

'You got a sec, Eric?' I asked.

'Sure.' He stamped out his cigarette and picked up the extinguished butt, as promised. He could smoke on my property, I'd agreed, but only outside, and only if no trace remained.

We walked by two young women I didn't recognize who were discussing how to position Chinese vases on a table. New temp workers.

'What did Wes want?' I asked without preamble.

He tossed his extinguished butt into a box half filled with trash. 'I don't know. He'd just introduced himself when you got there.'

I nodded. 'I can't tell you not to talk to him, or any reporter, for that matter. Do what you want. But I would ask that if you do talk to them, tell them the truth and tell me what you told them. Okay?'

'Sure. But I don't want to talk to that guy – or any reporter.'

'Well, don't, then.'

'It's hard,' he said, seeming embarrassed. 'I've seen them work. They keep asking things.'

His question made me realize how young he was, and how inexperienced. I nodded, and said, 'Yeah. Persistence is part of a reporter's job description. Say "No comment." Just repeat it over and over. Eventually they'll go away. You don't owe them cooperation.'

'Okay,' he said. 'I guess I can do that.'

'And if you want, you can always tell them they need to talk to me.'

'Yeah, that's good.'

'So how's it going?' I asked, gesturing widely toward the entire area.

'Good. We still have a lot to do.'

'Okay. I'll let you get back to it. If you want a break, there's some pizza in Gretchen's office.'

'In a little while, I might just.' I watched him head toward Paula.

Wes was still standing by the gate talking on his cell phone. There was a chance he could help, if he would, and if I could trust him. I stood and thought for a moment, looking for flaws in my thinking. *Hell*, I concluded, *why not?* I walked back and joined him at the fence.

He looked up as I approached, and smiled, pocketing his phone.

'I knew you'd see the light. Are you ready to talk?' he asked.

'May I ask you something?' I responded, all business.

'Sure. Shoot.'

'What does "off the record" mean?'

'Why?'

I grinned. 'Answering a question with a question, huh?'

He laughed, and said, 'Mea culpa. "Off the record" means I don't quote you and don't act on what you tell me until you tell me – if you ever do – that something is *on* the record. Why do you ask?'

'Are we off the record?'

He tilted his head to look into my eyes, squinting a little in the sun. It felt good to stand in the bright light. It was too early in the season for the sun to produce actual heat, but it created the illusion of warmth.

'Okay. I'll bite,' he said. 'Off the record.'

'I don't know how to investigate something and I'm betting that you do. If you agree to help me – off the record – I'll promise you an exclusive interview about the entire Grant situation after it's all cleared up.'

'From what I hear, it'll be cleared up with your arrest.'

I shook my head and paused, trying to judge if he was baiting me. I couldn't tell, so I decided to play it straight. 'No. I didn't do it. But regardless, I'll keep my word. An exclusive.'

'Who decides when it's all cleared up?'

'We do. I'm not trying to split hairs. We'll know when it's cleared up.'

He thought about it for a long minute, his eyes fixed on mine. 'What do you want to research?'

'Off the record?'

'You don't have to keep asking. Everything we're discussing is off the record until and unless you tell me otherwise, or unless I ask if something can be back on the record and you agree. Okay?'

'Promise?'

He look up, casting his eyes heavenward. 'Yes. Jeez. What are you on to? Did Grant steal the Hope diamond?'

'Okay, then,' I said, ignoring his question, which, if he only knew, might be a whole lot closer to the truth than he'd believe possible. 'Mr and Mrs Grant. I need to know everything about them. Where they were born. How they met. Schooling. Friends. Children. Everything. Starting way back when and continuing to now.'

'Why?'

'I don't have time to explain now. I will later. There's more.'

'Go ahead.'

'Can you access phone records?'

'Whose?'

'Mr Grant's.'

He made a whistlelike noise. 'Maybe you'd better fill me in now after all.'

'Later. Can you? Do you have a contact who can get us the records?'

'Local or long distance?'

'Both.'

He didn't answer but stayed still, looking at me, gauging I don't know what.

'Can you do it?' I prodded.

'Maybe. I'll try.'

I smiled, relieved. 'That's great. When will you have the information?'

'Hell, I don't even know that I can get it at all, let alone when.'

'Let me know as soon as you have a sense of when you'll get it,' I told him, ignoring the 'if ' in his sentence.

'Josie,' Eric called from the far doorway.

I turned and shielded my eyes from the sun. 'Yeah?' I shouted.

'Gretchen needs you in the office.'

'Tell her I'm coming,' I answered. I pointed to Wes, and repeated, 'Call me.'

Gretchen stood with her arms crossed and her lips tightly sealed, a picture of righteous outrage. 'Look at this,' she said, handing me a blue-covered folder. I nodded a greeting to Alverez, leaning against the front door, unsmiling.

I opened the papers, and started to read. The documents used legalese to tell me that a judge had authorized a search for stolen goods.

'Call Max for me, will you?' I asked her.

She marched to her desk to make the call, and I turned to Alverez, and asked, 'How would you like to proceed?'

'Do you have an inventory listing?'

'Yes,' I answered, 'mostly. It's not a hundred percent accurate.' I shrugged. 'We do our best.' I turned to Gretchen, and added, 'When you're done calling Max, please print out all of the inventory listings for Chief Alverez.'

'We'll need to look throughout the facility as well,' he said.

'Help yourself,' I responded, hating everything about the situation. 'We have an auction preview going on, so if you can try to stay out of the way of our doing business, I'd appreciate it.'

'We'll try,' he answered, and turned to confer with the three police officers who stood nearby.

Gretchen handed me the phone and began punching keys at her computer.

Max said, 'Are you okay?'

'Yes.'

'Does the warrant read home and business?'

I opened the folded document and reread the neatly typed words. 'Yes. And vehicle.'

'I'll talk to Alverez in a minute and remind him to make certain they leave everything as they found it. And I'll ask him if he wants you to accompany them to your house. Okay?'

I swallowed. 'Okay.'

In addition to Alverez and the three police officers in the warehouse, two more were standing by my car and two were seated in a marked cruiser nearby. Alverez and his team were working inside under

Gretchen's disapproving eyes as I left to join the two officers in the patrol car. I sat in the back, and as we pulled out of the parking lot, I looked over my shoulder and saw that one of the two standing near my car had already popped the trunk.

The two police officers, a middle-aged black man with a potbelly and thinning hair at the wheel, and a tall, thin redhead in her thirties sitting beside him, spoke so softly that I couldn't make out their words.

'That's it,' I called as we approached my house. He pulled in to the gravel driveway.

Never having observed an official search before, I watched with a kind of grim curiosity. They opened closets, drawers, and chests and moved things around a little bit, looking for I don't know what, maybe a tube containing another stolen painting. They examined the bottom of furniture, poked a long, narrow, needlelike tool into cushions, and lifted mattresses to see what was underneath.

'Any garage?' the woman asked me.

'No,' I answered.

'Toolshed? Anything else?'

I shook my head. I accompanied them outside and watched as they walked the grounds. Back inside, they surveyed the empty basement, poked their heads into the tiny attic, and then they were done.

They dropped me at the warehouse side entrance. I saw Eric talking to Paula, and the other two temps were setting up Plexiglas display shelving for the dolls and dollhouse section. Circling the fencing, I entered through the front door.

'Are the police still here?' I asked Gretchen.

'Yes,' she said, her contempt apparent.

'They're just doing their jobs,' I remarked, and shrugged.

'I don't care. I just hate it.'

Funny, I thought, since I was the chief suspect, and it was my property they were searching, that I was able to remain more philosophical about the process than Gretchen. On some level, she had no vested interest in the outcome. I wondered if her concern was personal, based on affection, because she liked me, or practical, based on the rational fear that if I were arrested, she'd be out of a job. Or maybe there was a simpler explanation: since Max had alerted me to the likelihood of a search, I'd had time to get used to the idea.

She handed me a note. Someone named Dana Cabot and her daughter, Miranda, were at the Sheraton in Portsmouth awaiting my return call. Gretchen had written the phone number and their room number.

'Who are they?' I asked.

She looked over her shoulder. We were alone. Still, she lowered her voice. 'Mr Grant's daughter and granddaughter.'

'You're kidding!' I exclaimed. 'What do they want?'

'I don't know. Mrs Cabot just said she wanted to talk to you. She said it was urgent.'

I stared at the paper, incredulous. Mr Grant's lawyer, Epps, had told her I was a shark. *What*, I wondered, with a shiver of anxiety, *could she possibly want with me?*

chapter nine

'Do me a favor, would you?' I handed Gretchen the note. 'Call them now and ask if I can call them after the preview – about nine-thirty tonight. Okay?'

Gretchen nodded and took the paper.

'Anything else?' I asked.

'Nope. Sasha said everything's AOK at the preview.'

I nodded. 'Okay, then. I'll be around.' I went into the warehouse and paused. Heading toward a rustling noise, I found Alverez standing with a uniformed officer. Following the instructions Max gave me on the phone, I kept away from them as they worked. Alverez selected an item from the shelf and read the numbers above the bar code aloud as the other man compared them to what was printed on the inventory.

I felt pulsating anxiety as I watched because even though I knew that I possessed no stolen goods, I was aware that whoever had snuck the Renoir into the crate might have left something else behind as well.

Alverez saw me and said something to the officer, who nodded in response, and turned away, toward the back of the warehouse. Alverez walked toward me.

'How you doing?' he asked as he approached.

'Okay.' I shrugged, and after a pause, added, 'It's pretty much a nightmare.'

He nodded. 'We're making good time. We'll be gone soon.'

'I didn't mean that,' I said. 'It's not just the search.'

'I know.'

I looked at him and felt a fresh wave of attraction. It was more than his appearance, although I was drawn to his weathered good looks. For some unknown reason, I felt that I could trust him, that maybe we could be friends.

'May I ask you something?'

'Sure,' he said.

'Did you check the schedule with Macon Cleaners?'

'Yes, I did.'

'And?'

'And they mopped the area by the crates two days before we found the Renoir, on schedule.'

'So the footprint could have been left anytime during those two days?'

'Right.'

'So, is it a clue?'

'I don't know.'

I nodded. 'Did you look for the wall safe?' I asked.

'Yes. And we've examined the bottoms of furniture, fake cushions, hidden holes in the floor, et cetera. Nothing.'

I shook my head, allowing mystification to show. 'Have you met Mr Grant's daughter?'

'Why do you ask?'

'No reason. Just curious,' I said, circumspect in the face of Max's warning about not volunteering information.

'Yes,' he said, 'I have.'

'What's she like?'

'What are you up to, Josie? Are you going to try and get work on the estate?'

I shrugged. 'I don't know. Do you think there's a chance?' Whatever Mrs Cabot wanted, I doubted it was to offer me work.

'You know that Epps recommended Barney?'

'Yeah. It'd be a long shot, I know.'

'Probably. There is something I can tell you. I don't know whether it'll help you get the job or not.'

I looked at him, brushed hair out of my eyes, and smiled. 'What's that?'

'She's thinking of bringing in a New York firm.'

'Makes sense, actually.'

'Because of the value of the items?'

I nodded. 'That, but not really. If the family wants to sell everything outright, they just have to contract with an outfit that's got access to that kind of cash. What I was thinking about is the uniqueness of some of the pieces. A lot of research will be required to optimize value.'

'Well, good luck with it.'

I smiled again. 'Thanks.' After a short pause, I asked, 'So what did Mrs Cabot know about the Renoir?'

He looked at me for several seconds, expressionless, then said, 'We're still investigating.'

'Josie?' Gretchen called from a distance.

'Back here!' I answered, and stepped into the main corridor so she could see me easily.

Gretchen glared at Alverez with icy disdain as she approached, and handed me a note reading 'You have an appointment to meet the Cabots in the hotel coffee shop at 9:30.'

'Excuse us, please,' I said to Alverez. 'Business beckons.'

He nodded and headed toward the other officer. I watched him walk, the confident stride of a man with a purpose. When he was several paces away, I turned to Gretchen.

'Meet them? I thought you were going to set up a phone call,' I asked in a low tone, surprised.

'They said they wanted to discuss Mr Grant's estate,' she whispered. 'I was sure you'd want to meet them.'

I nodded agreement. 'Good job.'

Mr Grant's family wanted to see me to discuss his estate? It hardly seemed possible, but maybe I still had a chance of closing the deal. Plus, perhaps I could work in a question or two about the Grant family's background.

When I reached the auction preview site, Barney Troudeaux was standing in front of a pair of George II mahogany drop-leaf tables with cabriole legs and ball-and-claw feet, his hands latched behind his back, looking like a military man at rest. He was big and broad, about fifty, with easy manners and a quick smile. Yet his smile didn't always seem to reach his eyes, and his kindness sometimes seemed calculated, not warm. I forced a grin as I approached him, knowing that the appearance of unconcern was an important business tool. My father always said that the more difficult the negotiation, the more important it was never to let them see you sweat.

'Barney,' I said. 'I'm glad you were able to get here.'

'Hi, Josie,' he said, offering his hand. 'I wouldn't have missed it. You've done a wonderful job with the display.'

'Thanks.'

'You date these tables from when, 1750?'

'Just about. Probably 1745.'

He nodded. 'They're beauties.'

'Yeah.'

'What do you expect they'll go for?'

I smiled. 'A lot, I hope.'

He smiled appreciatively, then remarked, 'Terrible situation about Mr Grant, isn't it?'

'Awful,' I agreed.

'I understand you've been talking to the police,' he said compassionately.

'Yeah,' I acknowledged, on guard.

Over the years, I'd found interacting with Barney consistently confusing, and this time, trying to understand his relationship with Mr Grant, and his interest in me, was proving to be no exception. He was always charming, apparently supportive, and seemingly sincere. Yet sometimes there seemed to be a disconnect between what he said and what he did. I worked at resisting the lure of his gentle and pleasing personality.

'How was it?' he asked.

I shrugged. 'Okay, I guess. I couldn't tell them much. How about you?'

'How about me, what?'

'Haven't you met with the police about Mr Grant?'

'Oh, that. Yes, briefly.' He shook his head. 'It's just so sad.'

'What were you doing for him?' I asked, feigning innocence.

'Mr Grant? We were discussing estate planning.'

'Really?' I asked, trying to sound both dumb and naïve. 'What kind?'

'Not clear. We hadn't gotten far in our conversation. His lawyer, Britt Epps, mentioned that Grant wanted to sell a couple of things. Do you know Britt?'

'We've met.'

'Great guy.'

'Do you know what Mr Grant wanted to sell?'

'Not for sure. Martha talked to him more than me.'

'Mr Grant? Or Epps?'

'Mr Grant. She just had a fondness for that old man. They enjoyed a great rapport.' He shook his head and looked sad.

The thought of Mr Grant being sweet to Martha Troudeaux made me crazy with jealousy. My fingers curled like claws. I silently chastised myself, repeating that it was completely stupid to feel jealous about a dead man's business dealings with a rival, no matter how much I disliked her. I looked at Barney as he smiled kindly at me. I wished I had the gift of mind-reading. *What*, I wondered, *did he really want? Was he trying to pick my brain? About what?*

Another mystery was what he saw in Martha. Their relationship bewildered me. How could Barney stand her? She was abrasive, aggressive, and greedy. The only answer I'd ever come up with was that they, as a team, had her play that role on purpose. Her job was to take the heat for him. Whenever a situation got tricky, like competing for business, or vying for the best booth position at a major antiques fair, Barney became unavailable, and I'd been forced to deal with Martha. Barney maintained his friendly, open manner, and she was the bad guy, his bastard, my father would have said. *Every leader has a bastard*, he'd told me. *In any negotiation, figure out who's in that role right away, greet them with a smile and a hearty handshake, and watch your back.*

I realized that Barney was waiting for a response about Martha's and Mr Grant's rapport. 'He sure was sweet,' I said finally.

'Yes. Horrific how he died.'

I shook my head. 'Terrible, just terrible.' I sighed, pretending to be upset, so Barney wouldn't think my question odd. 'When did you see him last?'

'Not for a few days before he died.'

'And Martha?'

'The same. How about you? I hear you saw him the morning he died.'

Who'd spread that diabolical rumor? 'No. I had an appointment, but I guess he was already dead by the time I got there.' I shivered.

'Yeah.'

We stood without speaking for a moment. I didn't know what to say. Finally, I asked, in as light a tone as I could muster, 'So, are you thinking of bidding on the tables?'

He smiled and winked. 'I might just.'

I knew, and he knew I knew, that it was extremely unlikely he'd bid on anything. Our research, unlike Martha's, was accurate and complete, so he couldn't expect bargains, and he knew it.

He walked down the aisle and paused at a white jade marriage bowl, dating from the mid-1700s.

'This is a special piece,' he said.

'Best of show,' I agreed.

He leaned over to better examine the underside. All of it was visible because it was positioned at an angle in a raised Plexiglas display case. Intricately carved with chrysanthemums, asters, and bamboo, it was a nearly flawless example of craftsmanship from the reign of Emperor Qianlong.

If the truth be known, I didn't expect much from the drop-leaf tables, maybe $750 each, if I got lucky. But the bowl was unique and might fetch as much as $50,000. And the Wilson executor had entrusted it to me. I felt a rush of pride.

At nine that night, Sasha and I said good-bye to the last preview customers, and locked the doors. The police had finished their search, and I'd felt vindicated when Alverez informed me that they were taking nothing away from my business, my home, or my car. Max had agreed, when I told him, that it was good news.

Sasha sank into a chair near the registration table and kicked off her loafers, wiggling her toes. She rubbed her eyes and sighed from exhaustion. She'd been at work for more than twelve hours.

I looked at her loafers. They looked to be about the right size. 'Do you wear size nine shoes?' I asked.

'Me?'

'Yeah.'

'Why?'

'Just curious,' I said.

She shrugged. 'It depends on the shoe. Eight and a half or nine, usually.'

'Narrow?'

'Yes.'

Her feet might be the right size, but if those footprints were hers, it had to be that she'd walked by in all innocence. No way could I believe that Sasha was involved in a crime. Sasha was a woman of scholarly ambition and, seemingly, little passion. She didn't seem to care about money, politics, religion, or even people. All she seemed to care about was art. That thought gave me pause. She'd care about a Renoir, all right.

'What's your sense of the preview crowd?' I asked, pushing away the uncomfortable thought.

'There seemed to be a lot of genuine interest,' she said, and yawned. 'But there were some people who came just because they were curious, about, you know, the Grant situation.'

'Like who?'

'A woman named Bertie,' Sasha reported. 'From the *New York Monthly*.'

'The *New York Monthly*? Why would they send a reporter?' I wondered.

'She said they're doing a piece on scandals in the world of antiques.'

'Oh, jeez. Just what I need. What did you tell her?'

'Nothing. I had to let her in since she was a registered bidder, but I didn't talk to her. I kept pretending I saw someone gesturing to me.'

I smiled. 'That was smart thinking, Sasha.'

'I couldn't figure out how else to get away from her,' she said, shrugging.

I shook my head sympathetically. 'Well, it's over now. You heading home?'

'Yeah. To a hot bath and bed.'

'Oh, that sounds delicious,' I agreed, my word choice reminding me that I'd had nothing to eat since the pizza hours earlier. 'Let's call it a night.'

We walked together to the front office. As I set the alarm, I watched Sasha drive off in her small car, and I was alone.

Unexpectedly, I began to cry. I felt awash in melancholy and I knew why. Hearing the *New York Monthly* reporter's name brought back the dreadful memories. After my boss at Frisco's arrest, but before his trial began, I'd confided my role as whistle-blower and confidential police informant to a co-worker.

Two hours later, when I stepped out for lunch, Bertie lay in wait, and even though I said nothing, not even 'No comment,' she was on a local television station within hours delivering an 'exclusive report.' That night, the siege began in earnest. Bertie and a dozen others were my constant companions for the three months of the trial. I never spoke to any of them. Not one word. I kept my head lowered, and never even made eye contact.

I was in the right, yet despite my ethical stance and stubborn refusal to discuss any aspect of the case with reporters, my colleagues treated me with icy disdain. It was as if it were I, and not my boss, who'd done wrong. And because they avoided me, I had no way to counteract their unspoken contempt. It was crippling.

I'd never before been shunned, and I hoped I never would experience anything like it again. No wonder many cultures use it as a punishment for errant behavior; I could see that it would be a potent tool to ensure conformity.

I'd learned a bitter lesson that year. I'd learned that I couldn't trust anyone but my father. And he was dead.

Standing at the door, Sasha long since gone, I realized that my sadness was aggravated by stress, hunger, and fatigue. And my growing anger helped still the tears. I was plenty tired of feeling sad, and so I greeted the anger with relief. I shrugged, trying to relax my shoulder and neck muscles, with no success.

I wondered what the Cabots wanted with me, and why it was so urgent. A glimmer of hope that the business might not be lost heightened my curiosity. Still, to cover myself, I called Max as the car warmed up, and got him at home. He sounded tired, but, as always, pleasant and interested.

'Max,' I said. 'I'm en route to meet Mr Grant's daughter and granddaughter. I figured I ought to let you know.'

'Good. I'm glad you called. What are you meeting them for?'

'I'm not sure. They said they wanted to talk to me about the estate.'

There was a long pause before he asked, matter-of-factly, 'That's a surprise, isn't it?'

'Yeah,' I acknowledged.

'Where are you meeting them?'

'A coffee shop in the Sheraton.'

'How do you feel about it?'

'Okay. Curious, I guess.'

There was another long pause. 'If they ask anything about the murder, don't answer. Say you don't know or can't comment. No matter what.'

'Okay.'

'And call me if you need me, all right?'

'Thanks, Max.'

Max's palpable concern communicated itself to me. As I drove out of the parking lot, I became fearful that they might blame me for Mr Grant's death. Another worry added to the rest.

chapter ten

I nearly fell asleep driving into Portsmouth. I found myself drifting into a kind of stupor as the taillights in front of me rose and fell, gently undulating with the grade of the road. It was hypnotic. I was hungry, tired, stiff, and worried. When I reached the brightly lit hotel parking lot, I sat for a minute, waiting for a second wind. It didn't come.

I found the coffee shop, mostly empty at this hour, and stood near the hostess stand, waiting. A large woman with crimped, silver-blue hair approached me.

'I'm supposed to meet the Cabots,' I told her.

'This way, dearie. They're waiting for you.'

She led me to a table around a corner, past oversized windows and tall palm trees. Two people sat across from each other. One, an attractive woman in her sixties with white wavy hair and an ivory complexion, sipped from a coffee cup. The other, a younger woman of about my age, shook a tall glass of what looked like the dregs of iced tea. I heard the jiggling of the ice as we approached. They sat in stony silence, as if they were strangers.

'Here she is, dearies,' the hostess said as she placed a menu on the table.

'Hello,' I said. 'I'm Josie Prescott.'

Both women looked at me. I suddenly felt conspicuously under-dressed and unkempt. I shouldn't have come straight from a long day at work. My jeans were dirty and stretched out, my plain Jane T-shirt was covered by an oversized flannel shirt, and my engineer boots were scuffed.

'I'm Dana Cabot,' the older woman said politely, without warmth. 'And my daughter, Andi. Miranda.'

'Hi,' I said.

Mrs Cabot said, 'Please, have a seat.'

The younger woman leaned back and stared at me. She looked and acted angry as she shook her glass, swirling the ice. Switching her attention to the hostess, she said, 'I'll take another.' She took a last, long drink and handed over the glass.

'And for you, dearie?' the hostess asked me.

'Give me a minute,' I answered, sitting down, looking from one to the other. They didn't look alike. Dana Cabot looked well coiffed, well dressed, and well fed. Her daughter, Andi Cabot, looked sick.

'Have you eaten?' Mrs Cabot asked.

'No, actually, I haven't. If you wouldn't mind, I'd love to get something.'

'Of course,' she answered.

I looked at the menu and, surreptitiously, at them. Mrs Cabot looked like an affluent matron who hadn't had a lot of worry in her life. Andi was too thin, the kind of thin that comes from a chronic, life-threatening disease, or maybe from doing a lot of drugs over a lot of years. Her eyes were clouded, her skin sallow, and she seemed enveloped in a cloud of resentment. Sitting next to her, I wanted to slide my chair a bit farther away lest I catch whatever ailed her.

'I'm sorry about your father,' I said. 'And your grandfather. I hadn't known him for long, but we'd had many pleasant conversations over the last week or so.'

'Thank you,' Mrs Cabot replied. 'My father had many good qualities.' She cleared her throat. 'You're probably wondering why I asked to meet you.'

'My assistant said you wanted to talk to me about your father's estate.'

'Yes,' she said, with a glance at Andi. 'You saw my father's house?'

'Yes. Everything is very beautiful. Not just the antiques. Everything. The house, the grounds. Everything,' I said.

She nodded. 'It's funny to be in New Hampshire and staying in a hotel. But we couldn't stay at the house. Not after ...' she trailed off.

'I understand,' I said.

The waiter arrived with Andi's drink and coffee to refill Mrs Cabot's cup. He poured a cup for me, too. I ordered a hamburger, medium, and asked for water, no ice. I wanted a martini, but knew that even one would put me to sleep, facedown in my plate.

Andi shifted impatiently in her chair, continuing to look irritated. I wondered if it was annoyance I was perceiving, or contempt. Maybe she took my sloppy appearance as a personal affront, as if I were indicating that she and her mother weren't worth the bother of cleaning up.

'I should have mentioned,' I said, 'that I came straight from work. Please excuse my appearance.'

'No problem. We understand completely, and are just pleased that you were able to come at all,' Mrs Cabot said.

I waited for her to continue, wondering if her polite words would mellow Andi's antipathy. Andi slapped her drink on the table, and opened her eyes wide at her mother. Having caught her attention, Andi wiggled her fingers. *Hurry it up, Mother,* she seemed to be signaling. *Get on with it.*

'Did my father talk to you about selling anything?' Mrs Cabot asked, jumping in.

'Why do you ask?' I was curious about Andi's role in the family. It almost seemed that Mom was following cues from her daughter.

She sipped her coffee, and I noted that she drank it black. 'I need to decide what to do about my father's estate. I'm trying to learn what my father intended.' She shrugged. 'Knowing his plans might help me decide what would be best to do at this point.'

I didn't see the connection. What did Mr Grant's former intention have to do with their current plans? Maybe she was a sentimental sort.

'Are you thinking of selling the contents of the house?' I asked, faking confusion, aware that I was avoiding answering her question. For some reason, it seemed smart to be cagey, but I wasn't sure why I was having that reaction. Maybe Andi's impatience and seeming disdain colored my view. Or perhaps it was Max's warning not to talk about the murder that made me wary. For whatever reason, my gut was telling me that until I knew more about what was going on, I shouldn't reveal too much.

'Perhaps. Did you look at everything?'

'I don't know about everything. I looked at some things.' I flipped a hand. 'If you're interested in selling, I'd be interested in buying, or auctioning, any or all of the goods. The items I saw were very special, and I'm sure you'll realize a large amount of money.'

'If I decide to sell,' Mrs Cabot asked, 'and if I ask you to help, how would the process work?'

I was spared the necessity of providing a quick response when the waiter brought my hamburger and asked if we wanted anything else. I asked for ketchup and he produced it from a pocket in his apron.

'How much do you know about the origin of the antiques?'

'Why?' Mrs Cabot asked.

I wondered if she was being cagey, too. 'It makes research easier,' I answered. True enough, but I had another reason for asking. I was trying to discover how much she knew about her parents' buying habits. From that information I might be able to discover more about the history of the Renoir.

'Not much, I'm afraid. I left home when I married, forty years ago.'

I nodded. Learning anything useful had been a long shot. So much time had passed since the Renoir had been hidden, according to the Web site I'd consulted, in an Austrian barn. Memories fade and witnesses die.

'How much will you give us for the lot?' Andi asked abruptly.

'Andi!' her mother protested.

'Oh, come on, Ma. What's the problem?' To me she added, 'Well? How much?'

'I don't know,' I answered calmly, addressing Mrs Cabot, not her daughter, while spreading ketchup on the bun. 'As you know, your father hadn't actually retained my company's services before he died. What that means is that I didn't do a complete appraisal. If you'd like, I will. Then I can make you an offer, tell you how much you'd be likely to get at auction, or discuss other possibilities, like a consignment sale arrangement.'

'How long would *that* take?' Andi asked, irritated.

'A few days. Not even,' I replied, remembering that I still had the videotape as reference.

'How much do you charge for the appraisal?'

'You probably don't need a written appraisal.' I shrugged. 'For me to get enough information to make you a fair offer, no charge.'

'Thank you. That's very clear,' Mrs Cabot said. 'May I ask you ... do you know my father's lawyer, Mr Epps?'

'Yes,' I said.

'This is a little awkward, but I need to know, well, would you comment.... Let me ask you.... Did you know that Mr Epps was recommending that Mr Troudeaux help my father sell some items?'

I felt pinned by Andi's eyes and turned to look at her. Her antagonism was directed at me like bullets from a rifle, and I found myself getting angry. What on earth, I wondered, did I ever do to her?

'I wouldn't know,' I answered, turning my attention back to Mrs Cabot.

'What do you think of Barney Troudeaux?' Mrs Cabot asked, ignoring her daughter.

I shrugged. 'He's well respected in the industry.'

'Assuming our choice is between you two, why should we use your services instead of his?'

I took a bite and chewed. It tasted knee-weakeningly good. 'I don't know how to answer that without sounding immodest.' I shrugged and smiled. My father once told me that the secret to pitching new business was to avoid adjectives and generalities which only sound like marketing hype, and to stick to the facts. And to keep it short. 'Barney's well respected, but I have on staff researchers whose work will ensure that you get the highest prices. Barney doesn't. As to the rest, well, I'll be glad to give you references.'

I took another bite. I could tell that when I was done eating, I was going to have trouble staying awake.

Andi made a contemptuous clicking noise with her tongue and looked away as if to show that she thought my pitch was completely lame. Usually, I'd want to strike out against her display of rude belligerence. For some reason, though, witnessing her behavior just made me feel sorry for Mrs Cabot.

'The money,' Andi said as if she were talking to a four-year-old. 'If we give you the job, how soon would we get the money from the sale?'

'It depends on the deal we make, whether it's an outright sale, consignment, or an auction.'

'Andi,' her mother said kindly, 'don't let's get ahead of ourselves.'

Andi pushed back her chair. 'Whatever. Let's not make it more complicated than it has to be. We should let them do their appraisals, submit offers, and take the highest bidder. Period.' She stood up and turned to her mother, adding, 'I'll be upstairs when you're done.' She stomped out of the restaurant, her anger poisoning the air.

'Please forgive my daughter. She's never learned patience.'

Either Mrs Cabot was in complete denial, or that was a masterful example of understatement. I wasn't sure how to reply. I looked at her, but her attention was focused on the far distance. She probably didn't even realize that I was watching her. There was a hollow sadness in her voice that I recognized, and deep in her eyes I sensed a vulnerability that echoed within me. My father had died unexpectedly, too, so I thought I understood part, at least, of what she was feeling.

After the initial shock of his death had worn off, a barren loneliness set in, and was with me still. True, in the last several weeks I'd felt flickers of hope that happiness could again be mine, but those moments were brief and transitory. The big difference was that for the first time, I believed that things would get better. Mrs Cabot was still in shock; for her, the bitter aloneness hadn't yet begun.

'It's okay,' I said, finally.

'I don't know what to do,' she said in a whisper.

*

Just after eleven that night, showered and wrapped in my favorite pink chenille robe, I sat on a window seat in my kitchen with my feet tucked under me, sipping, at last, my first martini of the day. The creamy cold gin soothed and calmed me.

Staring across the silver-lit meadow that backed into a thick forest, it occurred to me that I could picture Andi somehow being involved in sneaking the Renoir into my warehouse, and maybe even in her grandfather's death. While it seemed absurd to think that Mrs Cabot would have snuck into my warehouse and hidden behind my crates, I could easily picture Andi skulking about, her face pinched with anger. But why would she have done so? Nothing added up.

Still, her anger seemed beyond reason. Could she really be involved? *No,* I told myself. *Such a thing would be incredible!* Yet even as I silently spoke the word, a picture of her blazing eyes and sneering lips came to mind. Maybe. I shook my head, incredulous at the thought. Maybe it was true.

I realized that if I'd been thinking like a detective, I would have looked at her feet. As it was, I hadn't once noticed either Mrs Cabot's or Andi's shoes, so I had no idea whether their sizes might be nine narrow.

I needed to stop thinking.

'Chicken,' I said aloud, and smiled. 'I'll make Monterey chicken tomorrow night or Sunday.' I liked to cook, and I was good at it. Whenever I want to improve my mood, I cook.

When I was thirteen, just days before my mother's death from lung cancer, she'd made a ceremonial presentation of her recipe box. Her handwritten index cards contained a treasure trove of family favorites, and I'd made them all, adapting the proportions so I could cook for two, and lately, for one.

I'd make Monterey chicken tomorrow or the next day, but tonight my mind wouldn't be silenced. I sipped my drink and thought about Mr Grant's paintings, the Jules Tavernier garden scenes.

It wasn't unheard of for a curator or owner intent on protecting a treasured canvas to arrange for an artist to paint a second image over the first, secure that the priceless original would remain safely disguised. Once the danger had passed, the second layer of paint could be removed. But Tavernier had died in the 1800s, so he couldn't have worked to disguise paintings stolen by the Nazis. Yet there was something about those paintings that seemed out of whack.

I reviewed what I knew about them. They were among the least valuable of Mr Grant's possessions. Yet they were the most valuable of all the artwork I'd seen. The other paintings were inexpensive reproductions, and there weren't many of them. It's odd, I thought, that the Grants would have reproductions in that houseful of treasures. And not many of those. Mostly the walls were decorated with family photographs. There was something else, but whatever it was escaped me.

I sipped my martini and stared out into the silvery night. Seeing the light shimmer on the fluttering tall grasses reminded me of a toast my father coined, meaningless, but pleasing nonetheless: *To silver light in the dark of night*, he'd say, and raise his glass. I mouthed the words, lifted my drink, and was relieved that I didn't cry. *Progress*, I told myself. If I could repeat my father's toast and stay dry eyed, I was definitely making progress.

As I watched the gently shifting shadows caused by the pale moonlight and a light breeze, I realized that, as the crow flies, Alverez was probably less than five miles away. Fox Point Road, where he lived, was on the other side of the meadow, past the stand of birch and maple trees that flanked the forest on the edge of the property, on the other side of a small tributary called Knight Branch.

I wondered if he was sleeping, or if perhaps he was wakeful, looking out of his window, thinking of me. Remembering the magnetism we'd shared, I became tearful, grateful that my ability to respond to a man and feel womanly, which for so long had been attenuated, was intact.

It was close to midnight when I took a last sip of my second martini, finally relaxed enough to sleep. Just as I was swinging my feet to the floor, the phone rang, startling me.

'Hello,' I said, braced for trouble.

'How ya doing? It's Wes. I hope I'm not calling too late.'

'No,' I said. 'I'm awake.' *Wow*, I thought, *Wes does quick work. Could he have answers to my questions already?*

'About what I said, that I'd like to interview you. I wanted to let you know that if you changed your mind, I'll be at the paper tomorrow morning after nine.'

'What are you talking about?'

'You know,' he said, 'the interview.'

'What interview?' I felt as if I'd wandered into a hall of mirrors. Nothing was as it appeared. Had I gone insane – agreeing to an interview with Wes Smith? It wasn't possible.

'Yesterday. You asked that I call you.'

And with those words, I finally understood that Wes was being discreet. He knew I hadn't agreed to an interview – he was being careful, which could only mean that he was assuming that my phone was tapped. Whether it was tapped or not, he was smart to presume that it was, and I was stupid not to have thought of it before.

'Ha, ha, Wes. I told you,' I said, playing along, 'I won't talk to you. Besides which, I have the auction tomorrow – and the tag sale.'

'When do they start?'

'I need to be there by nine.'

'Okay. I'll be at the Portsmouth Diner at seven.'

'Is that the place by the Circle?' I asked, thinking that we weren't doing a very good job of being circumspect, and that anyone listening to our conversation would know we were arranging to meet.

'Yeah, that's the joint.'

'Well, I've told you that I won't talk to you,' I repeated, wanting to be on the record, in case the call was, in fact, being taped, and Max ever needed to defend me against a charge of interfering with an official investigation.

'I understand,' he answered. 'Just in case, write down my cell number.'

I did, told him good night, and hung up.

Wes sounded confident, even excited, and it was contagious. That must mean that he had answers he knew I'd be glad to hear. I couldn't imagine what they were, but I allowed myself to feel optimistic.

I smiled as I climbed the stairs, and I was still smiling as I fell asleep.

chapter eleven

Wes was leaning against an old dark blue Toyota in the parking lot of the Portsmouth Diner when I pulled in just before seven. It was thickly overcast and cold, and he wore a red-and-black checked woolen jacket buttoned to his chin.

I pulled up near the front in response to Wes's signal. I lowered my window and he said, 'Go ahead and park. I'll drive.'

'Where are we going?' I asked.

'You'll see.'

'Wait a sec!' I called as he walked away. From the back, he appeared rounder than he had from the front. If he wasn't careful, he'd be fat before he was thirty. 'What about breakfast?'

'Later.'

I pulled into a space and hurried to his car. Looking in, I spotted crumpled-up coffee cups, candy wrappers, and fast-food bags covering the floor in back, stacks of papers haphazardly placed on the backseat, and a portable CD player wedged between a scuffed, old briefcase and a battered CD storage case. It was a pit.

Reaching across from the driver's side, Wes swept crumbs from the front seat on to the floor. Gingerly, I sat down and latched my seat belt, wrinkling my nose with distaste. The metal was sticky.

Wes revved his motor and accelerated as if he were on a race track, then, when he came up on a slower moving vehicle or red light, pounded the brakes to stop. And he did it over and over again. It was nauseating. Reaching Portsmouth Circle, a rotary that served as the unofficial entrance to the city from the interstate, felt like a major accomplishment. Wes swung south on I-95, and at the next exit, reeled east toward the ocean.

'If we're going far,' I said, turning to look at him, 'let me drive.'

'What's the matter?'

'You drive like a maniac.'

Amazement showed on his face. 'What are you talking about? I'm a good driver.'

'Oh, God. Slow down, will you? You're not a good driver – you're a jerky driver. If you don't stop it, I'm going to get sick.'

'Okay, okay.'

He slowed to a reasonable speed, but his driving stayed staccato. I readjusted my grip on the overhead handle, and hung on.

Fifteen minutes later he slammed to a stop at the edge of the dunes in Hampton Beach. The sky was overcast and thick. It looked like rain. I held on to the dashboard for a moment, relieved that we were uninjured and no longer moving.

'Wow. Whatever's going on, I sure as shooting hope it's worth what I just went through on that ride.'

'So,' Wes said with faux concern, 'are you always cranky before breakfast or only when you're with a new man?'

'Oh, God, save me from fourteen-year-old race-car drivers.'

'I'm twenty-four,' he protested.

'Well, you look and drive like you're fourteen.'

'You're getting old. The older you are, the younger other people look to you.'

'Did you bring me to the beach so you could insult me?'

'No,' he said, opening his door and stepping out. 'That's just an added benefit. Come on, don't get me started. Follow me.' He handed me the portable CD player he'd extracted from the backseat. 'Take this.'

'What in the world? ...' I began, but he disappeared behind the car and opened the trunk. He pulled out a scraggly woolen blanket and a scuffed red-and-white Playmate cooler and locked the car.

'Ready?' he asked.

'For what?'

'Come on.' He scrambled up a dune, pushing through tall grass, and with a sigh and a shrug, I followed.

Wes headed toward the ocean, and looked around. He selected a fairly level spot about ten feet from the surf. Snapping the blanket to lay it flat, he smoothed it out and sat down, gesturing that I should join him. The wind off the blue-black ocean was bitter, and I shivered as I sat down, lifting the collar of my pea coat and rubbing my hands together.

As I got settled, I looked around. Wind-whipped whitecaps rippled across the ocean surface. The beach was mostly deserted. I saw someone sitting about a hundred yards to the north, huddled in a lawn chair staring at the ocean, and far to the south, a man was throwing driftwood to a golden retriever. Each time the man tossed the branch, the dog dashed away and retrieved it, trotting with a jaunty swagger, to drop it at his master's feet.

Wes turned on the CD player, and Frank Sinatra began to sing 'Fly Me to the Moon.' 'I have no reason to think you're wired, and I damn well know I'm not,' he whispered, leaning toward me. 'But I'm going to be quoting a police source, so I can't take any chances. With the ocean sounds and the CD, if we whisper, we should be fine.'

'Are you serious? You think I might be wearing a wire? You've been watching too many movies.' I noted that even as I expressed incredulity, I whispered.

Wes leaned back, resting his weight on the palms of his hands. 'You might be right. So what? Indulge me, okay?'

I shrugged. 'Sure.'

He pulled a thermos of coffee, two plastic mugs, and a box of doughnuts out of the Playmate. I couldn't remember the last time I'd eaten a doughnut. I took a honey-glazed and nibbled. It didn't taste like food. It tasted like dessert. Wes took an oversized bite of a chocolate-glazed doughnut. He used the back of his hand to wipe away smudged chocolate from his cheek.

'What do you want to hear about first?' he asked. 'Phone, prints, or background?'

'It doesn't matter. Phone, I guess. Were you able to learn who called Mr Grant?'

Wes nodded. 'Basically, no one.'

'What do you mean, "basically"?'

'His daughter, a widow named Dana Cabot who lives in Boston, called several times. So did his next-door neighbor and his lawyer, Epps. Also, there were two business calls.' He shrugged. 'Other than that, no one but you and another dealer, Barney Troudeaux, called him during the last month.'

'What kind of business calls?'

Wes reached into his jacket pocket and pulled out a single sheet of lined paper, folded into a small square. Consulting it, he said, 'His doctor's office. And Taffy Pull, a candy store on the beach.' He refolded the paper and placed it on his lap.

'Nothing there seems to stand out, does it?'

He shrugged. 'Not to me. The police are checking them out.'

'Do you know what they've learned?'

Wes pursed his lips. 'No.'

'Your source won't tell you?'

'My source says he – or she – doesn't know.'

'Do you believe him – or her?'

He turned both hands up and gave me a 'my guess is as good as yours' look, then smiled, and said, 'I'll keep pushing.'

I nodded. It was hard to imagine that calls from a candy store or his doctor were relevant. The former was probably a sales call, and the latter was most likely routine.

'Did Mr Grant make any calls?' I asked, thinking that perhaps he'd initiated one or more of those calls.

'No one but you, Troudeaux, and his lawyer.'

'Not even his daughter?'

'Nope. No other calls.'

'Was he in frequent touch with his lawyer? Mr Epps?'

'Doesn't look like it. There were a couple of calls, but earlier in the month. Nothing from, or to, Epps in the last week.'

'How about Barney? When did Barney last call him, or vice versa?'

He smiled. 'Are you ready? Troudeaux called Mr Grant at seven-thirty-two the night before he died.'

'The night before,' I repeated. I turned toward the ocean, and watched as water rushed in, then slowly seeped away. 'What does he say they talked about?'

'Changing an appointment.'

'What appointment?'

'Did you know Mr Grant kept a diary?'

'Yes. My appointment to see him the morning he was killed was in it.'

'Right. Well, apparently, so was Barney Troudeaux's. Troudeaux had an appointment to see Mr Grant the morning he died, too.'

'That morning? You're kidding!'

'Yeah, at nine. Except that Barney said he called Mr Grant and changed it.'

'How do you know?'

'My source tells me that Barney said that Mr Grant agreed to change the appointment to three that afternoon.'

'Why the last-minute change?'

'A board meeting for the association Barney heads up.'

'But he would have known about a board meeting sooner than the night before,' I objected.

Wes shrugged. 'Looks like he screwed up and double-booked himself.'

'Were there any calls on the day Mr Grant was killed?'

'Yeah. From you, his daughter, and his neighbor. That's it.'

'But then how did Barney learn that Mr Grant was killed?'

'I don't know. Does it matter?'

I shrugged. 'I'm just wondering ... did he show up at the Grant house for his appointment that afternoon?'

Wes looked intrigued, wiped his chocolate-sticky fingers on his jeans, and wrote a note on the folded square of paper. 'Good question,' he said. 'I'll check it out.'

'What about fingerprints?' I asked.

'Apparently yours were everywhere. Barney's were around, too, but not as many as yours.'

I smiled. 'I'm more thorough.'

'I'll keep that in mind when I'm ready to sell my family's treasures.'

'Does your family have treasures?' I asked.

'Hell, no. I was joking.'

'Too bad. I would have made you a good deal.'

Wes shook his head, grinning a little. 'There were other prints, too. Miscellaneous and explainable. Grant's wife, for instance, obviously from before she died, a house cleaner who came in periodically, and a delivery boy from a grocery store in town. There was one set of prints in the living room that is still unidentified.'

'Can they tell anything about who left them?'

'No, not to quote them on. They're adult prints, but smallish, so based on the size, they may be from a woman.' He shrugged. 'But there are small men, too. And large men with small hands.'

'Doesn't it seem incredible that no other prints were found? I mean, what about his daughter and granddaughter? Or other delivery people? Or friends?'

'I guess he lived a pretty quiet life.'

I shook my head, wondering what prints they'd find in my house if they looked. I wasn't a bad housekeeper, but I wasn't a nut about it either. It made me wonder whether maybe one of my dad's prints was still somewhere, maybe on the side of a dining room chair, a remnant from one of the scores of times when he'd sat, idly tapping a beat, waiting for me to serve the meal.

'Anything else scheduled for that morning?' I asked, focusing on Wes, chasing away the memory. 'Besides me?'

'Just Barney Troudeaux's nine o'clock appointment.'

'I thought he changed it when he called the night before.'

'That's what he says, but it was still in the diary.'

'Maybe Mr Grant hadn't gotten around to changing it before he died,' I said, saddened at the thought.

I recalled the day that I'd made a mistake in my schedule, realizing it only after I'd left the Grant house. I hurried back and knocked on the door. When he answered, I apologized for my error, he assured me it wasn't a problem, and escorted me back to the kitchen. I could picture him sitting at his kitchen table, erasing the mistaken entry, turning pages to find the correct date, his callused index finger running down the center of the page until he located the time slot he wanted. He smiled then, and using a freshly sharpened pencil, he wrote my name.

'We'll never know, I guess,' Wes said.

'Yeah. And probably, it doesn't matter. Because Barney was at the board meeting, right?'

'Right.'

Bright sunshine unexpectedly illuminated the beach from a sudden break in the clouds. I heard the dog bark, and squinted into the sun in time to see him run a circle around his owner as they made their way up the dunes. I took another bite of doughnut. My coffee had cooled enough so it was comfortable to sip.

'How about Mr Grant's background? Were you able to learn anything about him or his family?'

Wes nodded. 'Yeah. Quite a story, actually. He was born in Kansas, the only son of successful ranchers. He came east to go to prep school, and never lived in the Midwest again.'

'Was he in the war?'

'Yeah. He joined the army in 1942, and for a lot of the time, he was stationed in France. That's when he met his wife. According to all reports she was a piece of work. A tough old bird with a temper. She was maybe French, maybe Belgian, maybe who knows what.'

'What do you mean, "who knows what"?'

He shook his head, and gestured that he had no idea. 'I know that her name was Yvette. Or at least that's what she called herself. I couldn't even find a record of her maiden name.'

'How can that be? What does that mean?'

'Probably nothing. Maybe she was a Jew on the run. Maybe she was a Nazi sympathizer. Who knows? Back then, there were lots of good reasons to change your name and reinvent yourself.'

I thought about that for a long minute, watching as shards of sunlight dappled the sand and water. Gretchen had wanted to reinvent herself, a fresh start, she'd called it. I wondered if Gretchen was her real name, or if, like Yvette, she too had changed it. No matter. She was Gretchen to me, and I felt grateful that her desire for a fresh start had led her to my door.

After a sip of coffee, I asked, 'What did Mr Grant do after the war?'

'He settled in Rocky Point and started a painting contracting business.'

'And?' I prompted.

'And he made a fortune. Everyone I checked with said he was a ruthless SOB, but likable. The kind of guy who could sell tulips to a Dutchman.' He shrugged. 'Apparently he was a good talker and a terrific negotiator. But you'd better be careful every step of the way because if there was anything he could exploit, he would.'

'Why? What does that mean?'

'You know ... it means that he was a smooth operator, a guy who knew the angles and never missed an opportunity to make a profit. He built his business by winning federal contracts until it became the biggest company of its kind in New England, then sold out to a national firm. That was about fifteen years ago.'

That sounded like both the Mr Grant I'd met and the one I'd gotten to know after his death: charming and shrewd. 'How big a fortune are we talking about?' I asked.

Wes glanced at the folded square of paper. 'Somewhere around thirty million dollars, depending on who you ask.'

'Wow.'

'Yeah,' he agreed. 'Wow it is.'

I remembered that Max had planned to ask Epps who would inherit Mr Grant's estate, and wondered if he had done so. From my conversation with Mrs Cabot yesterday, I assumed she inherited everything. It occurred to me that Wes might know.

'Does his daughter inherit everything?' I asked.

'Nope. Fifty-fifty split with the granddaughter. Nothing to anyone else.'

'No siblings, uncles, cousins? No other family?'

'No. Mr Grant had a sister who died in her teens back in Kansas. Mrs Grant – who knows what family she might have had. According to my source, no one else has surfaced yet.'

I nodded. That would account for Andi's impatience. Fifteen million dollars would buy a lot of independence. I wondered whether she cared that she had such a small family. As the only children of only children, apparently Andi and I shared a common legacy – small families that grow smaller with each generation.

'Anything else of note?' I asked.

'Something about the daughter's leaving after high school. Mrs Cabot. She left to get married in ... let me see here ... 1964. It seems she and her father had an argument sometime during the summer after her high school graduation that was heard for miles around.'

'What about?' I asked.

'No one remembers. But they sure remember the shouting. The fight started on the beach, and continued through the village. Dana marched into the house, packed two bags, and, with her mother pulling at her and begging her to stay, left.'

I stared at Wes. Was it possible that a forty-year-old argument had anything to do with Mr Grant's death? It was hard to believe that a long-ago altercation could be relevant today. Turning my attention to the sea, I looked at the whitecaps shimmering in the now-bright sun. I remembered Max asking Alverez why he was interrogating me about the jewelry in my safe. Alverez had said that until he knew what was going on, it was impossible to know what was a tangent and what was a clue. Dana's departure had been so remarkable, it was etched in the community's memory even after forty years. An event that memorable might, in fact, have repercussions that rippled through the generations.

'That kind of breach between parents and a child, it's sad, isn't it?' I asked.

'Yeah,' Wes answered with a shrug, seeming not to care much one way or the other. 'I guess. But I bet that her half of thirty million dollars will help heal a lot of wounds.'

'Don't be cynical,' I said. 'It's sad, and that's that.'

'Yes, ma'am.'

'I gotta tell you, Wes, that my head is spinning a little from all this information. But I'm not sure whether any of it is relevant.'

'Me either. I just provide the facts, ma'am. Just the facts.'

'Good point.'

'Plus which, there's more.'

'What?'

The sun was warming the air, and Wes paused to unbutton his jacket. I followed suit. He offered me some more coffee, and I accepted a little. He poured himself a full mug. 'Stardust' resonated through the speakers.

'Want another doughnut?' he asked.

'No, thanks.' Three-quarters of my first one rested on a nearby napkin. 'So, what else?'

'Seems Mrs Grant ran a tight ship. One of the things she did was keep a detailed record of purchases.'

'What kind of purchases?'

'Everything. Appliances, antiques, dry cleaning. Even milk, bread, and gasoline. Everything.'

'Wow.'

'Yeah, a little anal, wouldn't you say?'

'She probably grew up poor. You know what I mean ... like how for some people who survived the Depression, watching pennies was a way of life.'

'Yeah, whatever. The point is, she listed everything in big ledgers. By category, in chronological order by date of acquisition.'

'So?'

'So the police experts have accounted for everything on the ledger except two things.'

'What?'

'Two paintings – one by Cézanne and one by Matisse.'

'You're kidding!' I exclaimed.

'Nope.'

'What paintings?'

Consulting his notes, he said, '*Apples in a Blue Bowl with Grapes*. That's the Cézanne. The Matisse is called *Notre-Dame in the Morning*.'

I shook my head. 'Think about it ... a Renoir, a Cézanne, and a Matisse.'

'Good taste, huh?'

'When were they purchased?'

'September of 1945.'

'Where?'

Wes shook his head. 'Only initials. Apparently Mrs Grant used a kind of shorthand. I guess since she knew where they bought things, she didn't bother spelling everything out.' He shrugged. 'According to my source, the paintings were purchased from an "A.Z." '

I nodded. 'Sounds like a private party. You know, some person's initials. Were all three paintings bought at the same time?'

'Yeah.'

'It's hard to picture, isn't it? At the end of the war, with everything going on, can you imagine buying art?'

'Who knows the circumstances? Things were completely chaotic over there. Maybe the Grants were helping a friend by taking the paintings off his hands when he needed hard cash, not art.'

I nodded, letting Wes think he was making a valid point. I was willing to bet that the Cézanne and the Matisse would be on the Swiss Web site's listing of pillaged art, alongside the Renoir, and flirted with the idea of telling him about it. I decided to stay quiet. My knowledge of the

Renoir's provenance was the only leverage I retained. Once revealed, its usefulness was gone. At some point, I might need to parlay what I knew for something, so it made no sense to offer it for free. Right now I had nothing to gain and, potentially, everything to lose.

'Maybe,' I answered finally. 'How much did they pay?'

'Ten thousand each. In U.S. dollars. Cash.'

'Wow. They paid in cash?'

'Right. I bet most transactions in Europe at the end of the war were in cash.'

'That makes sense. But would they be in U.S. dollars?'

'I guess the U.S. dollar was primo even back then.'

'Interesting,' I mused. 'But only ten thousand dollars? Even for sixty years ago that sounds like a bargain. I wonder how much that would be in today's dollars?'

'I looked it up,' Wes said, unfolding his paper to check the figure. 'Close to a hundred grand. Each.'

'That's unbelievable.'

'Cheap, huh?'

'Just a little,' I responded, opening my eyes wide and shaking my head, astonished.

'How much are they worth today?'

I shrugged. 'I'd need to do research to be sure. There are lots of variables. But in 1999, a Cézanne sold at auction for more than sixty million.'

Wes stared, disbelieving. 'You're kidding.'

'No. So if you bought a Cézanne for a hundred thousand dollars today, it would be fair to say that you got, ahem, a good buy.'

'But we don't know the going price for a Cézanne back then.'

'No,' I acknowledged. 'If I remember right, though, in the mid-1940s, a master would have sold for something like a few hundred thousand dollars.'

'In other words, it's safe to assume that ten thousand dollars was low.'

'Probably, but not necessarily. Sometimes art appreciates exponentially, sometimes prices stay flat, and sometimes, prices even decline. It's pure capitalism. Art sells for what a buyer will pay, and no more.' I shrugged. 'The bottom line is that there's no way to tell without extensive research what Cézannes sold for back then.'

'If it's that complicated, how do you set prices?'

'Recency is a big factor. I can do a good job of accurately predicting today's values by looking at sales of similar items over the recent past – unless something has occurred to impact value – up or down. For instance, if a great artist's studio burns to the ground along with half of his works, whatever still exists is likely to shoot up in value. On the other hand, if an artist painted in a certain genre or style that falls out of favor, who knows why, the marketability of the paintings might plummet. That said, if all things are equal, the fact that a Cézanne sold for sixty million dollars in the last few years tells me that a similar piece is likely to go for many millions now – even if sixty million dollars is an aberration. But there are so many other factors to consider – provenance, historical value, condition, and so on.' I flipped a hand. 'The point is that not knowing what Cézannes typically sold for during the war, I have no way of knowing whether the Grants got a bargain or not.'

He nodded. 'And the Matisse? How much would it have sold for?'

I shook my head. 'I don't know. A lot.'

Wes leaned back and soft-whistled. 'The things we don't know about our neighbors.'

'Yeah,' I agreed. 'Makes you wonder, doesn't it?'

'Where do you figure the Grants got thirty thousand dollars cash back then?'

'Who knows? Didn't you tell me Grant came from money?'

'Successful ranchers, yeah, that's true,' he agreed, and stretched. 'So, what do you think?' he asked, putting his square paper away in an inside pocket. He smiled and half winked. 'Did I earn my exclusive?'

'If we forget the winklike thing you just did … yes.'

'What "winklike thing"?' he asked, sounding hurt.

'That thing you just did with your eye.'

'That wasn't a "winklike thing," ' he protested. 'That was a suave move.' He waved his hand dismissively. 'Forget about it. So? Did I do okay?'

'Yeah. Wes, you did more than okay,' I said, meaning it. He'd done an amazing job of discovering facts and uncovering hidden memories, and he'd done it quickly. I was impressed.

With a lopsided grin, he reached up to high-five me, and I looked to the sky, embarrassed, but high-fived him back. Jeez Louise, kids today.

'Ready?' he asked.

'You bet.'

He stood up, scooped up my mostly uneaten doughnut with a napkin, and dropped it in the Playmate while I shook sand from the blanket. We made our way through the shifting sand to the dunes. As we approached the street, the CD player still on, Frank Sinatra began singing 'They Can't Take That Away from Me.'

The drive back to Portsmouth was as bad as the drive to the beach had been. Wes jumped a red light in the center of the small downtown, and as I braced myself for the inevitable quick stop that I was certain would follow, we passed a sliver of storefront called the Taffy Pull, the candy store that had come up in Mr Grant's telephone records. *Funny,* I thought, *that I'd never noticed it before.* I didn't have much of a sweet tooth, maybe that was why.

I looked back as we sped by. At this hour, it was locked up tight. The entire block of tourist-oriented stores was deserted. Come July, even at 8:30 on a Saturday morning, the place would be hopping.

'What's our next step?' I asked.

'I follow up,' he said, patting the pocket where he'd placed the paper with his notes. 'How about you? What will you do?'

'I'm not sure. There's so much to think about. You'll call me when you learn more, right?'

He assured me that he would, and when we arrived, he pulled up near my car and added, 'I believe you, you know.'

'Believe me about what?' I asked.

'I believe that you didn't kill Mr Grant.'

I swallowed, oddly touched by his unsolicited vote of confidence, and tried to smile. I reached over and touched his shoulder. 'Thanks, Wes. That means a lot.'

My stomach grumbled and I decided to get a real breakfast. I sat at the counter, ordered bacon and eggs, and shut my eyes. I heard voices, but no conversations, rustlings as people turned newspaper pages, and the clatter of coffeepots. In the midst of life, I felt cocooned and able to focus on Wes's revelations.

I felt restless, anxious to be up and doing, not sitting and eating. But I wasn't sure what to do. The Grants owned a trio of paintings of nearly inestimable artistic and monetary value – where did the Cézanne and Matisse come from and where were they now?

A deepening sense of dread colored my outlook, yet my growing fear was nonspecific. It was as if I'd wandered unawares into Act II of a three-act drama, but didn't know my lines or even the role I'd been assigned to play.

I opened my eyes and took a long drink of orange juice. I had more questions than before, and no idea about how I could get answers. Nothing made sense. In fact, it seemed that the more I learned, the less I knew.

chapter twelve

I didn't get back to the warehouse until almost 9:30. Greeting
Gretchen on the fly, I ran upstairs to my office to change into my
uniform. I, like everyone else on staff and all temporary workers, had
to adhere to a dress code on auction and tag-sale days. We wore
maroon collared T-shirts with the words Prescott Antiques printed in
small white letters on the pocket and black slacks and shoes.

Only Tom McLaughlin, the auctioneer in for the day from upstate,
was allowed to wear whatever he wanted. The first time he'd driven
down to work for me, about eighteen months earlier, I'd asked him if he
wanted to wear a Prescott T-shirt. His sour look had been answer
enough.

Tucking in my shirt as I hurried down the stairs, I went directly to the
auction site, where the final preview hours were about to begin. Sasha
seemed to have everything under control.

'Ready?' I asked, entering through the back.

'As ready as I'm going to be,' she answered, trying for a smile.
Responsibility was new to her, and she took to it awkwardly, but with a
quiet determination to succeed.

'You'll do fine,' I said, responding to her underlying message, not her
words.

'Thanks,' she said with a quick smile.

'Anything I need to know about?'

'I don't think so. We're ready to open up on schedule. Katrina's
outside signing in the early birds.'

I nodded. 'Good.' Katrina, a part-time worker with a year's experience, would be with Sasha all day helping her register bidders, pass out
catalogues, record winning bids, and run errands.

'Tom is here,' she said, pointing toward the front.

I spotted him near the podium, scowling at the catalogue. Today, as always, he wore a rumpled brown suit and a glum demeanor. I didn't care that he was routinely surly before and after the auction. With a gavel in his hand, he was transformed. He worked the crowd with seemingly effortless ease, exuding goodwill and confidence, and creating eager bidders. With a nod to Sasha, I headed toward the stage, calling to him as I approached. He turned and frowned at me.

'Do you have everything you need?' I asked.

He snorted. 'Not unless you have a check for a million dollars in your pocket.'

I smiled politely. 'I wish. You have the catalogue, I see.'

'Did you do the research?'

'No. Sasha did it. And wrote the descriptions.'

'It's good.' Words of high praise from a man who knew.

I smiled my thanks. 'She and Katrina will be here all day if you need anything.'

He nodded and waved me away. I told Sasha I'd be back in a while, and left. I stuck my head into the office, and called, 'Gretchen? I'm going to dash over to the tag sale to be sure we're ready to open. Anything for me first?'

'Yes,' she said, standing up and turning to face me. She wore her Prescott T-shirt with flair, looking as stylish as always. 'Mrs Cabot is here to see you.'

Mrs Cabot, Mr Grant's daughter? In a dazzling flash of hope, I imagined that she'd selected me to handle her father's estate. I caught myself beginning to hyperventilate at the thought and quelled my impulse to hoot and holler and kick my heels in the air. *Stop, Josie,* I admonished myself. *Stop, breathe, and think.* Forcing myself to slow down and think, I took a deep breath. And another. Okay. I was ready.

I stepped inside. Mrs Cabot sat in an upholstered guest chair near the front, her feet firmly on the ground, gripping her handbag tightly.

'Mrs Cabot,' I said, smiling as I walked forward. 'I didn't see you.'

As I got closer I could see that her eyes were moist and reddened. I knew the look; she'd been crying.

'Hello,' she said quietly, pushing herself upright. 'I'm sorry to disturb you.'

'You're not disturbing me. Not at all. You met Gretchen?' I asked.

'Yes,' Mrs Cabot said with a nod and half smile.

'Absolutely,' Gretchen responded. Turning to Mrs Cabot, she asked, 'Would you reconsider about coffee?'

'No, thank you, though.'

'Are you sure?' I asked Mrs Cabot.

'I'm fine. Thank you.'

'What can I do for you?'

She cleared her throat. 'I was hoping ... do you have a few minutes to talk?'

'Sure.' Her look of relief piqued my curiosity.

As I was about to invite her to sit down again, her eyes flitted toward Gretchen, and I read the unspoken request. 'Come up to my office. We'll be more comfortable up there. It's private.'

'Thank you.'

I gestured that Mrs Cabot should walk ahead. 'Gretchen,' I said, 'will you go find Eric at the tag sale and make certain he's okay?'

'You bet,' she answered.

My priorities had shifted in an instant. At that moment, nothing was more important to me than talking to Mrs Cabot.

Mrs Cabot, wearing a royal blue suit, sat on a bright yellow love seat. I took a chair across from her and waited for her to speak.

'It's hard for me to be here,' she said softly.

'I can see that you're upset,' I said. 'Are you sure you wouldn't like some tea? Or some water? Something?'

She shook her head and cleared her throat. 'I'm here to ask you to help me. I have no reason to think you will, and I'll certainly understand if you say no. But I thought ... it occurred to me....' She glanced down and twirled her gold wedding band. A widow who still wore her wedding ring. A sign, I assumed, of a happy marriage.

'Please ...' she continued, 'I hope that you ... I mean I am asking that you ... I'm here because I don't know whom else to ask.' She finished in a rush, as if she wanted to get the words out before she changed her mind.

'Help you do what?' I asked, wary.

'First, I must tell you that I'm not going to offer you the sale of my father's estate. I've decided to bring in a New York firm, Dobson's.'

I felt a stab of such great disappointment that I had to look away. I took a deep breath, my father's warning against letting people see my emotional reactions to business frustrations resonating in my mind, stiffening my spine, and enabling me, after a moment, to look back and smile.

'I understand. There's a lot of research to be done. Dobson's is top drawer.'

She nodded. 'Your role will be key. And your fee will be more than fair.'

I stared at her for a moment. 'My fee for what?'

'For helping me.'

'Helping you do what?' I repeated, uncertain of my ground. On the face of it, it sounded as if Mrs Cabot was trying to bribe me. And I figured that the longer she took to get to the point, the more troubling her proposal would be.

'It's important that you understand why I chose you. I understand you moved from New York not long ago. I checked you out. You have an excellent reputation.'

'Thank you,' I said. Definitely a bribe, I thought. I couldn't imagine what she wanted me to do, nor could I think of anything I possessed that she might want to buy.

'I'm paying not just for your knowledge but for your integrity. What you did to help the police during that price-fixing trial, you know, coming forward and testifying, well, I was impressed.'

Maybe what she said was true, and she wasn't offering a bribe after all. If she was speaking the truth, and not setting me up somehow, it would be a huge relief. I found myself wanting to believe her and to smile. I was surprised at how pleased I felt that she knew about my past. It occurred to me that perhaps I'd discovered a reasonable litmus test of trust – be aware of my involvement in the Frisco price-fixing scandal and think well of me because of it. Still, I didn't know how to respond, so I stayed quiet.

After a long pause, she continued, 'Chief Alverez has told me that he expects the technicians to be done by tomorrow.'

'Which technicians?'

'The ones investigating my father's cause of death. And the scientists who've been working at the crime scene.'

'So they can release the body?'

'Yes.'

'And you can hold the funeral.'

'That's right. It will be on Monday.'

I shook my head a little, the way people do to show empathy.

'Chief Alverez said the scientists have finished investigating the murder scene.'

'So that you can enter the house?'

'Yes.' She cleared her throat. 'Everyone is very impatient.'

I paused for a moment, thinking what to say. 'Are you referring to your daughter?'

She nodded, a small movement, then half smiled. 'I hate being hurried. Sometimes my daughter thinks I'm indecisive, but it's not that.'

I nodded, understanding, I thought, what she was trying to express. 'You just like to think things through before you act.'

'How nice of you to put it that way,' she said with more of a smile. 'It's true, though. I'm methodical, not impulsive. I never have been.'

I wondered about her sudden departure forty years ago. *Wasn't that an impulsive act?* Maybe not. Maybe she'd planned to leave all along, and the shattering scene Wes had described was coincidental. I wanted to ask her about it, but the timing was wrong.

'Well, no matter,' she said, refocusing her attention. 'I need to tell you about my mother's lists.'

I waited for her to continue.

'I don't know if my father showed you her ledgers? The inventories?'

'No, he didn't.'

She nodded. 'He showed them to Mr Troudeaux.'

I shrugged.

'That isn't a compliment to him.'

'I don't understand.'

'No, how could you.' She sighed and shifted her position slightly. 'I knew the ledgers existed. All my life, I knew. I'd see my mother update them every evening.' She shook her head. 'She tracked everything. It was a kind of obsession with her.' She opened her purse and extracted a sheaf of papers, stapled and folded in thirds. 'These pages were copied from the ledger that detailed household goods. As you'll see, most of what's listed are antiques.'

She handed the document to me. I reached across and accepted the pages. Flipping through, I saw a list of furniture, artwork, and decorative items detailed in a fine up-and-down hand. The first entry was dated April 3, 1943; the last on the 15th of March, a year ago.

I looked up. 'What do you want me to do?' I asked quietly.

'Confirm that everything is there, and as described.'

'In other words, you want a detailed appraisal?'

'Yes. What I want you to do is make certain that everything my mother listed is there, intact, and genuine – that her list was accurate and is complete. And I want to know how much you think I can expect to receive when the items are sold.'

'I can provide you with a range of values.'

'That will be fine,' she said.

'What will you do with the information?' I asked.

'Ensure that Dobson's does a proper job.'

I considered whether she was telling me the truth. This approach, sending the auction house an independently authenticated listing, was smart. It helped keep everyone honest. But given the situation, I couldn't help wondering if that was her only motivation. 'Why did you say that your father showing the list to Mr Troudeaux isn't a compliment to him?'

She paused and looked away. 'I can't be certain, but I'm concerned that my father was ... perhaps he thought he could....' She seemed to shake off her uncertainty. Taking a deep breath, she said, 'Perhaps he was talking to Mr Troudeaux about a private sale so he could avoid paying taxes. I'm not sure, of course, but knowing my father, it's certainly possible. I don't know Mr Troudeaux, so I hesitate to imply that he might be involved with something unethical. But I did know my father, and I must confess that he had been known to skirt rules more than once or twice.'

'Oh, my.'

She nodded. 'Yes. A bit dispiriting.'

She'd referred to Andi, her daughter, as impatient, when she was, in fact, a termagant. Now she was describing her father's dishonesty as 'dispiriting.' Another masterful example of understatement. I glanced at the papers wondering what to do about the missing Cézanne and Matisse. I knew the paintings hadn't yet been found, but I didn't know whether she was aware of it or not. Surely, I thought, the police had told her. Taking a deep breath for courage, I asked the question that was foremost in my mind. 'What if something's missing?'

Looking at me dead-on, her eyes clear and her focus intense, she answered, 'I trust that you'll find it.'

I wondered what she thought I could do that the police hadn't done. I tilted my head, watching her watch me think it through. I had a startling thought. I wondered if she thought the paintings were hidden somewhere in the house, somewhere an antique dealer would know about, but that the police might not discover.

'Did the police tell you that I helped them look for the Renoir?'

'No. What did you do?'

'I remembered having seen a partners' desk. And I knew that it was pretty common for the old English partners' desks to have hidden cabinets.' I shrugged. 'I found the secret cabinet, but not the painting.'

Speaking slowly, as if she were carefully choosing her words, she said, 'There may well be other places you will discover.'

I nodded. We continued to look at each other, and I was struck by her composure. I stood up and stretched, then walked to my desk for a bottle of water. I looked out of the window. A big old maple sat right outside, and it looked fine. Last summer, a huge branch fell in a thunderstorm, and I had worried that the tree would die.

'Does Andi know that you're hiring me? And Dobson's?' I asked, my back to her.

'No. I thought it best ... that is ... I'll explain after ... no.'

I didn't know what to say. I would have bet big money that even if she knew where the paintings were hidden, she didn't want to tell me. If she found the missing paintings on her own, Andi would try to bulldoze her into selling them privately. If she helped me find them, Andi would go ballistic. But if I located them, no matter how many fits Andi threw, there'd be no choice but to return them to their rightful owners. My best guess was that Mrs Cabot wanted to bring me in to help her do the right thing in the face of nearly overwhelming familial pressure.

'Thank you for explaining the situation,' I said, turning to her.

I could see the relief on her face. 'Thank you. Thank you so much. I'll give your name to Dobson's. And no matter what,' she said, clearing her throat and looking down, 'I won't let Andi disturb you.'

I nodded, wondering how she could stop Andi from disturbing me. *Probably*, I thought, *Mrs Cabot held the purse strings, and used the threat of withholding money to keep Andi under control*. I bet she hated her role as enforcer. And heaven only knew what havoc Andi would wreak once she got her hands on her share of her grandfather's fortune. Poor Mrs Cabot. I shook my head, feeling sad for her and powerless.

For some reason I thought of Eric, maybe because he needed money, too. I recalled the day that I'd driven by his house en route to a buy. His mother was sweeping the walkway and I'd waved as I went past. She'd glared at me, perhaps not recognizing me, but still, her glower was uncalled for and odd. When I got back to the warehouse, I mentioned that I'd driven by and had seen his mom outside. I was immediately sorry that I'd spoken.

He was embarrassed, explaining inarticulately, 'Mom works so hard taking care of the place. I plan to fix it up, but, you know, everything costs so much.'

'I hadn't noticed that anything needed fixing,' I said politely. 'All I noticed was how big and beautiful the house is. And those apple trees! I can taste the pie now!'

'Yeah,' he responded. 'My mom makes a great apple pie, that's for sure.'

I got the sense at the time that he was grateful that I ignored his dilapidated house and crabby mother. But now it made me wonder what he would do if he inherited a fortune. Would he fix up the house and buy mom luxuries? Or, like many nineteen-year-olds, would he flee, deserting both the rundown structure and the fractious woman who held him close?

My father once told me that money didn't buy happiness, it bought freedom. The trick is to decide what sets you free. I didn't know with Eric. I sometimes thought that there was a lot I didn't know about him, hidden layers of his personality.

Mostly though, I thought he was just what he appeared to be – a devoted son, a nice guy who was good with his hands and loved his dogs, an able worker who lacked ambition.

I realized that Mrs Cabot was waiting for me to comment. 'I'll plan on getting started on Monday,' I said.

'About your fee ... what would be reasonable, do you think?'

'The identification of items is easy. The verification is tough. Assessing value is time-consuming and detail oriented, and requires a lot of judgment. Finding missing items, if there are any, might be impossible.'

She nodded, and paused. 'How's twenty-five thousand dollars as a retainer?'

I swallowed. That was more than my company grossed in a month during most of the year. 'That will get us started,' I said. 'And the final fee? How should we set it?'

'You'll know how hard you worked, and what was involved. At the end, you'll bill me, and I'll pay it.'

'I'll be fair,' I assured her.

'I know you will. Remember,' she said, smiling again, 'I checked you out.'

While she wrote a check, I printed out my standard letter of agreement. She read it carefully and signed it without comment. She also gave me a key to the Grant house and a note authorizing me and my staff to enter at will.

We stood just outside the front door in the parking lot. The sun was steady now, and bright. I noticed two dozen or so cars, a good omen since it was barely ten and both the preview and the tag sale had just opened.

'I'll call you Monday evening. Is that all right?' I asked.

'Yes, thank you. I won't be leaving until Tuesday.'

'And then you'll be back in Boston?'

'Chestnut Hill, yes,' she answered, naming an affluent suburb just west of the city.

A black Lincoln pulled up, and a small Asian man got out, leaving the engine running. He nodded at me and opened the back door for her.

'Does your daughter live in Boston, too?'

'No,' she said. 'New York. Why?'

'Just curious. One more thing,' I said, changing the subject. 'I was just thinking that I might stop by the house tomorrow, if it's all right.'

'I don't know. You'll need to check with the police.'

'May I call them directly?'

'Yes, certainly. In this endeavor, you're my representative.'

I smiled. 'Thank you, Mrs Cabot. I won't let you down.'

'I know you won't.'

'What's your room number at the Sheraton?'

'Room three-nineteen.'

I nodded. 'Thank you.'

She turned to step into the car, then paused. As she swung her feet inside, I noticed that they were average sized, and at a guess, her shoes were about a seven.

'How long do you think it will take you?' she asked.

I wondered which task she was referring to – generating an independent inventory, verifying authenticity, assessing value, or finding the missing paintings.

'*If* I can find everything, and *if* it's all as described, no more than a couple of days for the inventory itself. For the verification, a week to ten days. For the appraisal, another two to three weeks.' I shrugged and made a Murphy's Law joking grimace. '*If* this, *if* that. *If* it rained in the Sahara, it wouldn't be a desert. You know how that goes.'

'Of course. I understand. Obviously time is of the essence. I know you'll work as quickly as you can.'

I nodded. 'Realistically, I expect it will take a month to six weeks, soup to nuts. I'll do my best to speed the process along.' Wes had told me that the police had made an inventory. I wondered if she was aware of it. 'One thing that might save time,' I added, pleased at my boldness, 'is if we can work off an existing list. For instance, do you know if the police made an inventory?'

'Ask Chief Alverez. As I said, in this matter, you're my representative.'

She reached out her hand and we shook. Her entire attitude conveyed something more than the confirmation of a business deal with a new partner. There was that, but there was also a melancholy resignation, as if she was proceeding along the best path she'd found, but that while it might be the best, it was none too good. I had the sudden realization that, to her, anything I discovered was likely to be bad news. If I found the paintings, Andi would be furious. If I didn't, Andi would go crazy, perhaps accusing me or others of stealing them. An ugly scene was almost guaranteed, regardless of the outcome.

I stood for a moment and watched as the car drove away. Walking inside, I wondered if Mrs Cabot had already planned how she'd handle Andi's explosion when it came.

'Good news?' Gretchen asked when I stepped inside.

I grinned. 'Well, we didn't get the estate sale, but we get to appraise everything.'

'Yowzi! That's great!'

'And it's interesting work, too. Sasha's going to love it.'

'Congratulations.'

'It's a tribute to us all.' I waved it away. 'Tell me both the preview and tag sale are open.'

'Yup. On time, and looking good.'

'Great. I'm going to the tag sale. Would you go ask Tom if he'd like a cup of coffee?'

'Okay,' she said, whining, stretching out the last syllable for effect. 'Only for you.'

'He's not that bad,' I argued.

'Yes, he is,' she responded, laughing. 'He's a jerk! But he's our jerk, right?'

'He's talented,' I said, wanting to quash her open expression of dislike and remind her of his value. I shrugged. 'I don't care about his personality. He does a great job for us.'

'I know, I know. I wouldn't say anything to anyone else, even joking. For your ears only.'

Not for the first time, I was struck by her loyalty. 'Okay, then,' I said with a smile, and added in a whisper, 'Just between us, he's a huge jerk.'

She laughed again, and I smiled back, grateful that her breezy, sunny spirit lightened my load.

I headed to the tag sale to make sure Eric was okay. He served as on-site manager, and that was a lot of responsibility for a relatively young man. I trusted him, but thought it made sense to keep in fairly constant touch.

My father always encouraged giving responsibility to young people. When I'd got the job at Frisco's and expressed wonder that they'd entrust both valuable antiques and clients to me, an untested and unknown twenty-one-year-old, he'd remarked that we, as a nation, entrusted our security to eighteen-year-olds with guns, and that that strategy had worked out pretty well for us so far.

As I pushed open the door from the warehouse into the tag-sale section, the first thing I saw and heard was Martha Troudeaux making herself obnoxious.

'But it's mislabeled,' she said, her voice shrill.

'Hi Martha,' I said calmly, approaching with a smile.

'Ah, Josie. I'm glad you're here. There's a major problem with your pricing.'

'Really? I'm surprised. We try so hard to get it right. What's the problem?'

'This stool. It's not from the Empire! Why is it priced as if it were?' She sneered, her self-righteous tone of outrage making me long to slap her face.

I looked at the small bamboo stool. The tag, tied on to a leg, stated that it was a reproduction. The price was twelve dollars. If it were genuine, dating from around 1890, a stool of this size and quality would fetch more than ten times twelve dollars. Rude and ignorant. What Barney saw in her mystified me. It occurred to me that maybe she was neither rude nor ignorant; maybe she was trying to create a scene, to make me look bad.

Out of the corner of my eye, I noticed that Barney stood not far away, his back to us, near the boxes of art prints. He seemed absorbed in a conversation with Paula, the blond part-timer who preferred T-shirts with messages to the Prescott one, but wore it as instructed. Barney was probably trying to weasel the name of my art source out of her, but she couldn't tell what she didn't know, so that was no worry.

Turning back to Martha, I spotted Alverez half-hidden by a post near the mechanical toys section. I bristled. Alverez's presence was more troubling than Barney's. I glanced around, considering whether customers knew who he was and thought less of me because of his presence. I also wondered whether I should call Max and report his unexpected arrival.

Focusing instead on Martha's nasty aspersions, I forced myself to smile. 'Perhaps you didn't see the word "reproduction," ' I said politely.

'The price is too high!' she complained.

I tilted my head to really look at her. She was a pretty woman, tall and thin. Her very short, almost black hair was layered and suited her. It was unfortunate that her eyes were calculating, with no hint of warmth, and that her tone was always strident, never pleasant. She was eminently unlikable.

'Then don't buy it,' I said, smiling a little, trying to convert her attack into a semipleasant interaction.

She was having none of it. 'It's not worth more than five dollars, and I wouldn't buy it even at that price because it's in terrible condition. And one more thing....'

I listened to her for a moment longer, my attention drifting to Alverez who seemed to be watching me while pretending not to, and to Barney, still talking with Paula. I scanned the venue. There were about fifty customers, par for a nonholiday weekend at this time of day. I noted that Alverez had moved on to housewares and appeared to be interested in a stainless-steel bar set from the '50s.

'Excuse me, Martha. Someone's calling me,' I fibbed. I headed straight to Alverez.

'Hey,' I said, approaching him.

'Josie,' he answered. 'Things look great.'

I felt the familiar tug of connection, the inexplicable chemistry we shared, but ignored it. 'Interested in barware?'

'Not really,' he answered, grinning.

'What are you doing here?' I asked, not smiling.

'Isn't this open to the public?' he asked, gesturing broadly.

'Yes, but that doesn't answer my question.'

He paused. 'That's the only answer I have to give you right now.'

'Should I call Max?' I asked.

'Why? Because I came to a tag sale?'

'Don't play with me. I'm upset.'

'I can tell you are, but I'm not sure why.'

'Oh, never mind. I have work to do.'

I glanced back over my shoulder as I walked away. He stood watching me.

'Hey, Eric,' I said, joining him at the cash register. Only Eric and Gretchen were authorized to haggle or accept money. And me, of course. Our standing policy was that dealers who were known to us or who had proper bonafides got a 10 percent professional courtesy discount, but that we didn't offer discounts to consumers. As closing time approached, however, we'd been known to bend that rule, especially if we had the opportunity to move hard-to-sell inventory, like mismatched china or undistinguished volumes of old books.

A part-timer was wrapping each piece of a six-part set of Sandwich glass in old newspaper and I noted with mingled pleasure and pride that there was a line waiting to pay.

'I can help you here,' I called to the next person in line. As I wrote up the sale and scanned the bar code on the 1970s silver-plated tray, a real bargain at four dollars, I looked back toward the furnishings area, and was pleased to see that Martha was gone. Paula was helping a customer, so I guessed that Barney had left with Martha. I noted that Alverez was nowhere to be seen either. Confirming that all three were gone made me feel good, empowered somehow, as if I'd succeeded in chasing them away.

With both the tag sale and auction preview under control, I went back to the office to talk to Gretchen. She was on the phone when I arrived, and eavesdropping, I was pleased to hear her tell Roy, one of our best pickers, that he should come on by now.

'Roy?' I asked, when she was off the phone.

'Yeah. He says he has some interesting books.'

'Good,' I said. 'Have you made a copy of the Grant tape yet?' I asked. As policy, all tapes are to be copied immediately – just in case.

'Yeah. All done.'

'Make a copy for Sasha, okay?'

'You got it.'

'And these,' I said, pointing to the ledger-page copies that Mrs Cabot had left with me. 'Make a copy for each of us, and keep this with the file.'

'Okay.'

'Also, keep an eye on Eric,' I said. 'He had a little queue a minute ago at the checkout line. If it gets busy, you may need to help him.'

'Sure thing.'

'I'm going up to my office,' I told her. 'Buzz me at one if I'm not down by then, okay?'

'Should I bring you a sandwich?'

Since we provided food for the staff during public events, and Gretchen would be coordinating distribution, bringing me a sandwich would serve two purposes – her delivery would alert me to the time, and I'd be certain to get something to eat. Gretchen, my caretaker, at work.

'Good idea,' I said.

As soon as I got upstairs I called Max and got him on his cell phone. I could hear street noises in the background, a horn blaring, and, in the distance, a siren. I wondered if he was out and about running errands with his children.

'Max,' I said, 'a couple of things.'

'Okay. I'm ready.'

'Mrs Cabot has hired me to appraise Mr Grant's estate before sending the goods to auction in New York.'

'What do you think of that?'

'I think it's a great opportunity.'

'Good, then.'

'She thinks I can get into the house tomorrow. Can you check for me? Or should I call?'

After a pause, Max said, 'I'll do it. I'll call Alverez.'

'Thanks.'

'You're welcome. What else?'

'Could you ask him if they inventoried Mr Grant's possessions, and if so, how it compared to Mrs Grant's ledger? In other words, is anything missing?'

'I'm making a note. Okay. Anything else?'

'Well, it was kind of funny, but ... Chief Alverez was here just now.'

'Where?'

'Here. At the tag sale. Looking at stuff.'

'Did he say anything?'

'He acted like he just was at the tag sale for the tag sale. But I didn't believe him.'

'I'll ask him about it when I call him.'

'Thank you, Max. One more thing. Did you ever ask Epps about who inherited from Mr Grant?'

'Yes, the daughter and granddaughter – a fifty-fifty split. Didn't I tell you?'

'I don't think so. It doesn't matter. I was just curious.'

'Well, anyway. Yes, I asked him, and yes, they split it all.'

Confirmation. I allowed myself to relax a notch, relieved to learn that Wes had told me the truth. And it occurred to me that maybe, if one thing he reported was true, so too was everything else.

I turned on my computer, and when it had booted up, I went directly to the Web site where I'd learned that Mr Grant's Renoir was stolen. My heart pounding with anticipation, I entered 'Apples in a Blue Bowl with Grapes' and 'Cézanne' in the Web site's search engine, and felt no surprise when, within seconds, the listing appeared.

I leaned back in the chair and read the brief description. According to the site, the painting had been the property of the Viennese collector and businessman Klaus Weiner and his wife, Eva, who were forced to sell it in 1939 to pay the 'Jew tax' imposed by the Nazis after the Anschluss of 1938. The site asked that anyone with knowledge contact a man named Jonathan Matthews, a trust officer with the Imperial Bankers Trust, a private bank in Dallas, and promised a no-questions-asked $1 million reward for the painting's safe return.

I opened a bottle of water, thinking about the ethics of offering a reward for the return of stolen goods. Wouldn't that simply encourage more theft? I shrugged and dismissed the thought as irrelevant. Rewards had been offered and accepted for the return of lost or missing items forever. 'I'll cross that bridge if and when,' I said aloud, then added, 'Not my issue. At least, not right now.'

I turned back to the computer and typed in 'Matisse' and 'Notre-Dame in the Morning.' Another hit. According to the site, it had been owned by the Rosen family, who had lent it to a small museum in Collioure, a French village on the Mediterranean, in 1937. In February of 1941, the curator reported it stolen along with seventeen other works. No explanation of the museum theft was given. The contact was listed as Michelle Rosen. The address was in the sixth arrondissement in Paris.

Three paintings, three stories of loss. And starting tomorrow, I'd have free rein to search for the two that were still missing. I couldn't wait. I felt an exhilarating excitement and wished I could head over to the Grant place now. But I couldn't. I took a deep breath and forced myself to think instead of act.

One decision I had to make was what to tell Sasha – and when. Another decision was to create a protocol for our work. Just as cleaning a house required an answer to the question *When is it clean enough?* so too did research demand an answer to the question *When do you know enough?* Sometimes I consulted a specific number of sources. Sometimes I aimed to achieve a certain depth of information. Other times I insisted on answering particular questions. No one approach was best for all circumstances. I needed to determine what was best in this situation. And I needed to figure it out before we began or we'd waste time and energy.

I was eager to get under way, yet I felt anxious, too, fearful of what I might learn as I examined the Grant antiques for clues about the missing paintings, convinced that if I found the art, I might also discover a secret that had led to Mr Grant's murder.

chapter thirteen

The day was a success. At the auction, everything sold, and we beat our estimates; several people told me they were impressed, including a woman who made an appointment for an appraisal; and Bertie, from the *New York Monthly*, looking for fodder for her article on scandals in the antique business, learned nothing.

The tag sale went well, too. Revenue from sales was flat, but three people invited us to make offers on selling miscellaneous household goods to spare them the hassle of running yard sales. Anyone in the antique business will tell you that buying is tougher than selling, and the search for quality goods is constant. So to have opportunities to acquire inventory was all that was needed to transform a good day into a megawinner.

Max called around seven that evening, just as we were getting ready to close up.

'I finally reached Alverez,' he said.

'And?'

'And it's okay for you to go to the Grant place anytime.'

'That's great.'

'He mentioned that they're maintaining a loose patrol, so if you're questioned, it would make your life easier if you had some kind of written permission on hand.'

'I have a letter from Mrs Cabot.'

'Good. Go ahead and fax it to me, and carry it with you. Moving on … I asked him about the inventory.'

'And?'

'And everything is accounted for except two things. You've seen Mrs Grant's ledger, right?'

'Yes.'

'Then you know about the Cézanne and the Matisse?'

'Yeah, I saw.'

'Well, those are the only two items missing.'

I was prepared for the news. So far, Wes's source, whoever it was, was batting a thousand. 'Pretty amazing, huh?' I said.

'Just a little,' he said dryly.

'Yeah.'

'Also, I asked him about being at your place today.'

'And?'

'And he said he went to your tag sale because he likes tag sales.'

I paused. 'Did you believe him?'

'Sure, why not? I like tag sales, too. And you should see my wife.'

'I don't know … he just doesn't strike me as a tag-sale sort of guy.'

'Well, whatever his reason was, I wouldn't let it worry you.'

'Okay,' I said, willing to stop discussing it, but unconvinced. 'Any other news? Did he indicate they're making progress on the investigation?'

'No news. He said they're still following up on several promising leads, whatever that means.'

'What do you think it means?' I asked, not liking the sound of it.

I could imagine Max's shrug. 'Probably just what it says. That he's following up on several promising leads.'

The phrase 'following up on promising leads' chilled me. Somehow, the wording sounded ominous.

We agreed to talk on Monday after I'd been through the Grant house, or sooner if I needed him. His rock-solid support was an enormous comfort to me. I pictured him sitting in his suit and bow tie, his brow furrowed as he listened, and I wished I was nearby to touch his elbow, to thank him for helping me navigate this uncharted sea.

As I hung up, Sasha came into the office.

'We're all set,' she said, looking exhausted.

'You did a great job, Sasha,' I told her.

'Thanks,' she answered, blushing, her awkwardness at being complimented manifesting itself in a quick hair twirl.

'New project,' I said, changing the subject.

'Oh, yeah? What?'

'The Grant goods. We've been hired by Mrs Cabot, Mr Grant's daughter, to verify, authenticate, and value the contents of the house. You and I will work together, but you'll be doing most of the research.'

'That's great!' she exclaimed, her eyes blazing at the prospect, exhaustion a thing of the past.

'The first step is for you to watch the tape I made. And read the inventory Mrs Grant kept. Review them before Monday, okay?'

'Absolutely. This is so exciting! Thank you, Josie.'

'You're welcome. It's great, isn't it? Let's meet at the Grant house at, what? Nine on Monday morning? Is nine okay for you?'

'Sure, nine is good.'

'Okay. Make sure you have the address.'

She smiled and thanked me again. From her perspective, I was offering a rare treat. She was visibly excited at the prospect of spending her weekend studying the tape I'd made of Mr Grant's antiques and poring over the inventory. Lucky me.

I slept until noon on Sunday. When I awakened, I felt discombobulated, uncertain of the day or, even, momentarily, where I was. No remnant of a dream lingered, so I couldn't blame my confusion on that. Shaking off the amorphous discomfort proved tough, and it wasn't until I showered and ate eggs, cooked just the way I like them, scrambled soft with tomatoes and onion mixed in, that I began to feel more like myself.

At three, dressed in jeans and a lightweight sweatshirt, I headed for the Grant house planning to stop at a grocery store on the way back to buy the ingredients I needed to cook Monterey chicken. I took the scenic route, glad for an excuse to drive along the shore.

It was a warm day, the bright sun hinting at summer. I rolled down the windows, relishing the ocean breeze. As I drove, I spotted several sailboats coursing along, running parallel to shore. I'd never sailed, and I decided that once I was clear of the Grant situation, I'd learn. Why not? I asked myself.

Driving through the village, I saw that the Taffy Pull's door was propped open, and impulsively, I swung right into a vacant parking space. According to Wes, someone from the Taffy Pull had called Mr Grant shortly before he'd been murdered, and I wanted to know why.

I stepped out and looked around. The street was deserted, but there were several cars scattered along the stretch of Main Street where the shops were nestled.

The Taffy Pull's front window was decorated with displays of small piles of sand, artistically arranged to suggest the beach. Miniature lawn chairs dotted the sand piles. Brightly colored saltwater taffy pieces somehow connected to fluffy clouds dangled on nylon threads from the ceiling. It didn't make logical sense, but it was whimsical and cute.

I took a deep breath for courage, and entered the store. I blinked several times, trying to hurry my eyes along as they adjusted to the dim inside light.

A blonde stood with her back to me, stretching to pull down a small white box of candy from a high shelf.

'Hi,' I said, looking around, glancing at the woman's back.

'Hello,' she answered over her shoulder.

Box in hand, she turned, and I'm certain surprise showed on my face. 'Paula!' I exclaimed.

Paula, my part-time tag-sale employee who wore T-shirts emblazoned with her political views and causes, responded, 'Josie?'

'I didn't know you worked here.'

She grimaced, just a little. 'Family business. Today's my turn.'

'Got it.' I smiled. I wanted to say something nice. A family business required a compliment even if she had made a face in telling me about it. 'The display window's cute.'

'Thanks. That's my mother's touch. She's the needlepoint and scrapbooking type, so her window displays are always "cute." '

She spoke the word 'cute' as if it were vulgar, or at least embarrassing. I flashed on a memory from when I was about nine or ten, with my mother. My dad was busy with business, and the two of us had driven out to the Norman Rockwell Museum in Stockbridge, about two hours west of Boston.

'It isn't just his craftsmanship, Josie,' my mother told me later that night, as we sat eating dinner at the Red Lion Inn. 'Obviously, Rockwell's a brilliant technician. But it's more than that. It's the emotion. He captured the moments in life exactly. You look at what he painted and you know how the people in his pictures felt about whatever situation he put them in. That's an amazing talent.'

To this day, I loved Norman Rockwell. But I was willing to wager that Paula, like many of the hip, so-called sophisticates I'd run into during my years living in New York scorned him, viewing his illustrations with disdain. 'White bread,' they called his work, dismissing it as banal. Too bad for them. I could just imagine the picture Rockwell would have created showcasing Paula's mother pridefully putting the final touches on the display window.

Paula seemed the same as always, cordial but not friendly. Solemn, as if she bore the weight of the world on her shoulders. Today's T-shirt read Mind Your Own Religion. Appropriate dress, I guessed, for an atheist with an attitude to wear on a Sunday.

Given her reaction to the window I'd just described as cute, I felt the need to clarify my comment. 'I meant it as a compliment.'

She paused, apparently unused to hearing positive remarks. 'Oh. Sure. I'll tell my mother. She'll be pleased.'

I smiled. 'So you sell saltwater taffy, do you?'

'Yeah. And other stuff. We sell all sorts of handmade candy.'

'Can I ask you something?'

'Sure,' she said, placing the small white candy box on the counter.

'You know how a man named Mr Grant was murdered?'

'Yeah, I heard. Terrible.'

'Was he a customer?'

'A customer? I don't think so. I don't know. Why?'

'Did you know him?'

Her look of surprise at what must have struck her as an out-of-the-blue question seemed genuine. 'No. Why?'

I shrugged, not wanting to explain. 'No reason. He's a local, that's all.'

A man entered the store holding hands with a girl of about seven or eight. They were laughing.

'Hi,' Paula greeted the newcomers.

'Hi,' the girl answered sweetly. 'Oh, look, Daddy....' and she led him to a display of pink-wrapped taffy.

There was no point in asking any more questions, even if I knew what to ask, which I didn't. I didn't feel right not buying something, so I pointed to the small box she placed on the counter, asked if I could buy it, and when she said yes, paid in cash. As I was about to leave, I turned back and got her attention. 'You did a great job yesterday.'

She seemed taken aback. 'Thanks.'

'I'll see you next Saturday.'

Paula almost smiled. 'You bet.'

Getting in my car, I placed the little white box of candy on the seat beside me, noticing the kind-of-hokey, kind-of-sweet tag line under the logo: Made with pride by the Turner family.

The smell of ocean salt and musky seaweed swept over me, and I decided to walk to Mr Grant's. I estimated it was less than two miles, and it would feel good to stretch my legs. There were no parking restrictions on Sunday, so I could leave the car where it was.

As I headed south, the ocean on my left, I found myself thinking about Paula. I realized I knew very little about her. In fact, I realized, feeling slightly guilty, I'd never actually thought about her as an individual at all. It was habit more than desire that led me to keep employees at a distance. Idly, I wondered if that professional reserve was wise. I shook my head. No way to know the answer to that one.

I knew more about Paula than before. I knew she had a family, and was involved enough to honor her responsibilities to the family's business. Still, discovering her there was odd. Maybe it was just a coincidence that one of my employees worked at the Taffy Pull. But if I'd named all the people I might have expected to find there, Paula Turner wouldn't have been on the list.

The Grant house, an icon of a gracious age, had been built around 1920 and beautifully maintained ever since. As I approached, I spotted a policeman in uniform sitting on the porch, gently rocking in a weathered Adirondack-style chair. I recognized him. He was the middle-aged black man who'd led the search of my house. His belly hung over his pants. I was sure we'd been introduced, but I didn't remember his name.

'Hello,' I said as I started up the flagstone walkway.

He stood up, hitching his pants and taking a step forward. He nodded.

'I'm Josie Prescott. We've met.'

'I remember.'

'I'm authorized to go inside.'

'You got a letter or something?'

I dug into my purse, pulled out Mrs Cabot's note, and handed it to him. He read it slowly, turned it over, I don't know why, and gave it back to me.

'You going in now?'

'Yes. Is that all right?'

He shrugged. 'Sure, why not? I was just checking on things. Nothing much going on.'

My guess was that he was more interested in relaxing on a sunny spring day than he was in checking on things, but all I did was nod. 'I'm going to look around back.'

'I'll be heading out now, but I'll back in a while. You going to be here for long?'

'I don't know. Not too long, I don't think.'

I watched as he headed slowly toward the alley. That's why I hadn't seen his car, I realized. He was parked along the side. I looked around. Things looked fine. Someone, probably a landscaping service, had been maintaining the yard, for the lawn was freshly mowed. A stranger walking or driving by wouldn't know that the house was unlived in.

I circled the grounds slowly, looking for I don't know what, anything, I guess, that struck me as unexpected or out of whack. I saw nothing unusual, no recently excavated plot of land, no outside structure like a shed or tree house that might conceal two canvases laid flat or rolled. Entering with the key Mrs Cabot had given me, I stood for a moment in the vast hallway and listened to the sounds of nothing.

Not even the ticking of the grandfather clock disturbed the quiet. No one, I supposed, had wound it. I walked toward it, shaking my head in admiration.

It soared more than seven feet tall, a beautiful example of a Pennsylvania Queen Anne grandfather clock, circa 1785, with a walnut casing burnished to a glossy sheen. The flat-top bonnet featured an arched door with free-standing turned columns enclosing the hand-painted faces. The illustration showed the phases of the moon, and at the bottom, an inscription read Jacob Spangler York Town. I stroked the side, relishing the feel of the satiny wood.

I turned toward the kitchen, visible through the open hall door. It was creepy. I considered leaving, but I wanted to remind myself of the layout, so when Sasha and I met tomorrow, I could direct her efficiently. I walked through every room. Shadows stretched through old-fashioned slanted metal Venetian blinds. A musty odor of disuse permeated the air, my footsteps echoed, a lonely sound, on the hardwood floors, and a thin layer of dust lay undisturbed on every flat surface. I felt my normal Sunday melancholy descending on me like a shroud.

An oversized leather trunk in the basement caught my eye. Sitting on wooden planks about six inches off the concrete floor, it had probably been made in the 1920s. The cordovan-colored leather was butter soft and only slightly scuffed. I'd opened it when I'd surveyed the house for Mr Grant, so I knew it was designed in two parts. On top was a tray, about eighteen inches deep, sized to rest perfectly on a small ridge. When I'd removed it, a larger section, maybe four by six feet, was revealed. Mr Grant had used it to store stacks of old clothing. What had just occurred to me was that there might be a third section below the other two. Some old traveling trunks were built with a narrow but deep drawer at the bottom. Under the dim light cast by the single overhead bulb, I couldn't see well enough to tell, so I stooped down and used my flashlight to examine it carefully, and there it was. Two slots had been fabricated on the front side of the trunk, about 4 inches from the bottom, and in each slot, a metal handle lay flush with the leather surface.

My heart began to race. I couldn't believe my eyes. It was a perfect hiding spot. I reached down and wedged my fingers under the handles, and pulled. It resisted my efforts, and I tugged harder. The drawer slid out smoothly, and it was empty.

I felt deflated, but less so than when I'd sat on the floor in front of the partners' desk and cried. Then not finding the missing paintings had left me disconsolate. Now the hunt got my dander up.

I stood and stretched, turned off my flashlight, and stowed it on my belt. I looked around. The basement was a labyrinth of small rooms, and most were empty of items that would go to auction. One room housed the oil burner, another the washer and dryer, and a third was lined with wooden shelves filled with Mason jars of homemade preserves and pickles.

In a small workshop, presumably awaiting Mr Grant's attention as a handyman, stood a nonworking lamp, a chair that needed caning, and two pieces of a broken china platter. I doubted they were worth our time, but decided to examine them more closely tomorrow. Next to the platter, on the chipped surface of the worktable, was a three-sided wooden frame painted black with a plywood backing, waiting, I guessed, for the final piece to be attached. Sitting nearby were plastic containers of screws, nails, and bolts.

I switched off the light and was ready to head upstairs when I heard a creak, the sound of a floorboard bearing weight. I felt my heart suddenly stop, then thud so hard I almost felt sick. I froze. I didn't know what to do. I stood and listened. Nothing.

I shook off the concern, telling myself I was still skittish. *Don't be a silly-billy*, I chided myself, *you know very well that floorboards frequently make settling noises long after they're trodden upon, so what you're hearing is the aftereffect of your own presence.* I smiled, wondering if I'd gained a pound or two.

At the top of the stairs, halfway in the kitchen, I heard a soft scroop as the front door latch clicked home. Shocked, I recoiled and almost tumbled down the steps. Then I froze again. Someone was in the house.

As the footsteps moved confidently and quickly away from the door, heading, I guessed from the direction of the sound, to the study in the front, I moved forward, trying to glide, my boots leaden as I moved. I tried to think who it could be, but no one made sense. It certainly wasn't Mrs Cabot. And she'd assured me that she'd keep Andi away. Could the police officer have returned? Maybe.

I left the basement door ajar, not wanting to risk the sound the latch would make if I closed it, and listened. I heard what sounded like drawers opening and closing. A loud scrape startled me, and I tried to imagine what could have caused it. Something big, I thought, like a chair or an ottoman, being dragged across the floor would sound like that. Then I heard a soft thud, as if the item had tipped over and landed hard on a thick carpet. *No*, I said to myself, *whoever it is, it's not a policeman.*

I thought of calling 911, but quickly dismissed the idea. *No.* I'd make too much noise rummaging through my purse to locate my cell phone, and my voice would carry easily through the empty rooms.

All I could think of was how to get out. I headed for the back door, aiming to keep as much distance between me and the intruder as I could. I stepped gingerly into the mud room, and paused to let my eyes adjust. I had trouble catching my breath. In the gathering twilight, I could barely see the doorknob, and a rush of fear streamed over me. My heart hammering, tears welled in my eyes, making it hard to see. I brushed them away, forcing myself to focus on the problem at hand – getting out – and not think about my anxiety.

As soon as I could make it out, I reached for the doorknob, turned it, and pulled. Nothing. I tried again, pulling harder, then spotted a latch and turned it. Still, the door didn't budge. I looked at it more closely, and felt my stomach lurch as I realized it was a dead bolt and required a key to open, even on the inside. I was trapped, with no way out.

Peeking around the corner, my mouth was so dry, I struggled not to cough. I saw and heard nothing.

I slipped back into the kitchen and crept forward, and stood beside the refrigerator, shielded from view. Purposeful steps headed in what sounded like my direction, and looking around wildly, I ran across the room to a door that swung into the butler's pantry, connecting the kitchen to the dining room, and unsure where to go or what to do, I crouched down.

Even tucked away in a small room in the middle of the house, I heard a car pull up in the alley and stop. I could picture it. My thighs began to ache, but I seemed paralyzed with dread. Heavy steps approached the back door, and I heard the faint click of the dead bolt turning. Someone was entering the door that had held me prisoner.

A moment later, I heard a rush of scurrying steps, then a long moment later, a car starting and squealing away. I stayed huddled in the butler's pantry, rocking a bit, tears running down my cheeks unchecked.

'Josie?' I heard. I recognized Alverez's voice.

I sat down, hard, nearly fainting with relief, dropped my head forward, and began to cry in earnest. 'In here,' I called faintly after a moment, my voice muffled with tears. I tried again, using as much willpower as I could muster to stem the flow. I swallowed. 'I'm here.'

I heard a soft whoosh as Alverez pushed open the swinging door from the kitchen. I looked over and saw faded jeans and brown boots. I didn't have the energy to lift my head higher.

'What happened?'

'Someone,' I said, my voice cracking. 'Someone was here. They left out the front.'

'Are you all right?'

I nodded, and struggled to speak, but before I could translate my scattered thoughts into a coherent explanation, he was gone, running toward the front. 'Stay there,' he called.

I stayed, unmoving, listening. I heard his running steps, heavy thumps, then silence. After several minutes, he again pushed his way into the pantry and squatted beside me. 'Can you tell me what happened? What's wrong?'

I hated that he was seeing me like this. I felt mortified. 'I don't know. Someone was here. I heard noises and I panicked. I tried to leave, but I couldn't get out.'

I started up, wiping away the remnants of my tears. 'I never used to cry. You must think I'm a mess.'

'No, no,' he said. He helped me stand, holding my elbow. 'Let's get you a glass of water and you can tell me what happened.'

Meekly, I followed him into the kitchen and stood silently while he let the water run and opened cabinet doors until he found a glass. He filled it with water and handed it to me.

'Thanks,' I said, accepting it. I took a sip.

'I called for backup. People will be here in a minute, but in the meantime, I'm going to call the lab and get some technicians up here. Don't move.'

'I don't mean to sound wussy, but don't leave me alone. Okay?'

Alverez smiled. 'Okay. I'm just heading to the front door. Tag along if you want. But don't touch anything.'

I followed him, carrying my water, taking an occasional sip. The front door was wide open.

'I take it you closed the door when you came in.'

'Of course,' I said. 'I can't believe it. I just can't believe it.' I shook my head, the evidence of the open door startling me. I shivered.

'Was the door locked when you got here?'

'I guess. I used the key. I assumed it was.'

He nodded. I listened as Alverez called someone and issued a series of instructions. When he was done, he went into the study and glanced around. Nothing looked different. The books lining the shelves were orderly, the blotter on the partners' desk was centered, and the chairs were angled as I recalled.

'It looks the same, right?' he asked.

I nodded. 'Yeah. But whoever it was wasn't here long.'

'Right.'

He gestured that I should lead the way out, and we stood in the foyer, waiting.

'How did you know I was here?' I asked.

'Griff told me.'

'Griff?'

'The officer you spoke to.'

'Oh, I didn't remember his name. Why did you stop by?' I asked.

He paused, then said, 'Just checking on things.'

Was he checking up on me? At the auction, thinking he was following me had made me mad. Here, I had a different reaction. For whatever reason, it was easier for me to believe that he was just doing his job than it was to think he was trying to trap me somehow. I guessed it was adrenalin-fueled relief that allowed me to trust him.

'Feel free to sit down,' he said.

I went into the living room and perched on a French Provincial chair upholstered in blue-and-yellow fleur-de-lis chintz. He leaned on the doorframe, keeping an eye on the front door.

'So, are you okay enough to tell me what you're doing here?'

He didn't sound accusatory or judgmental. I looked up and our eyes met and held fast. The attraction I felt was deeper than before, more personal, based on my response to his actions, not just his looks. I felt myself relax and despite the anxiety of my situation, for a moment, all I experienced was the delicious, mysterious connection between an interested man and a willing woman.

A car door slammed and broke the spell. I looked away, disoriented, but calmer, and no longer frightened.

'So,' he repeated, 'what were you doing here?'

I shrugged. 'Nothing. I was looking around. You know, getting ready for tomorrow.'

'What's tomorrow?'

'Sasha and I begin the appraisal. You heard, right? Mrs Cabot has hired me to do a full appraisal.'

He nodded. 'Yeah, Max told me. Congratulations.'

I smiled. 'Thanks.'

'So exactly where were you and what did you hear?'

'It just occurred to me that I ought to call Max.'

Alverez nodded. 'Sure. Do you have his number?'

'Yeah. On my cell phone.' I retrieved my purse from the butler's pantry where I'd deserted it. Max answered on the first ring.

'Max, I'm sorry to disturb you on a Sunday.'

'No problem, Josie. What's up?'

'I'm here at the Grant house with Chief Alverez. I'm fine. But it looks like there was a break-in while I was here and he was asking me about it, so I thought I ought to call you.'

'A break-in! Are you all right?'

'Yeah, I'm fine. I didn't see anything. But I heard footsteps and it pretty much scared me to death. Then Alverez came in and found me huddled in a ball crying my eyes out. Pretty embarrassing, all things considered.'

'Let me speak to him,' he said. He didn't sound like he found my attempt at lightheartedness amusing.

I handed the phone to Alverez, who took it, and said, 'Alverez.'

He rested against the wall, calm and seemingly at ease. I sat on the chair and watched and listened.

'She seems fine. She was spooked, was all.... I haven't checked yet.... Understood.... I'll be reinstituting security.... Yeah, absolutely. Okay ... okay ... here she is.'

I accepted the phone, and said, 'Max?'

'Did you see or do anything you don't want him to know about? Just answer yes or no.'

'No.'

'Do you have any idea who it was who entered?'

'No.'

'Do you know why someone would have broken in?'

'No. Well, maybe.'

'Why?'

'Can I say openly?' I asked, my eyes on Alverez, watching him watch me.

'No. Keep him in sight, but get out of earshot.'

I repeated Max's instruction and Alverez said he'd step outside. I watched through the kitchen window as he walked toward the ocean. When he'd stopped and was standing with his hands in his pockets and his back to me, I told Max I was ready.

'So, why do you think?' he asked.

'Maybe to find the missing paintings.'

'Right. Got it.' Max paused. 'Why would someone risk breaking in if you were there?'

'I don't know. I was in the basement, so they wouldn't have heard me walking around. And the workshop is on the far side of the house, so they might not have noticed the lights being on.' I shrugged. 'The bulbs are pretty dim down there, anyway.'

'What about your car?'

'I left it in town. I walked.'

'That explains that,' Max acknowledged. 'And you didn't hear the person drive up?'

'No. But if I was in the basement, I don't know that I would have heard a car.'

'In any event, you didn't?'

'No.'

'Did you see anything – a shadow, a reflection in a mirror ... anything?'

'No. Nothing.'

'What did you hear?'

'I heard a floorboard, on the porch, I guess. Then I heard the front door opening. Then more footsteps.'

'Where did the footsteps go?'

'It sounded like to the study, but I can't be sure.'

'That's all?'

'I heard noises. I thought it was someone moving around, pulling open drawers, maybe knocking over a chair. Then footsteps heading toward the kitchen.'

'Then what?'

'Then I tried to get out. And couldn't. And flipped out.'

'You did fine, Josie. What else did you notice?'

'Nothing. After Chief Alverez arrived, I heard running steps, then a car roar off.'

'And that's it?'

'That's it,' I said.

Max paused, digesting, I guessed, what I'd told him. 'What were you doing in the basement?'

'Looking around. I looked at a trunk and was deciding whether the broken things in Mr Grant's workshop were worth including in the appraisal.'

'What broken things?'

'You know, a lamp that needs a new cord, a plate that needs to be glued. Things like that.'

'What did you decide?'

'Probably they're not worth including. I mean, there's no market for glued china, you know? I thought I'd have Sasha look at the lamp, but that's about it.'

'Okay. You can tell him what you've told me. If he asks anything out of range of your experience today at the Grant house, don't answer. I told him I'd give you this instruction, so all you have to say is that you want to wait for me. If he needs more information, we can meet tomorrow. Okay? Are you clear?'

'Yeah. I am. Thanks, Max.'

'Just remember, short answers. One-word answers are best.'

'I remember.'

I hung up and slipped the phone back into my purse. I made my way outside and when Alverez turned toward me, I smiled. 'I'm all yours. Max said.'

I heard the sirens, and before he could answer, two marked cars had pulled up, their red lights spinning in the night.

chapter fourteen

After Chief Alverez finished questioning me, he told me that he needed to talk to the senior technician for a minute, and then he'd drive me to my car.

'Okay,' I said, feeling shaky and weak, glad for his offer, embarrassed to admit that independent little ol' me didn't want to walk alone in the dark to my car.

We rode without speaking. All I heard were the comforting sounds of the droning engine and the soft claps of waves as they washed ashore.

Approaching the strip of stores where I'd left my car, I noted that the Taffy Pull was closed and dark. My car was the only one parked nearby. The entire area looked deserted.

Alverez said, 'How are you feeling?'

'Embarrassed.'

'Well, you don't need to be. Why wouldn't you get upset when someone breaks in to a recently murdered man's house?'

'I guess,' I acknowledged. I shrugged. 'I'm okay.'

'You did fine,' he reassured me.

'Well ... no, I didn't. I used to pride myself on handling crises well. Now look at me. I'm a mess.'

'Jeez, Josie. Don't be so hard on yourself.'

My father used to say the same thing to me, that I had to give myself a break. Hearing Alverez speak similar words comforted me.

'Thanks,' I said, trying for a smile. 'Also, thanks for driving me.'

'You going to be okay on your own tonight?'

I swallowed, fighting sudden tears. 'You bet,' I said, aiming for perky.

He paused, then said, 'If anything else occurs to you, don't wait. Call me right away. Even in the middle of the night, okay?'

I shivered at the urgency conveyed by his words, and turned to look at him. In the glinty white moonlight, I could see the outline of his features, but not his eyes.

'Okay.'

'Here,' he said, reaching into his pocket. 'Take another card so you'll have my number handy.'

I took it and slipped it into my purse. After a pause, I asked, 'Do you know how the person got in?'

'Looks like they just popped the lock.'

I shook my head. 'I can't believe it's that easy.'

'Yeah,' Alverez said. 'That lock is probably original to the house. A credit card would do it, no problem.'

'But the back lock requires a key.'

'Yeah,' he said, nodding. 'Apparently Mr Grant didn't use the back door much, so he thought it ought to be secure.'

'Really? How can you know that?'

He paused, then said, 'It's what I do, actually. I find things out. Like, for instance, the grocery-store delivery folks always came to the front door, by request.'

I nodded. 'Funny, isn't it? We're in the same business. We both are paid to find things out.'

'Yeah. Same, but different.'

'Yeah.' I thought about what he said about the lock. 'Should I tell Mrs Cabot to change the lock?'

'Absolutely. I plan on telling her, too. We'll be providing security until we figure out what's going on. But she might want to add more, like an alarm system. Until the contents are removed.'

'That'll be pretty soon, I guess. In a week or so, probably Dobson's will take control of everything and put it all in storage in New York. So they can do their own research.' After a short silence, I added, 'Well, I guess I better go.'

'Will you be all right to get home?'

'Sure. I'm glad to be away from the Grant place, I've got to tell you.' As I spoke, I decided not to be alone there again. 'When you said you're going to be providing security, does that mean that you're going to station men at the Grant house?'

'Why?'

I shrugged. 'Call me crazy, but I don't really want to be there on my own again. And I don't think I ought to let Sasha be alone there, either.'

'Makes sense. For the foreseeable future, I'll have someone there.'

'Good. We're scheduled to start the appraisal tomorrow morning. Will it be all right for us to enter?'

'Yeah, no problem. The technicians are just about done already. They'll be out of here within an hour. I'll tell the man on duty that you're expected.'

'Thanks. Well, then....'

'You need me,' he interrupted, 'you call. Okay?'

'Okay,' I agreed, grateful for his attention, yet still feeling self-conscious about my emotional spectacle. He came around the car to hold the door for me as I jumped down from the SUV. When I had my motor running, I waved a quick 'See ya,' and he nodded and stepped back. As I pulled out and drove north, I glanced in the rearview mirror, and saw him, standing still, watching me.

Home again after spending more than fifty dollars at the grocery store, I put on a CD of Vivaldi's *Four Seasons* and made a martini. I broiled a hamburger and ate it with sliced tomatoes standing at the kitchen counter.

I was feeling better, more energized and less fearful. Even though it was approaching 10:00, I decided to proceed with preparing Monterey chicken. I was definitely not ready to rest, and it tasted better if it sat overnight in the refrigerator before baking anyway. I was grating Parmesan cheese for the breadcrumb mixture when Wes called.

'Hey,' he said. 'Let's meet tomorrow. Same time, same place, okay?'

'What do you have for me?' I asked.

'Another doughnut.'

'Please, God, no,' I said, understanding that he wasn't going to give anything away on the phone. 'Seven? At the beach?' I asked to confirm.

'Yup.'

'I'll drive myself.'

'Ha, ha, ha.'

'See you then,' I said.

I turned back to my butterflied chicken breasts, white-hot curious about what he had to tell me. While I prepared the recipe, I went over everything I knew about Mr Grant's murder and the missing paintings. Where would Mr Grant have hidden the masterpieces? I wondered if I had walked past them secreted somewhere and not even known it.

I ran water over my hands, rubbing my fingers to rid them of the breading mixture I'd used to coat the rolled chicken breasts, and stretched the plastic wrap taut over the roasting pan. I smiled as I placed it in the refrigerator and saw a carton of eggs. Tomorrow, I'd bring breakfast and show Wes an alternative way to eat. I put water on to boil.

Twenty minutes later, hard-boiled eggs and fruit salad ready to go for the morning, I finished wiping down the counter, turned the dishwasher on, and with my mind still absorbed in thinking of possible hiding places, I went to bed.

But sleep eluded me. I was exhausted, yet fretful and exhilarated as well. Tossing and turning so relentlessly that I jelly-rolled myself in the sheet, I finally gave up and turned on the light.

I decided to read for a while, to try to relax. I selected a favorite romance that I knew well, *The Reluctant Widow*, by Georgette Heyer.

It didn't work. I found myself staring into space, pages unturned, for minutes at a time. Suddenly, just before two in the morning, I found the answer I'd sought.

I put the book aside and sat up in bed. I had it. I thought it through, methodically working through the various issues involved. Satisfied, I nodded, convinced that I knew where the paintings were and how they were hidden.

And I had a plan to protect them.

I smiled, satisfied, and to the mournful whine of a screech owl, my still-active brain succumbed to my body's fatigue, and at last, I slept.

When the alarm went off, I hit the snooze button repeatedly until I finally forced myself out of bed, dawn's light seeping into the room through ill-fitting curtains. When I saw that it was after five, I panicked, and flew into the shower.

I planned to secure the missing paintings and set the protocol we'd use in the appraisal before meeting Wes, and that required that I get to the Grant house by 5:30.

I didn't make it. It was closer to 5:45 when I pulled up in front. A police officer stepped out on to the porch as I got out of my car. He was one of the young men I'd seen at the Rocky Point police station during one of my interrogations, and he looked tired.

I started up the walk, smiled, and said hello. 'I'm Josie,' I said.

He nodded. 'Chief Alverez said you'd be coming by.'

'And you are? ...' I asked.

'Officer O'Hara.'

'May I enter?'

'Sure.' Officer O'Hara stepped aside and I went in.

'I've got to tell you,' I said to O'Hara, looking back with a smile, 'I'm really glad you're here.'

He looked surprised, as if he was more used to people objecting to him or something he was doing than he was to receiving thanks. Or maybe he thought I was being cagey, a murder suspect trying to lull a cop into believing in her innocence.

'I'll stay out of your way, but I'll be around,' he said matter-of-factly.

'Okay.' I shut the door, and through the window, I saw him sit on a bench and stretch his legs out in front of him.

I hurried into the study, turned on the lamps, and looked at the three Taverniers sitting side by side on the far wall, hanging from the crown molding on metal brackets. Reaching up, I lifted the painting closest to the door off its brackets, and gently lowered it until it rested on the carpet and against the wall. I examined the frame carefully, rotating the painting one turn at a time, carefully searching all sides. I twisted it so I could see the back, spotting nothing unusual in its construction, except that it was oversized, perhaps four or five inches deeper than it needed to be. The second Tavernier seemed to be constructed in the same way. I saw nothing odd. The third one, when I lifted it down, was noticeably lighter than the first two, and as soon as I positioned it against the wall, I saw a gap, as I expected.

The three-sided structure in the basement was designed to slip into the top of this frame like a drawer, sliding into place, meshing perfectly. No doubt, that was where the Renoir had been stored.

Returning my attention to the first painting, with its three-sided removable frame still in place, I tried to pry it loose. Nothing happened. I couldn't see how to wedge it free. There was no handle or pulling device visible.

I unhooked my flashlight and leaning back on my heels, I examined the frame inch by inch, and there it was. On the top, in the center, was a tiny square plastic button, painted black to match the rest of the frame, and inlaid so perfectly, it was only by the closest examination that it ever would be found.

I pushed the button, and felt the spring-loaded apparatus nudge the top of the frame upward. Enough wood was now available that I could get a handhold and pull.

The frame was too large and heavy for me to extract standing up, so I laid the painting on the carpet and pulled it out that way. 'Oh, my God,' I whispered as the Cézanne came into view. The cobalt blue and muted shades of orange and green were indescribably breathtaking. I shook my head, dazed.

I heard a scuffing sound, realized that Officer O'Hara could enter at any moment, and rushed to lay the other Tavernier down on the rug. I pushed the button releasing the hidden drawer and slid the Matisse out of its secret place. It was gorgeous, the perspective complex, and the colors vivid.

Both canvases lay flat against plywood backing, clamped at the top to hold them in place. I was easily able to release them, lift them out, and roll them up. Sliding the three-sided structures back in place, I left the paintings leaning against the wall.

As I passed through the hall, I was relieved to see O'Hara perched against a porch column, staring at the ocean, smoking a cigarette. I headed for the basement, cradling the two rolled paintings. I shivered a little as I entered the cooler, darker environment, whether from the chill of the cellar, the memory of yesterday's panic attack, or the thrill of my discovery, I couldn't tell.

I tenderly placed the paintings on the top of the leather trunk, and squatted down to open the hard-to-find bottom drawer. It slid out smoothly, and unrolling the paintings, I laid them one on top of the other in the oversized space, closed the drawer, and ensured that the two handles were snuggled into their openings.

Standing, I realized that I'd been hyperventilating, and I forced myself to take several slow, calming breaths. I wasn't out of the woods yet. I grabbed the three-sided frame from the workbench and held it upside down. Under the targeted beam of my flashlight, I could see the small spring. From the top, when nuzzled in place, it was essentially invisible. I carried it upstairs, inserted it into the opening in the third painting's frame, and pushed it home.

I was done, and I sat down on the floor to catch my breath. 'Whew,' I said aloud.

When I'd first examined Mr Grant's treasures, all three Tavernier frames were intact. I wondered what the police had thought when they'd looked at the gap. Probably nothing more than that a piece of a frame had broken off.

Last night, with sleep eluding me, I concluded that Mr Grant had intended to destroy all three of the fabricated frames as soon as the stolen paintings had been sold, thus eliminating evidence of his deception. He'd taken the Renoir from its hiding place, and since he never intended that it would return to its home behind the Tavernier, he'd brought the three-sided frame to his workroom to demolish. No doubt he'd eventually expected to reframe the Taverniers, and I was willing to bet that somewhere, in the back of a closet, or in the attic, for instance, we'd find three traditional gilt frames ready to go.

I stood up, took a deep breath, and rehung all three paintings. It was exhausting.

I allowed myself a private grin and an 'atta girl.' I brushed hair out of my eyes, excited that I'd discovered the missing paintings, and proud that I'd found a way to keep them safe.

But my pride was mitigated by icy fear. Another thought I'd had last night, as I'd struggled to sleep, was that maybe someone had killed Mr Grant in order to have unfettered access to the Cézanne and the Matisse.

If Mr Grant hadn't liked how the negotiations over the Renoir had gone, and had decided not to proceed, killing him had been the only way of getting the art. Or maybe, I thought, Mr Grant was killed not because he'd withdrawn his offer to sell the Renoir but because his death allowed the killer to avoid receiving only a small percentage of the proceeds of its sale. With Mr Grant out of the way, the murderer could take it all. But only if he – or she – could locate the missing paintings.

It seemed obvious to me that the Renoir had been stolen at the same time that the murder occurred. What a disappointment it must have been for the murderer to realize that everyone seemed to know that the Renoir existed. Too risky to keep, and too risky to sell, it must have seemed clever to the killer to plant it at my warehouse in order to try to frame me for Mr Grant's murder.

I shook my head, sickened at the thought that someone could do such a thing to me. Whoever it was, I could imagine their growing frustration. The Renoir might be off limits, but if Mr Grant had mentioned the other paintings, perhaps dangling them as a carrot during the negotiations, and if the killer hadn't known that Mrs Grant's ledger would reveal the paintings' existence to the police, the murderer might think he – or she – was sitting pretty.

Of course, a search couldn't be undertaken while the house was under police custody as a crime scene, but as soon as the authorities unsealed it, someone had entered and had, apparently, started to hunt for the paintings while I was in the basement.

My final conclusion, and I shivered with fear at the thought, was that if someone had murdered once to acquire priceless masterpieces, that person wouldn't hesitate to kill again.

It was almost 6:30 when I got to my office. I ran inside, punched the code to turn off the alarm, and dashed upstairs to my office.

The best way to establish protocols is to actually do research. Otherwise, your decisions are based only on theory and can be arbitrary. Still, research only isn't enough. Setting reasonable price ranges requires knowledge, intuition, and street smarts. You have to consider factors such as the condition of the piece relative to other examples that have sold, current market demand compared to what economic conditions existed when other similar pieces were auctioned, and unique factors such as a distinctive provenance – and determine which ones matter most.

Two of my office walls were stocked with various guidebooks and auction catalogues. In addition, we subscribed to several Web sites that tracked and reported auction results worldwide.

As a test case, I selected the now-silent Queen Anne grandfather clock standing in Mr Grant's hallway. I wanted to see how long it took me to set a price. It was a reasonable test selection, since it was representative of the bulk of the items in the Grant estate: valuable, but not unique.

Noting my starting time, I quickly sorted through the American furniture catalogues that filled about a quarter of my bookshelves and found two clocks that were similar to Mr Grant's. One had been sold by a Florida dealer, Shaw's Antiques, in 2003. Mark Shaw described it as 'magnificent.' Barney's firm, Troudeaux's New Hampshire Auctions, had auctioned the second in 2002. M. Turner described the clock's condition as 'very good.' Which meant it wasn't 'magnificent.'

Most antique dealers used 'excellent' or 'mint' to indicate pristine condition, but some were more poetic, and used terms like 'magnificent.' The bottom line was that there was no standardization in the industry, so it was important for buyers to know how a dealer used words. 'Magnificent' implied perfection. 'Very good' usually meant there was some minor or normal wear.

Shaw's had estimated that the clock would sell for $9,000 and it had actually sold for $10,300. Troudeaux's had expected the clock to bring in $10,500, so its sale price of $6,750 must have been a huge disappointment. That was quite a spread – the Florida clock fetched $3,550 more than the one Barney sold.

Big differentials in prices between two similar items usually reflected differences in quality – which was, I knew from experience, impossible to define precisely. In this case, however, it seemed obvious why Shaw's clock did so much better. First, it was in better condition than the one Barney sold. Second, according to Shaw's description, the clock had been owned by a former governor of Georgia. That kind of connection often led to higher prices. Prestige by association. Besides which, Barney's estimate might reflect wishful thinking or whimsy. His firm's research was always suspect; whether from indifference or sloppiness, his estimates were wrong more often than they were right.

Searching through the Web sites we subscribed to, I found another similar clock, described as being in 'excellent condition.' It had sold at a Pennsylvania auction six months ago within its range. Estimated to fetch between $7,000 and $8,500, it had brought in $8,100.

From a low of $6,750 to a high of $10,300. Calculating both the average and the median, and considering the effect of condition and the Georgia governor's prior ownership, I estimated that Mr Grant's clock should sell for $7,000 to $9,000. Maybe more if Dobson's got lucky.

I typed out the description, including the estimated price range, and glanced at the clock on my computer. From first look at my bookshelves to the completed catalogue entry, half an hour. Not bad. In a separate document, I specified the details of my calculation.

The protocol was set: I would require that we research three sales of comparable items within the last five years. I e-mailed the file to Gretchen and Sasha, and printed out a copy for me to take. I smiled with satisfaction. Step one of the appraisal, done.

I called Wes en route and told him that I was running late.

It was twenty after seven when I pulled to a stop behind Wes's old Toyota. He was leaning against the hood, smiling like the Cheshire Cat.

'Sorry I'm late,' I said, hurrying to join him, the bag of food in my hand.

'If only you knew what I know, you would have been on time,' Wes said, popping a handful of mixed nuts into his mouth.

'Don't be a tease, Wes. Tell me.'

'Let me turn on the radio.'

'Wes, you're not still thinking I'm wired, are you?'

He chuckled, a snorting sort of sound, and ate more nuts. 'Nah, but I got news, and I'm not taking any chances.'

Wes sat down, and leaving the car door open, turned on the motor and punched a button for an oldies station. I got settled in the passenger seat and pulled plastic-wrapped hard-boiled eggs out of the bag, laid out napkins on his dusty dashboard, and handed him a plastic fork.

'What's this?' he asked.

'Food,' I answered. 'You ought to try it sometime.'

'What are you talking about?'

'I looked in the back of your car, remember? I ate your doughnut. You don't eat food. You eat junk. An egg and fruit salad. That's food.'

He looked skeptical. 'Thanks,' he said, but made no move to eat.

I unwrapped my share and took a bite of egg.

He gestured that I should lean closer. Accompanied by the familiar, gotta-dance rhythm of 'Under the Boardwalk,' he whispered, 'Barney kept the three P.M. appointment at Mr Grant's house. Alverez was the one who told him about the murder.'

Either Barney was telling the truth and had called the night before to change his appointment from 9:00 to 3:00 or he was lying, and had called for some other reason altogether.

Goose bumps rose on my arms as I had the startling realization that maybe Barney had shown up at 9:00 and killed Mr Grant. There was plenty of time for him to cover his tracks. It was simple. All he had to do was leave and return at 3:00, pretending he was there for his rescheduled appointment.

I stepped out of the car and walked a few steps, starting up the dune, wanting to see the ocean. I watched the frothy waves make rivulets as they rushed along the sand.

Wes stepped out of the car, and called, 'What are you doing?'

After a moment, I came back and sat down again.

'What do you think?' Wes asked, watching me consider options.

'Interesting,' I said.

'That's one of those comments....'

'What do you mean?'

' "Interesting," ' he said, mocking me. 'Don't give me that. Tell me what you're thinking.'

'I'm thinking that it's interesting,' I insisted, aiming to look and sound sincere. 'What do you think I mean?'

'Give me a break.'

I shook my head. I took out my plastic container of fruit salad, popped the lid, and ate some pineapple and cantaloupe pieces. 'Anything else?' I asked.

Wes sighed loudly. 'You owe me. You know that, don't you? You owe me big.'

'Wes, you and I both know we owe each other. You'll get yours.'

'I better. That's all I've got to say. I better.'

'You will. So, what else?'

He sighed again. 'What the hell. You know those two business calls?'

I nodded. 'Yeah. Mr Grant's doctor and the Taffy Pull.'

'Right. Well, the doctor made that call to tell Mr Grant about the results of some tests he'd taken a week earlier.'

'And?' I prodded.

'And,' he said, drawing it out, enjoying his moment, 'Mr Grant received a diagnosis of late-stage pancreatic cancer.'

'You're kidding! That's terrible.'

'Yeah. Apparently, it's terminal about ninety-six percent of the time. It looks like Mr Grant had only weeks or months to live.'

'Really?'

'Yup.'

'Wow. That's so sad.'

I felt unsettled, hearing yet another example of my not being able to trust my instincts. The older I got, the more I realized that the chasm that exists between perception and reality is huge. I shook my head, disheartened at the thought. I pictured Mr Grant standing in his kitchen, jovial and lively. It was hard to think that at that moment, he'd been deathly ill. Sadness swathed me like fog clouding a distant view. Taking a deep breath to clear my mind, I looked up and saw Wes waiting for me to speak.

'When was that call made?' I asked.

Wes pulled out his much-used notepaper. 'March twelfth.'

I nodded. 'Just before Mr Grant called me. That must be why he decided to sell everything – and why he wanted to move so quickly.'

'Makes sense,' Wes acknowledged. 'But what does it mean?'

'I don't know. I'm just trying to understand everything I can.'

'How about you? What have you learned?'

It seemed low risk to confide that I'd been retained by Mrs Cabot. It wasn't a secret, and if he published it, I'd get some good press. 'You didn't get this from me. All right?'

'Sure. What?'

In a hushed voice, I told him what Mrs Cabot hired me to do, sticking to the in-the-open reasons: to verify, authenticate, and value the estate.

Impressed, Wes shook his head a little, and whistled. 'What a coup. What are you going to do about Troudeaux?'

'What do you mean?'

'Good ol' Barney's gonna be pissed.'

I hadn't thought of that, but he might be right. 'It's just business,' I said with a dismissive shrug.

'You wish,' Wes responded with a grimace.

If he was right, it was a real problem because Barney had the power to hurt me. A rumor here, an innuendo there, and my business would be ruined. Just in case Barney would resent that I won the job, I had to anticipate and block an attack. I remembered my father talking to me about barriers to competition, and tried to recall what he'd said.

The echoing, lonely sound of a sea gull startled me. I looked up and saw it spike and dive.

'What do you think?' Wes asked, recalling me to the conversation.

'You might be right,' I admitted. 'So I'd better prepare for the fallout, huh?'

'What can you do?'

'I don't know. I have to think about it.'

149

'Let me know, huh? It might make for a good story.'

'Wes, you're something else.'

'Thanks.'

'That wasn't a compliment. You're like an ambulance chaser, you know, looking for ways to find a nicely battered accident victim.'

'Man, you're brutal in the morning, aren't you? All I'm doing is my job. I don't make anyone a victim, you know?'

'Yeah, I guess.' I shrugged and smiled a little. 'I didn't mean anything by it. Nothing personal, anyway. It's a comment on the breed, not on you as an individual, okay?'

'Yeah, whatever. Back to the subject at hand.... Don't forget – when you find the Matisse and the Cézanne, I'm your first phone call, right?'

I thought for a moment about what to say. I needed to remember how I'd felt before I found the paintings, and consider how I would have acted around a reporter. I looked back toward the rising dunes. Upbeat and noncommittal, I decided. 'Keep your fingers crossed that I find them,' I said, trying to for a casual tone.

'And then you'll call me, right?'

'You know I can't promise that.'

'Why not? I'm the guy that clued you in to Mrs Grant's ledger, remember? You owe me.'

'I'll tell you what I can when I can. And that's a promise.'

He sighed loudly and tried to look hurt. I laughed. 'Wes,' I added, 'you're a hoot and a half.'

'A "hoot and a half"?' he asked. 'What's that?'

'You're a good reporter. Persistent. But we're done now. Unless you learned anything about the Taffy Pull phone call.'

'Not yet.'

'How about who left that fingerprint in Mr Grant's house?'

He shook his head. 'Still unidentified.'

We shook hands, and agreed to talk if and when.

I arrived back at the Grant house a couple of minutes before Sasha and sat in my car, glad for the chance to rest. She pulled up and parked in back of me. As I got out to greet her, I spotted the Taffy Pull box that had sat on the passenger seat overnight.

'Do you like taffy?' I asked her.

'What?'

'I have a box of taffy, but I don't really care for it. So you can have it if you want.'

'Sure, thanks. I like it.'

As I handed her the box, I thought of Paula and her family business. I wondered what she and Barney had been discussing on Saturday at the tag sale.

'Are you ready?' I asked.

'Absolutely. I can't wait! I knew that the Grants had special things, but I had no idea.'

'I know. It's unbelievable. Wait 'til you see. First thing we'll do is walk the house so you can get a feel for the layout. Then I'll go over the research protocol and we'll discuss procedures. Then, off we go!'

Sasha smiled, her eyes sparkling with anticipation. 'Will you be here the whole time?'

'No. I need to follow up on some of the buying leads we got over the weekend. But I'll be available whenever you need me.'

Officer O'Hara was still standing on the porch. 'Hi,' he said as we approached.

'Hello,' Sasha said shyly, looking down.

I introduced them, took her inside, and began the tour. Sasha followed along in stunned silence. It's one thing to watch a video and another thing altogether to see and touch the real thing.

When we finished, we sat at the kitchen table, agreeing that Sasha would go room by room, starting in the living room. 'The only thing for you to look at in the basement,' I told her, 'is the lamp. I don't know if it's worth including in the auction. There's a leather trunk down there, but I'll take care of that. I've already begun some of the research.' It wasn't true, but I needed a good reason to keep her away from it.

'Okay. I'll look at the lamp later.'

'Should I get you a helper?' I asked.

'A research assistant would be helpful,' she said. 'There's so much to do.'

I nodded. 'That's what I was thinking.' I took out my cell phone and called Gretchen. 'Good morning,' I said. 'Everything okay?'

'You bet,' she answered, sounding chipper.

'Do me a favor, will you? Call Don in New York,' I said, referring to an executive recruiter I knew who placed a lot of curators and art historians in temporary and permanent positions, 'and tell him I'm going to need a researcher for a week. Explain about the Grant appraisal, and warn him that the collection is eclectic, so we'll need someone with a broad knowledge base. Tell him I'll call him later if he has any questions. And ask him to get the person up here today.'

'Got it.'

I hung up and turned to Sasha. 'Let me explain the protocol that I think makes sense,' I said, showing her the printout I'd prepared that morning, reviewing what I learned about the grandfather clock, and detailing the standards I'd established. She listened closely, and agreed that the approach was appropriate.

As Sasha and I sat and talked about the catalogue format we'd use in preparing the written appraisal, I heard a commotion outside. I was glad I wasn't alone, anxiety replacing the comfortable feeling of being in charge that I'd had all morning.

'Let me see what's going on,' I said.

I headed to the front and pulled aside the sheer curtain enough to see Andi Cabot, scary-skinny in a formfitting yellow spandex dress and French heels, righteous and rigid, arguing with Officer O'Hara. Her features were scrunched in anger.

'Let me in,' she berated. 'It's my grandfather's house and you have no right to stop me.'

I couldn't hear Officer O'Hara's reply, so I cracked the door, gesturing to Sasha, who'd begun to walk forward, that she should stay back.

'I demand to see that Prescott woman.'

'Calm down, ma'am,' O'Hara said. His words had the opposite effect, enraging her further.

'Don't you tell me what to do. Where is she?'

I stepped forward. 'I'm here. What do you want?'

Andi tried to push past him, to get to me, but O'Hara thrust out his arm and stopped her. 'Don't touch me,' she shrieked. To his credit, he didn't budge.

To me, she said, 'Get out, and get out now. You're fired.'

The angrier Andi got, the calmer I felt. 'You can't fire me, I'm afraid,' I said softly. 'I don't work for you.'

'Me, my mother ... it's all the same. I damn well can fire you. Get out!'

I shook my head, mystified about her motivation, but confident of my position. 'I don't know what your issue is, Ms Cabot. But you can't fire me and I'm not getting out. I have a signed paper authorizing me to be here. Do you?'

'How dare you speak to me that way?' she raged, trying again to push past O'Hara.

'Officer O'Hara,' I said, still calm, 'I'm going inside now. Would you like me to call Chief Alverez and tell him what's happening?'

'Yes, thanks,' he said, moving in tandem with Andi, keeping her in check as she tried to forge ahead.

'I'll get you,' she shrieked, 'you can't do this to me!'

chapter fifteen

Sasha stood in the kitchen doorway, big eyed and pale. I smiled to reassure her, and said, 'A tempest in a teapot. Why don't you head to the living room and get started?'

'Are you sure it's okay?'

'Absolutely. Just ignore the huffing and puffing.'

'Okay,' she said, 'if you think I should.'

'I do. Go!' I said, gesturing with both hands, whisking her away.

She walked slowly, as if she was giving me a chance to change my mind. When she was out of sight, I pulled out my cell phone, found Alverez's card, and dialed his number. He answered curtly, 'Alverez.'

'It's Josie.'

'Hey,' he said, changing his tone, seeming to relax a bit.

'You know what I said yesterday, about being a mess?'

'Yes.'

'Well, I have good news. I'm in the midst of a crisis, and I'm handling it well.'

'I'm pleased for you. But what's the crisis?'

'Being fired.'

'What?' he asked, startled.

'Well, not really, since Andi has no authority.'

'What's going on, Josie?'

'Andi Cabot, Mr Grant's granddaughter, is here, enraged and mean. She told me I was fired. I told her she couldn't fire me, that I didn't work for her, and came back inside. Officer O'Hara is wrestling with her as we speak, trying to keep her from charging into the house and physically putting me out.'

'I'll be right there. Stay inside.'

I heard the click as he disconnected and looked mockingly at the phone. 'Guess he had to run,' I said aloud.

Andi continued to harangue Officer O'Hara. I dialed directory assistance and got the Sheraton's number, and asked the operator for room 319. After several rings, Mrs Cabot said, 'Hello?'

'Mrs Cabot?' I asked.

'Yes.'

'This is Josie Prescott.'

'Oh, yes. How are you?'

'I'm fine, thank you. Mrs Cabot, I'm at your father's house. My chief researcher, Sasha, and I have begun the appraisal. But, well, I need to tell you that your daughter is here.'

'At the house? Now?' she asked.

'Yes, I'm afraid so. She's pretty angry.'

'Where is she?'

'Out on the porch. You know that the police are guarding the house?'

'Yes, Chief Alverez told me. He called last night.'

'Yes, well, a police office is keeping her on the porch. Actually, I can hear her from here. She's pretty upset.'

'I'm so sorry, Josie. I just told her that I'd hired you. I was confident that I'd convinced her that you'd get us the most money from the auction because of your expertise. I'm so sorry. Are you all right?' She sounded mortified.

'Yes, I'm fine. Do you know why she's so angry?' I hated to ask, but felt as if I needed to know what I was dealing with.

There was a long pause. 'Mr Epps, my father's lawyer, told us, when we met with him, that Mr Troudeaux was the person best equipped to assist us. That was when we first arrived. I think Andi heard his words and turned off her brain.'

I thought about what she'd said. 'Why?' I asked. 'What did Epps say?'

After a pause, Mrs Cabot said, 'You know that my father, apparently, asked Mr Epps for suggestions about selling the Renoir?'

'Not in any detail,' I said.

'Mr Epps said that my father called him and asked for suggestions as to who would best be able to arrange a private sale of the Renoir. He said he'd given my father Mr Troudeaux's name. Andi was very excited about the painting, and what it might fetch. Mr Epps told her that he didn't know, but he'd mentioned that he'd run into Mr Troudeaux at some meeting and had told him about the opportunity. I gathered from what Mr Epps said that Mr Troudeaux was interested, perhaps, in purchasing it for himself. Knowing my father, he would have liked that idea, since it would have implied that Mr Troudeaux was a man of means. My father admired the wealthy almost as much as he admired wealth.'

'And Andi was there the entire time?'

'Yes. She wanted to call Mr Troudeaux then and there and negotiate the sale as soon as the painting was released from police custody.'

'Why didn't you?'

'Well, besides the fact that I wanted to do more research before I authorized anyone to sell anything, Mr Epps pointed out that we'd have to go through probate first.'

I nodded to myself, taking in what she was telling me. 'Has Andi seen the police inventory? Or your mother's ledger?'

'No, I don't think so. I haven't shown them to her. She'd have no way of knowing about the ledger, I don't think. Why?'

As near as I could tell, that meant Andi didn't know about either the Cézanne or the Matisse. I didn't want to bring them up, and risk having to tell Mrs Cabot an outright lie. Soon, I'd talk to her about them, but not now. Not with Sasha in the house and the police nearby. Not on the day she was due to bury her father.

Nothing I'd learned explained what Andi had against me. Ignoring Mrs Cabot's question, I asked, 'Do you know why Andi's so anti-Josie?'

'This is so awful, isn't it?'

'Yes, it is. And please forgive my directness. I can't imagine how horrible this must be for you, having to answer questions like this hours before your father's funeral.'

'Thank you, Josie. But your directness is appreciated. I know my daughter is difficult. She's always been difficult. Lately, she's been more and more motivated by money. I don't know more than that. I don't think she's well. I mean, look at her. I think she has problems. But I don't think she's anti-Josie, as you put it. I think she's antianything that will delay her access to money.'

Everyone likes money. But her desire seemed more of a need. More of a craving. Gambling, blackmail, or drugs, I thought. Picturing her sick-thin look, I concluded drugs, and at a guess, crystal meth. When I was in college, there was a guy who looked and acted like her. Sunken cheeks, passionless eyes, temper on a short fuse, needing more and more money to pay for the crystal meth that kept him going. Maybe Andi shared his demon.

I heard a siren. Alverez was arriving. 'She told me I was fired.'

'Oh, my goodness. Please forgive her, Josie. Of course you're not fired.'

'Thank you, Mrs Cabot. May I tell the police that she doesn't have your permission to enter the house?'

A pause, then, 'Yes. Absolutely.'

'Thank you, I think Chief Alverez has arrived, so I'd better go.'

'Thank you for calling. I'll be here until eleven. Please call again if you need me.'

'Never a dull moment, huh?' I said to Sasha as I passed the arched entry into the living room, making a silly face.

'Is everything okay?' she asked, her voice barely audible, her lack of confidence conveying fear and angst. Poor Sasha, a shadow of a soul.

'Perfect. Our working papers have just been reconfirmed.'

As I approached the porch, the voices got louder. I opened the door and looked out. Alverez stood with his back to me, Andi's vociferous accusations buffeting him like waves powerful enough to wear glass shards to sand. He didn't speak, and seemed, from the back at least, to not even react.

'I'm going to have your badge, you fucking son-of-a-bitch asshole. And yours,' Andi screeched, turning to confront a hapless O'Hara. 'You groped me, you sick fuck. You son of a bitch.'

Switching effortlessly from hysterical attack to cajoling entreaty, she turned back to Alverez, and continued, 'Please, please, please. Okay, okay, if you won't let me in to my own grandfather's house, you won't. No problem. Okay, okay. I can live with that. But you don't need the Renoir anymore, right? Your technicians have examined it six ways to Sunday. They probably know everything about it. So you're done with it, right? Come on now, please. Let it out of police custody, and I'm gone. History. I promise. You'll never see me again. My mother has said I can have it, so there's no problem there, okay? What do you say, let's make a deal, okay?'

Whew. Definitely crystal.

'Chief Alverez,' I whispered from inside. 'I have relevant information.'

He leaned his head sideways, indicating that he'd heard me and understood my message.

'Wait here. O'Hara, keep her on the porch. Got it?'

I heard a grunt of affirmation.

'Stay here,' Alverez told Andi. 'I'll be back in a minute.' He swung around and strode inside, and led the way to the kitchen. 'What?'

'Having fun with Andi?' I asked, smiling.

'Not now, Josie,' he said, half smiling. 'Tell me what you know.'

I became all business, matching his mood. 'I just got off the phone with Mrs Cabot. She's reaffirmed that she wants me to complete the appraisal and has asked that you keep Andi out of the house. She explicitly stated that Andi has no rights or power in this situation.'

He nodded. 'Thanks. What's her number?'

I didn't bother to resend it. Instead, I got my cell phone, hit the Redial button, and told him to ask for room 319. I leaned against the sink and listened.

'Mrs Cabot?' he asked. 'Yes.... This is Chief Alverez.... Ms Prescott told me of your conversation.... Yes.... I wanted to hear it from you.... No ... no.... Are you sure?... Okay.... What about?... I understand.... Do you want her on the property at all?... Got it.... I'm sorry to disturb you.... Yes.... Yes.... No ... That's all right.... Is there anything else?... All right, then.... Thank you.... Yes.... I'll do my best.... Good-bye.'

He handed me the phone and headed out, brushing my shoulder as he passed, a kind of connection, hinting at intimacy.

I followed him and stood just inside the door with my back to the outside wall, out of sight, leaving the porch door open about two inches, wide enough so I could eavesdrop, but not open enough so I'd be seen.

Alverez said, 'No, you can't come in. No, you can't have the Renoir. That's it. If you don't like it, sue someone. But you have to get off the property now.'

I made a teeth-clenching face to the empty hall. Very impressive.

'I'll sue you,' Andi screeched.

'And the New Hampshire courts,' Alverez answered, his voice calm, not a hint of sarcasm apparent. 'Don't forget them. They're the ones that issue probate rulings.'

Without another word, Andi pulled away and tore down the path. The small Asian driver I'd seen with Mrs Cabot dashed around the Town Car and beat her to the back door before she got there. He opened it, and she charged in headfirst, fleeing from I didn't know what, but looking for all the world as if she were hunted.

It took about 15 minutes to reassure Sasha that everything was okay. Alverez told me that Griff would relieve O'Hara at 10:00, and that he'd be on duty until 4:00.

'Do you understand what's going on with Andi?' I asked.

'Sure,' he said. 'She's pissed.'

'But why?'

'What do you think?'

I paused, uncertain whether to open up, and well aware that Sasha was within earshot. I shrugged. 'I think she's eager to get money.'

'Yeah,' he agreed. 'That much, at least, seems clear.'

We finished our conversation, neither of us revealing anything that the other one didn't already know, and he left. Stepping into the living room, I found Sasha on the floor, using a flashlight to examine the underside of the inlaid chess table Mrs Grant had bought in Boston half a century ago.

'You're okay?' I asked.

'This is incredible workmanship,' she said reverentially.

'Yeah,' I agreed. She started to slide out from under. 'Don't get up. I just wanted to let you know that I'm taking off.'

'Oh,' she said, sounding fretful.

'You have your cell phone, right?'

'Yes.'

'Call if you need me,' I said, sounding chipper. 'And a police officer will be around. Okay?'

'Sure.'

'Keep your phone nearby. I'll call in a while.'

'Okay.'

At the front door, I looked back, and she was already absorbed by her task, examining the table's dovetail joints, searching for a Maker's Mark, and as always, alert for telltale signs of refinishing.

I called Gretchen on my way back to Portsmouth. Knowing her penchant for gossip – celebrity and otherwise – I wasn't surprised at her prodding questions about the Grant situation, and deflected them easily. All I told her was that I had left Sasha hard at work. Neither Andi nor Alverez's names came up. I asked what was going on and she told me that she hadn't reached Don, the recruiter I was counting on to send us a research assistant, but had left an urgent message with his secretary. Other than that, all was well. She was busy reconciling the receipts from the auction and the tag sale, and had just confirmed my appointment with the professor.

An English literature professor from the University of New Hampshire was retiring and wanted to sell his collection of books. Roy, the picker who'd called on Saturday with an offer of rare books, had let us down. He'd never shown up, and we didn't have a clue why. Probably another dealer had nabbed him en route. It happened all the time. So another lead on books, even if they weren't particularly valuable, was good news. Inventory was low. And buyers expected to see fresh stock every time they came to shop. If they didn't see new goods, they stopped coming.

At the warehouse, I said hello to Gretchen on the fly, grabbed the keys to the company van, and left. The van was old and blue, and clean and serviceable. I'd bought it for $3,000 when I'd first arrived in Portsmouth, a bargain at the time, and now, 110,000 miles later, an unbelievable find. It took us to book and antique fairs and buys without complaint, but it was a struggle to drive because it lacked power steering and was an absolute bear to park.

I found the professor's address on Ceres Street without a problem. There was even a space available pretty close to the single-family row house where he lived. It took me ten minutes to inch my way into the spot. It was a nightmare, but I did it. The professor greeted me cordially and led me straight into his den. A brief conversation and quick perusal revealed that there were no leather-bound volumes or first editions of note. It wasn't a collection of rare books, it was a book-lover's assortment of what are referred to as reading copies, undistinguished volumes of no particular value.

I randomly checked several books' title pages to confirm that there were no book club volumes, which, except on rare occasions, have no resale value. Finding none, I was ready to make an offer. I did a quick estimate by counting ten volumes to a shelf, six shelves to a unit, and fourteen units; 840 books. None of which would sell for more than a few dollars, most of which wouldn't sell at all.

The professor stood nearby, watching me work, his hands latched behind him. He looked sad. I needed to gauge his mood before I could begin to negotiate.

'Are you looking forward to retiring?' I asked. 'North Carolina, right?'

'Well, young lady,' he said, 'it's one thing to think about retiring and plan for it, and another thing altogether to sort through thirty-five years of possessions, donate clothes that haven't fit you for a decade, or sell books you love to a stranger. No offense intended.'

'None taken,' I said, and smiled. 'I think moving is the hardest thing in the world under the best of circumstances, and it's harder still when you have mixed feelings about doing it.'

'Exactly.' He sighed.

'I think you're going to be disappointed in my offer, but as an expert in English lit, you know there's nothing special here. That doesn't mean you don't love the books, but there's nothing that has a lot of resale value.'

'Really?' he said, surprised. 'What do you mean by value?' he asked.

I shrugged. 'There are very few books here that would retail for more than a dollar or so.'

'There are a lot of Civil War books there.' He pointed to a shelf on the right, near the door. 'They're worth more than that. I know because

JANE K. CLELAND

I bought them at a used bookstore myself. The prices are still in the front.' He reached for a volume and showed me the pencil mark that read twelve dollars.

I flipped through it. 'It's not in good enough condition to fetch a price like that anymore. Do you see?' I pointed to the gap in the binding. 'The spine is broken, and here, several pages are dog-eared.'

He began to get irritated. 'That's because it's been read. It's still a wonderful book.'

'I understand.' I gestured toward the shelves, sweeping my hand to indicate all volumes. 'They're all reading copies.' I smiled. 'I have shelves of books like that myself. But as a businesswoman, I can't offer you more than two hundred dollars for the lot.'

'What?' he asked, looking and sounding outraged, as if he couldn't believe his ears.

'I know you love them,' I said, meeting his eyes and speaking softly, 'and I'm sorry I can't offer more. Try other places, if you want. That's what they're worth to me.'

He paused, calming down, shaking his head, resigned. 'It's a shock, that's all, to learn that something you cherish has such limited market value.'

I nodded. 'It hurts.'

'You can have them for three hundred dollars,' he said, recovering from his disappointment enough to negotiate. Fancy that. I suspected mine wasn't the first bid he'd received.

I paused, as if I was thinking hard. I shook my head. 'I'm sorry. The best I can do is, maybe, okay, two hundred and ten dollars.'

'Ten dollars more! That's an insult.'

'You wouldn't say that if you knew my margins. I certainly didn't intend to insult you. I came up five percent from my original, fair offer.' I met his eyes and watched him think it over.

'Two-fifty, then.'

I smiled and headed for the door. 'Try other places if you want, but two hundred and ten dollars, here and now, cash on the barrelhead, that's all I can do.'

As I crossed the threshold, he called out, 'Wait.'

I turned. 'Okay,' he said. 'Take 'em away.'

He was a good guy. He might not know anything about the resale value of used books, but he agreed to let me send Eric to collect them in the morning, and he waved cheerfully as I drove away.

As I headed back to the warehouse, I allowed myself a grin. Those 840 books would flesh out our dwindling inventory of used books nicely, and I'd kept to the price limit I'd set of twenty-five cents a volume. All in all, a job well done.

I decided on impulse to go to Mr Grant's funeral. On the one hand, I wasn't a friend, or family, and I was a little afraid it might seem intrusive for me to show up. On the other hand, I wanted to show respect to Mrs Cabot, who was, I thought, fighting the good fight alone. Also, from a business perspective, I knew that it wouldn't hurt my reputation to be seen at a church event.

I hadn't planned well, though. I was wearing jeans and a flannel plaid big shirt over an ordinary tee. Hardly a proper outfit for a church funeral. I decided to go and at least make an appearance. Arriving at the church after everyone was seated, I scanned the names in the guest book, then added my own. There were only about twenty people total, including, to my surprise, Chief Alverez. I stayed in the atrium until the minister began to speak, then slid into a pew at the rear.

I spotted Barney and Martha, hovering as near to Mrs Cabot as they could. Barney leaned over Andi and whispered something to Mrs Cabot, apparently just a word or two. She didn't respond, but Andi turned and said something. Alverez sat near the back, his eyes on the move. He nodded in my direction when he saw me.

Epps, Mr Grant's lawyer, was sitting near Mrs Cabot. As if he sensed my gaze, he looked over his shoulder, saw me, and stared with disapproving eyes. I inferred that he still thought I was a shark. After a moment, he turned back to face the front, and from the tilt of his head, I guessed he was listening to the minister's invocation.

The minister's well-considered and well-delivered words only served to accentuate my grief, to remind me of my own loss, and to underscore that my wounds were still raw. After a few minutes, I left.

As I drove, I rolled down the window, allowing the chilly air to numb my skin. I wasn't sorry I'd gone to the church, but I was glad I hadn't stayed. It was too hurtful for me to hear words of mourning, and I'd learned in the years since my father's death that my best strategy to dull the pain was to insulate myself with work.

I returned to the warehouse and took some time reviewing the preliminary financials from the weekend's activities. Things looked good. I pushed the papers aside and turned to look out my window.

It was a bright day, but not very warm, and the tree remained barren. Wes was right. I needed to focus on the threat that Barney might present. He was competitive as all get out, and more by smooth talking than discerning judgment he'd won a reputation as an arbiter of quality. One bad word from him would be enough to cast doubt over my company's abilities. Not everyone would believe him, but some people would. Look at Epps. Mr Grant's lawyer believed I was a shark based on an uncorroborated indictment. If Barney intended to take me on, I needed to be ready. *Screw you, Barney*, I thought. *And the horse you rode in on.*

I used the toe of my right boot to pull open the bottom desk drawer far enough for me to perch my feet on comfortably. I leaned back, my hands behind my head. What could I do to create an effective barrier to competition? What could I offer that Barney couldn't? What value-added service could I provide that would create loyal customers and enhance my reputation?

I sat forward. *Bingo*, I thought. *What about an instant appraisal service?* A homegrown version of the PBS television show?

Sasha and I could take turns staffing a booth at the tag sale for an hour each Saturday. We could hook up a computer so we could use our subscription services to easily find values for the better items. I stood up and walked to the window, excited at the thought. Barney couldn't compete because he had no access to professional research. Martha's work certainly didn't count. I smiled devilishly.

Not only would I create a barrier to competition but I'd be able to make on-the-spot offers for items people might want to sell. We could call it Prescott's Instant Appraisals. We'd highlight that it was free.

I began to pace, my mind racing, coming up with ideas, discarding some and keeping others. I thought of how the ad I'd use to announce the new service should read. I considered what the booth itself should look like, and I planned how to control a crowd if we were lucky enough to get one.

The phone rang.

'Barney Troudeaux's on the phone,' Gretchen told me. 'He wants to know if he can stop by and talk to you. He said it's important.'

'Sure,' I said, my attention caught.

I couldn't imagine what Barney wanted to say to me that would be in the category of important. I tapped the desk, anxiety replacing confidence and creativity. I glanced at the computer clock and realized that Mr Grant's funeral was over. Mr Grant, a man I'd liked, yet apparently a thief and a liar. A man who'd been stabbed ... murdered – why? To protect the paintings? Or to keep the secret that the paintings had been stolen? What did Barney know, and did his coming here have anything to do with the murder? Increasingly apprehensive, my heart began to thud.

I paced. I stood in front of the window looking out. I sat down again.

Gretchen called up and told me Barney was there, and I asked her to send him up.

I walked to the spiral staircase and watched as he ascended.

'Hi, Barney,' I said, forcing a smile.

'Josie, great to see you! I love a spiral staircase! Clever use of space.'

'Thanks, Barney. That's right, you haven't been up to my office before, have you?'

'Never had the pleasure.'

'Well, come on in.'

I got him settled on the yellow love seat, offered him a beverage, which he declined, and holding my bottle of water in my lap the way a child holds a favorite blanket for security, I waited for him to speak.

'Josie,' he began, his beaming smile morphing into an oh-so-sincere, I-hate-to-be-here-but-duty-calls look, 'I'm here to offer help.'

'Really,' I said, unsure of my ground.

'This situation with the Grant estate … it's truly awful.' He shook his head sorrowfully.

'Yes,' I said, wary. Whatever was going on, the longer it took him to get to the point, the worse I figured the news would be.

'I understand you're helping Mrs Cabot.'

I thought about avoiding the question, but saw no point. It wasn't confidential. In fact, knowing Wes, it would be in tomorrow's paper. 'Yes, she's hired us to do an appraisal.'

He nodded. 'That's a big job.'

I smiled. 'Yeah.'

'Her daughter, Miranda, she's concerned about her mother. She's elderly, as you know.'

Dressing up her name from Andi to Miranda didn't make the bald-faced lie true. Andi had no thoughts for or about her mother. All she cared about was money. Money for Andi.

'Not so old,' I said.

'You can't always tell by looking,' he said, as if he were the bearer of bad news.

'Do you have a point, Barney?'

'Miranda feels obliged to challenge her mother's decisions about the Grant estate, I'm afraid.'

Well, well, well. Chief Alverez told her to sue. And I would have bet money she wasn't listening.

'I suppose she has the legal right to do so, but it's hard to believe that anyone would think Mrs Cabot isn't competent to handle her own affairs.'

'Well, luckily, that's nothing you or I will have to sort out.'

'True,' I agreed.

'Here's the thing. Miranda has hired me to help her sort through the complicated issues related to Mr Grant's estate.'

I felt like cursing him, but gripped the side of the chair instead. *No emotional display*, my father told me, and I took a long moment remembering his admonition. Breathing slowly, I was able to smile and stay silent, conveying, I hoped, disinterest and mild curiosity.

'I thought, and tell me if I'm out of line here, that maybe, just maybe, if you and I work together, we can help this mother and daughter find it in their hearts to settle their differences without resorting to the court system.'

The son of a bitch, I thought, half admiring his sterling ability to make his outrageous encroachment seem like a sacrifice he was willing to make for the greater good of others. I wished Alverez was here, confident that he'd share my appreciation of Barney's ridiculous and transparent offer, except it was probably a good thing that he wasn't in the room. If he were, I'd look up to share the joke, and once our eyes met, I doubted that I'd be able to keep a straight face. As it was, I was having a hard time maintaining professional decorum.

'Andi's going to do what she needs to do, including, I guess, hire you. Thanks for the offer, Barney, but we don't need any help.'

He stayed another twenty minutes, trying to find a wedge into my defenses. Finally he gave up. 'Josie, you're a stubborn young bird.'

'Hell, Barney, I'm not stubborn. I'm steadfast.'

He laughed, patted my shoulder, and left. But as he turned away, I noted that his eyes stayed hard. He was not amused at my refusal. *Too bad, Barney*, I said to myself as I escorted him out to his truck. *Too bad for you, you devious son of a hitch, but you don't get a piece of this one.*

chapter sixteen

Don, the recruiter, called with questions about the skill level required, and I explained that in addition to a solid foundation of knowledge, we were looking for half diligence and half common sense. He chuckled and told me he had someone in mind and would call back, he hoped, within the hour.

I realized that whoever Don found as our temporary researcher, he or she, as a newcomer, would need the appraisal protocol explained in more detail than Sasha had required. I sighed, resigned to doing what felt like busywork. It was too complex to delegate, but it had to be done.

'Gretchen,' I said, calling her, 'I need a binder. Would you bring one up?'

'Sure. Want some coffee? I just made a fresh pot.'

'Thanks,' I said, smiling. 'Good idea.'

I heard the clickity-clack of her heels on the steps, swung around in my chair, and saw her enter with a big smile, then accepted the steaming mug of coffee she proffered. She placed the burgundy binder, preprinted with our logo and name on the cover, on my desk.

'Can I help?' she asked.

'No, thanks. It's a research thing.'

'Well, let me know if I can do anything.' With a cheery wave, she was gone.

I thought for a moment about what to include in the binder. I started with a description of the grandfather clock and added the protocol itself along with the explanation of how I calculated the value. Since the researcher would be new to the region, I added a paragraph explaining my distrust of Troudeaux's research. Deciding that more information was better than less, I photocopied the title pages of the two catalogues I consulted, Shaw's and Troudeaux's, along with the pages containing the specific entries about the clock. I retraced my steps on the Web sites, found the information I'd discovered previously, and printed out the relevant pages.

I was trying to determine the best sequence when Max called, just before 1:00. 'Hey, Max,' I said, 'I was just thinking about lunch. Do you have time? I'll buy.'

'Thanks, Josie. I'll take a raincheck. Alverez called.'

I sat up straight, alert for trouble. 'What now?'

'I don't know. He wants to see us this afternoon.'

As if a switch had been flipped, I lost my appetite. Whatever Alverez wanted, I figured it must be dire if he was calling Max out of the blue. I began to shake, and swallowed twice to try to control my visceral reaction. 'Okay,' I said, as calmly as I could. 'When?'

'Is three o'clock all right?'

'Sure. I'll meet you there, okay?'

I hung up the phone and began to think about what might have led to this unanticipated request. Nothing came to mind, but I became increasingly disquieted and tense. *Stop it!* I told myself. Until I had cause, tormenting myself with unanswerable what-if questions was way south of pointless. I'd know whether I had reason to be concerned soon enough. Just as I was chastising myself and wondering how to stop worrying, Don called back and gave me the name of the researcher I was going to hire for five days at $400 a day, Fred Reynolds.

'He's perfect, Josie,' Don said. 'He's young and eager. Smart as a whip. With absolutely no social skills at all. But give that boy an antique and a computer and look out.'

I laughed, and it felt good. 'Thanks, Don. You're the best.'

Don told me that Fred was already en route. He was flying to Boston, where he'd rent a car, and with any luck, be at my warehouse by 4:00. I passed on the information to Gretchen, who made a hotel reservation at a small bed-and-breakfast in downtown Portsmouth.

As soon as I hung up the phone, anxiety returned. *Keep busy,* I admonished myself. I took a long drink of water, and turned my attention back to the protocol.

I played around a little, designing a jazzy title page on letterhead, and using a three-hole punch, thumped all the pages and inserted them into the binder. I flipped through, admiring my work, and smiled. I was ready to dazzle anyone. Don's researcher, Fred, would have an unequivocal understanding of what I meant by 'professional standards.'

Thinking about the schedule, I decided I'd better consult Sasha.

'Sasha,' I said, when I had her on the phone, 'how's it going?'

'Good. I'm working on the sofa, and have two tables and the plant stand to go.'

'That's great,' I said. 'You're working quickly.'

'I'm trying. There's so much.'

'Yeah. Listen, Don has called back. A young guy named Fred Reynolds, a terrific researcher, according to him, will be here by four o'clock or so.'

'Great.'

'I'm going to be out for most of the rest of the day. When Fred arrives, it might make sense for you to get him settled in at the extra desk near Gretchen, make sure he can get on-line, then show him around. Okay?'

'Okay. What about the protocol?'

'I'll do that. Are you okay to meet at the office at eight o'clock tomorrow?'

'Sure.'

'Arrange that with him, okay?'

'Okay.'

'You can watch the video with him first thing and show him how the tape relates to Mrs Grant's ledger. After that, I'll go over the protocol with him. Then we should be good to go.'

Hanging up, I realized that I ought to take the binder with me. I wanted to know the material cold when I reviewed it with Fred in the morning.

I headed downstairs.

Gretchen was on the phone arranging an appointment for me. From what I gathered as I waited for her to finish, a couple was downsizing after their kids had left for college. They were moving from a big Colonial in Durham into a small condo overlooking South Mill Pond in Portsmouth. She passed me a note reading '2:00 P.M. tomorrow?'

I nodded that 2:00 was fine. When she was off the phone, she said, 'This is a good one, I think.'

'Yeah? What do they have?' I asked.

'Loads of stuff, it sounds like.' She glanced at her notes. 'A set of china, nothing special. A dinette set from the '40s. End tables. Some hand-carved decoys. Japanese screens. A pool table, in pretty good shape. Boxes full of miscellaneous goods.'

'That's great! Where did the lead come from?'

'The tag sale. Eric got this one.'

'Excellent.'

I slipped the address she handed me into my purse.

'Eric's off today, right?'

'Right.'

Since we all work on Saturdays, everyone gets a weekday off. Eric usually took Mondays. Gretchen rarely did, since she was responsible for reconciling the weekend receipts. She and Sasha worked it out between them which day they took, so we always had coverage in the office. 'When are you off?' I asked.

'Wednesday.'

'When Eric gets in tomorrow, have him go to the professor's and pick up the books. He ought to have a helper. There's a lot of them.'

She nodded, jotted herself a reminder, and taped it to her computer monitor. 'I'll get a temp right now.'

'Good. I'm heading out,' I told her. 'When Fred arrives, remember that he's a stranger to these parts. Make sure he has everything he needs and that he can find his way to the B-and-B, okay?'

She gave me an of-course-I-will look.

'Yeah, yeah, I know, of course you will.' I smiled.

I stopped at a grocery store and circled their deli-style salad bar picking and chose whatever grabbed my fancy, drove to the beach, and ate sitting in my car. It tasted pretty good, but not as good as homemade. I missed cooking for someone. Rick, my former boyfriend, loved my cooking. It was one of his best qualities.

I wondered what Rick was doing now. When I'd called to let him know that I was leaving New York for New Hampshire, he'd told me that he thought it was a good idea for me to get away, that maybe the physical distance would help me put my father's death behind me. I didn't respond to either his insensitivity or his bitter tone. His lack of empathy was why we'd broken up a month or so after my father's death, and it still seemed incredible to me that he thought I ought, somehow, to simply turn the other cheek, and get on with things. I had wished him good luck, and hung up, relieved that I was no longer dating him.

I shook my head. We'd had such good times for almost two years, I still felt surprised at how quickly things had changed. In only a matter of weeks, we'd gone from cruising the farmer's market looking for the freshest produce to strangers laboring to maintain a conversation.

I leaned my forehead against the steering wheel, a sudden memory bringing tears to my eyes. I'd been making a Newburg sauce, slowly stirring sherry into cream, when he came behind me, his hands encircling my torso. He brushed my hair aside and began kissing my neck, his lips electric on my skin.

I sat up and pushed the memory aside. I didn't want to be with him, but I wanted to be with someone. I was aware that I was exerting a lot of mental energy coping with loneliness. I tried my best, without much success, to shake off my growing depression. I had a sense of impending doom. Not only was I alone but I was having to deal with being suspected of murder. I swallowed, fighting tears.

Whatever Alverez was going to say or do, I felt certain it would be bad news.

It was exactly 3:00 when I entered the Rocky Point police station.

Max was leaning against the counter chatting with Alverez. I saw the big blonde, Cathy, at a file cabinet in the rear. We walked down the now-familiar hallway to the interrogation room, and I took my usual seat. I doubted that I'd ever enter that room and see the cage in the corner without wincing.

Once we were settled, Alverez turned on the tape recorder, spoke the date and time, listed our names as those present, and then said, 'Thanks for coming in. Our investigation has progressed and I wanted to give you some information.'

'Okay,' Max responded.

Alverez leaned back, stretching out his legs. He looked the same as always, his demeanor providing no clue about his message. I was anxious, but braced to deal with whatever came my way.

'Unless new information comes up, which I don't expect, Josie has been cleared as a suspect.'

'What?' I exclaimed, stunned.

Alverez half smiled, and nodded. 'We don't think you were involved in the murder.'

Max gripped my shoulder for a long minute, a contained gesture of celebration. Tears welled up in my eyes, and I didn't try to stop the flow. I took a deep breath, realized I'd had a death-grip on the sides of my chair, and lifted my hands to the table top, clenching and unclenching my fists to relax. I reached over and put a hand on top of Max's, still on my shoulder, and squeezed, then reached into my purse for a tissue, and wiped away my tears.

As stress and anxiety receded, anger rushed in. I stuffed the crumpled tissue in my purse, turned to Alverez, and asked, 'Why didn't you call me?'

'What do you mean?'

'What do you mean "What do I mean"? You drag me down here to tell me that I'm no longer a suspect? Don't you think I might have been interested in hearing that news right away? Would it have killed you to have called and told me?'

He shrugged, and I took the gesture to mean that he thought I was overreacting. 'Sorry. There's something else I need to discuss, so I knew we'd be talking anyway.'

I looked at him and shook my head, his cavalier dismissal of my distress fueling my rage. '*You* needed to talk to *me*? How thoughtful of you to balance my needs with your own,' I added, unable to suppress the sarcasm.

'I didn't mean it that way. Sorry. Guess it was a little insensitive of me not to have called.'

'A little!' I exclaimed.

Max reached for my arm and squeezed, gently. 'Josie,' he said. 'Point taken. Let's move on.'

I shook off his hand. 'No, Max. This is too important.' I pushed hair aside. 'It seems I should be grateful that you have something else to talk to me about,' I said to Alverez. 'Otherwise I might have learned that I've been cleared – when? Tomorrow? The next day. Oh, I know! Probably you'd have given Cathy a note to call me when she got a chance, right?'

'Okay, Josie,' Alverez said, unsmiling. 'I get it. I was thoughtless. I apologized once and I meant it. I'm sorry. Can we move on now?'

Stop, I reminded myself. *Breathe. Think.* I took a deep breath and turned to Max. He was watching me with compassionate eyes. I looked out of the window. The tall grass that dotted the dunes waved in the light breeze. My anger dissipated as suddenly as it had arisen, leaving me spent. I felt exhausted and emotionally raw. Taking a deep breath, I looked at Alverez and smiled a little, a nonverbal offer of détente. His stern demeanor eased in response.

I felt awkward, uncertain what to do or say next. One emotion after another washed over me – the fatigue that had eclipsed my fury now gave way to an almost giddy volatility. I smiled again, broadly this time. Alverez smiled back, and I found myself admiring the flecks of gold that glistened in the brown of his eyes. His eyes were hypnotic, drawing me in. After a long minute, Max cleared his throat and the mood was broken. I looked away. 'Sorry about that,' I said. 'I guess this situation has made me a little emotional. I don't normally rant like a fishwife.'

Alverez smiled. 'It wasn't so bad. I've been called worse than insensitive.'

'Really? Like what?'

Alverez smiled and shook his head slightly. 'That'll be a topic for another time, if you don't mind,' he said, shifting in his chair.

'So,' I asked, pleased at his obvious discomfort, 'what made you realize I wasn't guilty?'

'That too can be covered later. We have something important to discuss now, if that's all right.'

'Sure. What?'

'The reason I asked you to come in is to ask for your help. We've reached a point in the investigation where we need an expert.'

'An expert in?...' Max asked.

'Appraisals.'

'Why Josie?'

'She's the logical choice. We can bring in an outside expert if we have to, but my plan is more likely to work if Josie will help us.'

'What do you need?'

Alverez cleared his throat and idly tapped his pen against the wooden table. 'A couple of things. First, what do you know about the Renoir? I mean, according to Mrs Grant's ledger, the three paintings, the Renoir, the Matisse, and the Cézanne were all bought from someone or something called A.Z. Do you know what, or who, that is?'

'One second,' Max said to Alverez, reaching out his hand to stop me from speaking. He leaned over toward me and whispered, 'Do you know what it means?'

'No,' I whispered back.

'Do you know anything about the paintings.'

I paused, then decided to tell Max the truth. 'Yes. Yes, I do.'

'What?'

'It's complicated.'

Max straightened up, glanced at the recorder, the red light indicating it was on, and said, 'Josie and I need to consult for a moment. We'll step outside and walk a little, if that's all right.'

'Sure,' Alverez said, narrowing his eyes. 'But you can stay here. I'll leave the room, like I did before.'

'I'd just as soon stretch my legs,' Max answered.

Alverez shrugged and hit the Off button. 'Let me know when you're ready to resume.'

Max and I walked across the street and stepped up on to the sandy dunes. I picked up a flat gray rock and hurled it toward the ocean. Clouds were rolling in from the west, white-topped waves rippling the ocean's surface. Max stretched and bent down.

'That's a relief, huh?' he asked, standing upright.

I choked on sudden tears. 'You have no idea.' I grasped his upper arm and leaned my forehead against his sleeve. 'Thank you, Max.'

He reached over and patted my shoulder. 'Sure, Josie. I don't know that anything I did had anything to do with anything, but it's a pleasure to work with you.'

I smiled as best I could given that I was still feeling emotional. My tears gradually abated, and I turned toward the sea. The salty air smelled fresh. I stood up, my smile broader, my confidence returning. 'How come you wanted to come outside?' I asked.

'Well, I wanted to make the point that we could. This time, we aren't here for an interrogation. You're being asked to do a favor.'

I smiled. 'Wow, that's right, isn't it?'

He shrugged, and looked mildly embarrassed. 'I wanted to crow a little.'

I tapped his shoulder and smiled again.

Max smiled back. 'So,' he said, 'talk to me.'

'I've researched all three paintings. They were stolen from Jewish families before or during World War II. The Matisse disappeared from a small museum on the Mediterranean. The other two were taken by the Nazis.'

'My God,' Max said, turning to look at me, shock registering on his face.

'Yeah,' I said, nodding, responding to his overall reaction, not only his words. 'I know. It's horrible. I think that's why Mrs Cabot hired me. I think her daughter, Andi, who's an immoral shrew, by the way, would make it impossible for her mother to return the paintings to their rightful owners. But if I find them, and announce the discovery publicly, well, Mrs Cabot will have no choice.'

He nodded. 'Makes sense.'

'Here's the thing. I've found them.'

'What?'

I nodded. 'Yeah.'

'Where are they?'

'I've got them safe.'

After a pause, Max asked, 'So why haven't you brought them forward?'

I looked away, turning to focus on the ocean as I struggled to get my jumbled thoughts in order. 'I'm not sure. Two reasons, I guess. First, I thought I ought to hold on to them in case I needed to use them to clear my name. And don't ask how they'd help me do that, Max, because I don't know. I don't have a plan. I just knew those paintings could somehow be an ace in the hole.' I shrugged. 'Or, they might be. It's the only thing I know that no one else does. Knowing their location is, somehow, an insurance policy.'

'What's the other reason?'

'I need to tell Mrs Cabot first. I just found them. And today's her father's funeral. It seems too awful to tell her today. I just couldn't do it.'

Max touched my arm again. 'You're a good egg, Josie.'

'A good egg?'

He smiled. 'What else?'

'That's it.'

'Where are they now?'

For some reason, I didn't want to reveal their location, but I couldn't justify not doing so. Max was my lawyer, after all. For reasons I didn't understand, I stayed vague. 'In Mr Grant's house. I moved them from one secret spot to another.'

He didn't prod further. Instead, he asked, 'How certain are you that someone else won't find them wherever it is you've hidden them?'

'No one but me has access to the house right now, and I've arranged it so none of my staff will go near them.'

'I don't like it, Josie. I think we ought to tell Alverez the truth, and let him take custody of them. Your exposure, your potential liability, if something happens to them, even, God forbid, a fire, is too great.'

I nodded. I hadn't considered that aspect of the situation before. He was right. 'There's one more thing,' I said, looking down, not really ashamed, but feeling awkward that money came into my reckoning.

'What's that?'

'There'll be a reward. It was posted on a Web site. I found them, so I want it. If I turn them over to the police, I'll lose my claim.'

'No, you won't. I'll make certain you're covered.'

I couldn't think of any reason not to do as he recommended. 'Okay, then.'

'You ready to go back in?'

'Are you sure I should tell him everything?'

He squeezed my arm again. 'Yes. I'll protect your rights.'

Alverez looked somber. His eyes were dark and intent. His manner was serious, even grave. He'd asked if we were ready to resume, Max said we were, and suddenly, the tape recorder light was red, indicating, that once again a record of our conversation was being created.

'Josie has a statement to make.'

'All right,' Alverez said.

'A couple of things before she begins,' Max said. 'She has acquired some knowledge of the missing paintings and is going to tell you what she knows.'

'Good,' Alverez said, his tone neutral.

'The paintings, we believe, were stolen. Josie expects to return them to their rightful owners, and if a reward is forthcoming, she expects to claim it.'

Alverez paused and I heard the soft whirr of the recorder. 'And?'

Max shifted in his chair. 'And we'd like to turn them over to you. But we want to be on the record that you acknowledge that but for the actions of Josie Prescott, you wouldn't have been able to take possession of the missing artwork.'

Alverez turned to look at me. 'Are you saying you have them in your possession now?'

Max said, 'Do we have your acknowledgment?'

'When you turn them over, I'll write you a receipt. I can make no comment about any other aspect of the situation.'

'That'll be fine,' Max said, but it didn't sound fine to me.

I leaned over to Max and whispered, 'That sounds bad.'

'Nah, it's standard operating procedure.'

'Okay,' I said, unconvinced.

'Plus, we'll have a copy of the tape.'

'Josie,' Max said aloud, 'tell Chief Alverez what you know about the paintings.'

Taking a deep breath for courage, I said, 'I found out that all three paintings were stolen.'

'How?' Alverez asked.

'A Web site.'

'We checked on-line.'

I shrugged. 'You checked law-enforcement sites, right?'

'Right.'

'Me, too. I didn't find the paintings listed there. I found them on a specialized site tracking Nazi thefts before and during World War Two.'

Alverez leaned back and shook his head. 'What are you saying?'

'You asked me before about Mrs Grant's ledger. The entry that indicated that Mr and Mrs Grant bought all three paintings from "A.Z.," right?'

'Right. Do you know who or what that is?'

I shook my head. 'No. Maybe a person. Maybe a gallery.' I shrugged. 'No idea.'

'What do you know?'

'I know Renoir's *Three Girls and a Cat* was one of several paintings taken from the Brander family home in Salzburg in 1939. Cézanne's *Apples in a Blue Bowl with Grapes* was stolen from a well-respected Viennese collector and businessman, Klaus Weiner and his wife, Eva,

also in 1939, except that they called it collecting the "Jew tax." Matisse's
Notre-Dame in the Morning was owned by the Rosen family. They'd lent it
to a small museum in Collioure, France, in 1937. In February of 1941, the
curator reported it stolen along with, if I recall right, seventeen other
paintings.' I shrugged. 'Maybe the Nazis got that one, too. I can't confirm
that. But I do know it was stolen, and it had been owned by a Jew.'

Alverez's eyes narrowed as he listened, and when I was done, he
shook his head.

'We figured they were stolen. Why else keep them under wraps?'

'Well, a legitimate owner might be afraid of theft,' I ventured.

He shook his head. 'Then you wouldn't leave a gimcrack lock on the
front door.'

'Good point,' I acknowledged.

'Where did you find them?'

'In a hidden compartment behind other paintings.'

'How did you know to look there?'

'Intuition? Luck? I don't know. I noticed a three-sided frame on the
workbench in the basement. A few hours later, tossing and turning in
bed, something clicked.'

'Where are they now?'

I turned to Max. He nodded encouragingly.

'I'll show you. I won't tell you.'

'Why not?'

'I want that receipt as I hand them over.'

He nodded. 'When we're done here, we'll go together.'

'And you'll give me a receipt?'

'On the spot.' He rat-a-tat-tatted the table with his pen. 'We need to
get the paintings authenticated.'

'Yeah.'

'I want to alert our expert that they're coming.' He pushed back his
chair and stood up.

'I thought I was your expert.'

He smiled. 'You are on appraisals. Not on authenticating art.'

'Who are you going to use for that?'

'Leo Snow from Dartmouth.'

I nodded. 'He's an expert, all right. Good choice.'

'I'll be right back.' He punched the Off button and left the room.

Max and I sat quietly. When he returned, he started the recorder, and
said, 'I got Dr Snow on the phone. He'll be here in the morning with his
chemistry set, and we'll have confirmation by the end of the day.' He
paused. 'Josie?'

'Yeah?'

'Congratulations on finding them.'

I smiled. 'Thanks. I was pretty pleased.'

He smiled back. After a moment, he asked, 'Change of subject. How do you set values?'

'You mean on the Cézanne or the Matisse?'

'Yes. Or anything.'

'It's complex,' I said, explaining the intricacies of the process.

'But,' Alverez objected, 'you're saying there's no intrinsic value to things.'

'That's true. Think of it as the last bastion of pure capitalism.'

'My God.'

'Why are you asking?' Max chimed in.

Alverez looked at us for a moment before settling back in his chair. He pushed it out farther from the table, and the scraping noise startled me. 'We have several suspects, and I'm hoping you'll help us narrow the field.'

'What do you mean?' Max jumped in before I could speak.

'If a junkie boosts a diamond pin and pawns it, I know how it would be valued. I could send in a guy undercover and he could hold his own in the conversation. With a Cézanne or a Matisse,' he said, gesturing hands-up, 'we're a little bit out of our depth.'

'You're thinking of asking Josie to do something undercover?' Max asked, incredulous.

'Or maybe to educate us, so we can do it. We have options.'

Neither Max nor I spoke.

'So, can you give me an example,' Alverez asked me, 'of how you'd set a price?'

Remembering the binder I'd prepared for Fred, I pulled it out of my purse. 'I just happen to have ... ta-dah!' I laid it on the table, opened the cover, and said, 'This is a summary of the protocol I established,' I explained, pointing to the first page. 'But, in a sense, showing you this first is bass-ackwards.'

Alverez looked amused.

'That's a perfectly good word, coined, as far as I know, by my mother. My mother was a lady who never in her life said a bad word. Given that standard, she found that she needed to be creative in order to properly express herself.'

'Of course. That explains it,' Alverez said, half smiling. 'Bass-ackwards. You were saying....'

'The first thing you do is look for comps. Just as in real estate, you need to find similar items with which to compare your piece. I found three. Two references came from printed catalogues that I had on my bookshelf. The third came from a Web site we subscribe to.'

'When you say catalogues, do you mean listings from other company's auctions?'

'Exactly.'

'Why do you have this with you?'

'We have a temporary researcher coming in to help us with the Grant appraisal. I thought I might want to review it later so I brought it with me.'

'May I see?' he asked, reaching for the binder. He flipped through the pages.

When he got to the title page from Shaw's catalogue, I stopped him. 'This page shows you which catalogue I'm referring to. One important thing to note is what, in the industry, is referred to as "recency." Obviously, the more recent the sale, the more valid the comparison. I decided five years is a reasonable window.' I turned the page and pointed to the catalogue entry itself. 'You see how this text details the factors that were used to authenticate the clock? And then the writer, in this case Shaw, added provenance information. That's very helpful in figuring out whether the price this clock sold for might be higher than others that sold around the same time.'

Alverez nodded, his eyes scanning the entry.

'What else is here?' he asked, flipping the page.

'Another catalogue entry.' Reading upside down, I said, 'You can see that this one is from one of Barney Troudeaux's auctions in 2002.'

After scanning the paragraph criticizing the quality of Troudeaux's research, he looked up, and asked, 'Why include it at all if you think it's so bad?'

I shrugged. 'Because it's there. I don't mean to be flippant. I'm serious. Troudeaux's sold a clock that was similar and we know how much it sold for, so we've got to include it. But it's also important to consider whether the clock might have sold for even more if the catalogue had provided better or more detailed research.'

Alverez nodded and flipped through the remaining pages. After a moment, Alverez asked, 'So if you wanted to set prices for the Cézanne or the Matisse, how would you go about it?'

'Same as I did here,' I answered, shrugging. 'I'd do research.'

'Can you give me a ballpark?'

'Millions, but I couldn't say how many millions.'

'Not even a wild guess?'

'No. I know a Cézanne sold for more than sixty million in 1999, but that was during the Internet bubble, so it's probably not relevant.'

He nodded. 'Just for the sake of argument, if ten million was a reasonable estimate for a sale of a Cézanne at auction, how much would you ask a private buyer to pay ... five million?'

'No way.'

'A million?'

I thought about it for a minute. 'I'm pleased to say that I have no experience in this arena. That said, I should think you'd have to offer an even greater discount ... say half a million, or even less. Think about it. You're limited to a certain kind of wealthy buyer. It has to be someone who is okay with never displaying the painting in public. In fact, they can never even admit they've seen it. I mean no disrespect when I say that a lot of collectors buy expensive pieces so they can display them. I mean, part of the fun is showing what you got.'

'So who would buy it?'

'I can only speculate. Someone who loves art and doesn't care about showing it to anyone else. Someone with a lot of cash – because I should think you've got to be careful about withdrawing that large of a sum from a bank account. Again, I don't know, but with the Patriot Act, after nine/eleven, I should think a big withdrawal sends up a red flag.'

Alverez nodded. 'Continue. What else would you assume about a private buyer?'

After a pause, I said, 'Well, actually, when I think about it, a rare masterpiece would be a pretty good hedge against inflation. And a good way to launder money.' I smiled. 'So, you're looking for a rich guy with a lot of cash lying around who wants to balance his portfolio. Or someone in the mob. Or a crooked dealer who knows people like that.'

Alverez drummed the table. 'Well, that narrows the field,' he said dryly. 'Here's the thing. I'm hoping that you'll research the value of either the Cézanne or the Matisse, and offer to sell it privately.'

'What?' I exclaimed. 'To whom?'

'Let me get this right—' Max began, but Alverez put up a hand and interrupted.

'Once we agree on Josie's involvement, I'll give you full details.'

'I can't advise Josie to put herself in harm's way,' Max said.

Alverez looked at me. 'You'll be in no danger,' he assured me.

I found myself unable to look away. His eyes were seductive, and I felt my breathing slow as I relaxed, gazing deeper and deeper into his eyes, feeling safe in his presence. I swallowed. 'I don't understand,' I said. 'You want me to research one of the painting's value, and then do what?'

He paused. 'Help us a catch a killer.'

chapter seventeen

I sat, stunned, unable to think of how to respond. After a moment, I turned to Max and raised my eyebrows, silently soliciting his reaction.

'Tell us about it,' Max said to Alverez.

Alverez leaned back, balancing his chair momentarily on two legs, then righting himself to address Max. 'Well, I've already told you that the first thing I need is for Josie to research the under-the-table sales price of either the Cézanne or the Matisse.'

Max looked at me, tilting his head, silently asking if I was game.

'Sure,' I said. 'I can do that.'

'How long will it take you?' Alverez asked.

'It depends on how easy it is for me to access relevant data. Anywhere from a couple of hours to a couple of days.'

He nodded and tapped his pen on the edge of the table. 'Obviously, sooner would be better than later.'

I nodded. 'I'll get started as soon as we're done. Do you have a preference – the Cézanne or the Matisse?'

'No,' he said, shaking his head.

'Then what?' Max asked.

'Then we'll make an offer that I hope won't be refused.'

'To whom?' I asked.

Alverez shook his head. 'One step at a time.' He stood up. 'Let's get the paintings back here.' He reached over and punched the Off button on the recorder and pulled out the tape. 'I'll get Cathy to make a copy of this while we're gone.'

Max and I waited outside under thickening clouds while Alverez spoke to Cathy. When he was ready, we drove in his SUV to the Grant house, greeted Griff, standing guard on the porch, and made our way down the basement steps. Walking through the shadowy light of the solitary hanging lightbulbs, we entered the small room that housed the leather trunk. Retrieving the two paintings was anticlimactic.

They lay untouched, as I'd positioned them. The three of us stood silently for several moments looking at the Cézanne, which rested on top. Alverez rolled them up, one at a time and placed them in a military-style duffle bag he'd brought with him.

I watched as Alverez extracted the receipt Cathy had prepared and Max had approved from an inside pocket. We watched as he signed it and handed it over.

'Fax me a copy,' Max said as I accepted it. 'Okay?'

'Sure.'

With no further conversation, we left. We said good-bye to Griff and walked around the house to the side alley. As Alverez drove along the ocean to the Rocky Point police station, I looked up at the sky. The clouds were leaden, and the air smelled like rain.

After depositing the paintings in the police station safe, Alverez followed us to the parking lot. Max patted my shoulder, shook Alverez's hand, and walked to his car. Alverez and I watched without speaking as he pulled out of the parking lot and headed toward Portsmouth.

'You okay?' Alverez asked.

I nodded. I thought I felt a drop of rain, but it was hard to tell. The air was thick with moisture. 'Yeah. Things just feel kind of strange, you know?'

'In what way?'

'Giving you the paintings. Not understanding what's going on.' I shrugged. 'I don't know. The entire situation.'

'Things will straighten out pretty soon.'

'You think?'

He nodded. 'Yeah, I do.'

I wondered whether he was offering standard-issue polite reassurance or if he meant it. I didn't know him well enough to gauge his attitude toward providing skittish women support. Maybe he mouthed words of comfort with the same insouciance that I answered 'Fine' when a stranger asked 'How are you?'

Glancing at him, I found his eyes on me, watching me intently. No, I thought, whatever else might be going on, I had to believe that his comments were personal to me, and that he intended me to feel safe and cared for.

I smiled. He smiled back, and we stood like that, leaning against my car, looking at one another, smiling, until the rain began in earnest.

'It's raining,' I said, realizing that I'd left my umbrella upstairs in my office. 'I'd better go.'

He held my car door until I was inside, then closed it. I lowered the window. 'You're getting wet,' I said. 'You should go inside.'

'I will. Call and let me know how the research is going. Okay?'

I told him that I would, and backed out of the space. As I turned north, I glanced back over my shoulder and spotted him still standing in the middle of the parking lot. I waved good-bye and turned my attention to the road. The rain was coming steadily now and streams of water threatened to block my view.

When I got back to the warehouse about 4:30, it was as dark as night, and the rain showed no signs of letting up.

Gretchen was showing a young man, Fred, I supposed, the corner where we kept the coffee machine, a microwave, and a small refrigerator. Sasha tapped the keys on the computer at the spare desk.

'Did you forget your umbrella again?' Gretchen asked as I ran inside.

'Yeah,' I said. 'And it's raining like the dickens.'

'It's gotten so dark, hasn't it?' Gretchen agreed, looking out of the window. 'Are you okay?'

'Yup. Just damp.' I turned to the man standing next to her. He was short and narrow chested, in his mid-twenties maybe, and he wore glasses in black squared-off frames. He looked like a nerd.

'You must be Fred,' I said, smiling and offering a hand. 'I'm Josie.'

'Hello,' he said vaguely, as if he wasn't quite sure who I was.

'Do you have everything you need so far?'

'Yes, everything's very clear.'

'Good. Hey, Sasha. Are you doing all right?'

Always shy and self-effacing, Sasha gave a quick grin, as if she didn't want to show pleasure, but couldn't help herself. 'Yeah. Great.' She turned back to the computer.

'I'll let you guys get back to it,' I said. 'I have some work to do upstairs. Fred, you and I will go over the research protocol in the morning, okay?'

'Sure.'

I climbed to my office and got settled at my desk, ready to research the paintings' value. Since Alverez had said that it didn't matter which painting I selected, I decided that I'd go with whichever one seemed to be the easiest to research.

A quick survey of our subscription sites suggested that there was a fair amount of activity surrounding Matisse's paintings and sculptures, so I decided to proceed with *Notre-Dame in the Morning*.

The data was confusing. Recent auction prices for Matisse paintings ranged from a low of just over $1 million to a high of $12 million, with no obvious reason for the disparity. After an hour of gathering more and more information, but not perceiving a pattern, I stretched, and decided I needed outside help.

I called a former colleague from Frisco's in New York, one of the few people who'd been decent to me during my last months in New York. She'd even called me once in New Hampshire, just to say hello.

'Shelly,' I said, when I had her, 'it's Josie.'

'Oh, my God. Josie! How are you? I can't believe it. Is everything fine? You're coming back, right? We miss you!'

I laughed, and said, 'You're so sweet, Shelly. Thank you. But, no, I'm staying put up here in New Hampshire. You have to come up and see my operation sometime.'

'Yeah, right. When the cows come home.'

'Don't be such a snob. New Hampshire's beautiful.'

'Next time you're in town, bring pictures.'

We chatted about personnel changes at Frisco's and Shelly's new apartment, my company and her boyfriend, vacation plans, and old friends' whereabouts. Finally, I explained why I was calling, and asked her how she would interpret the data.

All business, she asked prodding questions about which painting I was pricing, which I deflected, and finally, gave me the name of a London dealer, Ian Cummings, who was, she said, the leading expert in the field.

Hanging up, I was surprised to feel stabbing homesickness. I lowered my head and waited for the wave of isolation and loss to pass. *Get over it*, I told myself, *move on, stop thinking*. After a moment, I sat up and shook off the despondency that threatened to pull me down. I was rebuilding my life, I reminded myself, and doing so rather nicely. I looked at the clock. It was too late to call London, so I made a note for first thing in the morning.

Instead of calling the dealer, I called Mrs Cabot at the Sheraton, and got her. She sounded tired. 'We're making good progress with the appraisal,' I told her.

'Thank you, Josie.' After a short pause, she added, 'Has Andi spoken to you again?'

'Well, in a manner of speaking,' I said, hating that I needed to tell her of her daughter's perfidy. 'Apparently Andi has hired Mr Troudeaux to help her.'

'Help her do what?'

I cleared my throat and, with my elbow on the desk, rested my forehead on my hand. 'From what he said, I gathered that Andi intends to challenge your father's will.'

The silence that greeted my revelation lasted so long that I began to wonder if she'd ended the call, quietly cradling the receiver, and if she had, what I should do in response.

'Thank you for informing me,' she said, finally.

'I'm sorry,' I said, not knowing what else to say.

'I'll be leaving in the morning, as scheduled. Will you call me in a day or two and give me a progress report?'

'Certainly.'

'And my instructions stand. I'll call Chief Alverez in the morning before I leave. Andi may not enter my father's house or interfere with your work in any way.'

We ended by thanking each other, and when the call was over, all I wanted was a martini. I turned off my computer and went downstairs.

Roy, the picker with the great books who had been MIA on Saturday, was standing by Gretchen's desk while Sasha sorted through the boxes. Fred sat at the computer, absorbed by whatever he was reading on the monitor.

Roy was an old man, grizzled and uncouth. His clothes were streaked with grime, and he was agitated, bouncing from one foot to another as he spoke. 'He tol' me he's paying top dollar. I'm old, I tol' him, but I ain't no fool. You can't bullshit a bullshitter, I tol' him. I tol' him twice. No cash, no books. I ain't no fool.'

'Hi, Roy,' I said. 'What's going on?'

'You want the books, you pay me cash.'

'Sure. Just like always.'

'Yeah, that's what Barney tol' me, but he don't have the cash. I ain't no fool.'

Sasha was stacking the volumes on the desk. They were all leather bound, and I spotted a gold-tooled set of Shakespeare; a two-volume folio-sized Johnson's dictionary, certainly not a first edition, but an early copy, lovingly maintained; and what looked like a collection of a dozen or so medical reference books from the early nineteenth century. I met Sasha's eyes and they conveyed fiery excitement.

Leather-bound books sell to two separate markets: decorators who seek 'bindings,' as they're known in the industry, and collectors who care about the book itself as much as its cover, or who buy certain categories of books as investments. Bindings often sell by the yard, and the market is strong, but distinguished volumes fetch more when sold to a book lover or investor.

'How much?' Roy asked, turning from me to Sasha, then looking back again. 'How much you give me? How much?'

'I need to look a little more,' Sasha said.

'I gotta go. I gotta go. You want 'em?'

'Absolutely,' Sasha said.

We had a standing policy of offering any picker a minimum of five dollars a volume for decent leather-bound books, more when we knew the particular item was special. These all looked good. Sasha seemed hesitant so I approached her and whispered, 'Offer him eight dollars a volume, and go up to ten.'

'Is that all right? I think they're worth it, but I don't want to offer so much if you don't think I should.'

'No, do it. It's all right.'

I wished I could give Sasha the gift of confidence, but I couldn't. She was, it seemed, inherently insecure.

There were fifty-seven volumes in three boxes, all in excellent condition. At a glance, I spotted no incomplete sets, no volumes with missing pages, and no broken bindings. Roy, after fifty years picking, knew the value of what he had and held fast for twelve dollars a volume, an unbelievably high price to pay a picker for miscellaneous leather volumes.

I nodded over his head to Sasha, and swallowing, she made the deal. Gretchen slipped out to go to the safe we kept in a back corner of the warehouse, and returned with the cash. Roy counted it carefully, thanked Sasha, and left, his gait awkward and his steps slow. I figured he had to be approaching seventy-five, and maybe he was even older.

I wasn't concerned with the high price we'd just paid, since, at the least, we'd triple our expenditure. Gretchen and Sasha repacked the books in the ratty cardboard boxes Roy had hauled into our office, and set them aside to be researched and cleaned.

I told everyone good-bye, and, having forgotten my umbrella again, darted through the rain to my car. As I waited for the defroster to clear the foggy window, the windshield wipers clacking a steady beat, I decided to go to the Blue Dolphin. I still wanted a martini, and given the piercing homesickness I'd just endured, I decided that tonight was definitely not a night to drink alone.

Having wedged my car into a tiny spot on Market Street, I rushed through the drenching rain. I stood for a moment to catch my breath under the copper roof that shielded the restaurant's entrance, and listened to the echoing, staccato beat as the rain pounded the metal overhang. I was soaked.

Two hours later, it was still raining, and I was still at the bar, finishing my second martini. I was trying to prepare a cover story for the London dealer. I could tell Shelly that my interest in Matisse was general and vague, and, because we're friends, she'd accept that story with only a little push-back. No way would a big-time art dealer answer hypothetical questions from a stranger on a lark. I needed to have a credible reason for calling.

Home again, the unrelenting rain feeding my feelings of remoteness, I cooked the chicken I'd prepared earlier, and ate one of my favorite meals in lonely isolation.

I reached the dealer, Ian Cummings, in London as Sasha and Fred sat down to watch the video, a copy of Mrs Grant's ledger in hand. When I had Cummings on the line, I introduced myself, referring to Shelly, and thanked him for taking the time to talk to me.

'Right,' he said. 'So which Matisse are we talking about?'

'I can't tell you that, I'm afraid. My seller is still on the fence about whether to let it go. Of course, if she decides to do so, I'll call you first.'

'And you want price information?'

'Yes.' I detailed the range of prices I'd discovered, and explained that I was looking for guidance.

'Well, it's a little tricky without knowing which painting, but let's see. Is it an oil?'

'Yes.'

'On canvas?'

'Yes.'

'Quite. What subject matter?'

'A cityscape.'

'Paris?'

'Yes.'

'Size?'

I glanced at my notes. 'It's twenty-eight by twenty-one inches.'

'Provenance?'

'Various owners, all private, no one notable.'

'When was it last on the market?'

'I don't know. Not for at least a generation.'

'Well, I can't tell you anything for certain. But if I had to set a price right now, I'd probably aim to goose it just a little. I'd set a range of from one-point-three to one-point-six million pounds, and hope that I could persuade my seller to be satisfied with one-point-one million.'

I did a rough conversion. 'In U.S. dollars, then, you'd expect it to go for around two million.'

'Yes, with any luck, more. As much as three million dollars.'

'You've been very helpful,' I said. 'Thank you.'

Hanging up the phone, I sat for a moment, then put in a call to Alverez. I left a message on his voice mail.

I was about to head downstairs, ready to go over the protocol with Fred, when Sasha poked her head into my office and asked if they could come in.

'Sure. What's up?' I asked.

'I wanted to show Fred the catalogues.'

I gestured to the wall of shelves. 'Go to it.'

I listened as she explained how we organized them. 'We have a lot of catalogues of local dealers. It makes sense, since we all tend to carry similar merchandise.'

'Can you rely on them?' Fred asked. *A good question*, I thought.

'Well, it depends,' Sasha answered. 'Like anything else.'

As they started to leave, I asked if they were done with the video, and Sasha said, 'Part of it. Fred wants to study it, so I thought I'd show him how we typically research things while we wait for you. Then he can take his time reviewing the tape.'

'Good,' I said. 'I'm ready if you guys are.'

They moved chairs near my desk and I went through the steps I'd delineated as I took him through the binder. He nodded and scanned the pages.

'Is this one of the local dealers?' he asked, pointing to the Troudeaux title page.

'Yes,' I said.

'But we don't think very highly of their research,' Sasha added, twirling her hair. 'I mean we use them, but I'd want additional verification.'

'That's true,' I acknowledged. 'Martha Troudeaux does most of their research, and it's often sketchy and sometimes just dead wrong.'

'Who's this?' Fred asked, pointing to the editor's name: M. Turner.

I was about to say that I didn't know, when Sasha jumped in. 'That's Martha, too. Sometimes she uses her maiden name – Turner. I think it's to make the company look larger, you know, not a mom-and-pop outfit with everybody in the firm sharing the same name.'

Staring at the page, my mouth fell open. In a flash of clarity, the pieces of the puzzle fell into place. Barney, whose wife, Martha, did most of his research. And who sometimes used her maiden name – Turner. I pictured him at the tag sale, deep in conversation with Paula. Paula Turner. I was willing to bet that Paula was Barney's niece by marriage. That would explain the call that Wes had told me about, the one made from the Taffy Pull to Mr Grant. No one in the family would think it was odd for Barney to stop by his wife's family's store and borrow the phone.

Roy, the picker, had said that Barney didn't have the cash to buy the books. And a relatively small amount of cash it was. Less than a thousand dollars. Which must mean that Barney was broke. If Barney was broke, how could he afford the Renoir he'd intended to buy from Mr Grant?

Maybe he hadn't had any such intention. Perhaps he hadn't wanted the Renoir for pride of ownership or even for the commission a sale would bring. The Renoir might have represented a second chance, a way of raising enough cash quickly to save his business, to protect all that he had built up.

I realized that Sasha and Fred were engaged in a lively discussion about verifying research, and I'd missed it all.

'I think we're all set here,' I said. 'Any questions?'

'No,' Fred said. 'This is all very useful.'

'Great. Well, go and do.'

They left, still chatting. I'd never heard Sasha speak so much, or with so much enthusiasm. Maybe she'd met her match in Fred.

As their voices faded away, I thought of Mr Grant, and sadness swept over me. In all of our interactions, he'd been jovial, gregarious, and kind. I'd liked him, and he'd liked me. An image of Barney came to mind. I could picture him towering over the older, weaker man.

I shivered, upset and dispirited. *How could he have done such a thing?* I began to cry, and I didn't try to stop myself. Tears rolled down my cheeks and as they fell, I concluded that I needed to speak to Alverez.

To think that Barney had killed Mr Grant in order to steal the Renoir. I shook my head, astonished that I hadn't realized it before, and sickened at the thought.

chapter eighteen

By the time Alverez called back, about an hour later, I'd remembered what Max had said about not volunteering information, and had thought better of telling him what I knew about Barney. Instead, I simply stuck with the original reason for my call and said that I was done with the research and had the pricing information he'd wanted.

'Can you meet in an hour?'

I glanced at the clock. It was only 9:30. 'Sure,' I answered. 'If Max can.'

'I'll expect you here at ten-thirty then, unless I hear otherwise.'

'Okay,' I agreed, wondering whether I was imagining the urgency I perceived in his voice or whether, now that I had the information he needed, he was ready to act.

I reached Max at his office, and he told me that he could meet me at the police station at 10:30.

'Can we meet at ten-fifteen?' I asked. 'I'd like to talk to you first.'

'Sure,' he said. 'Our usual dune?' he asked in a joking tone of voice. 'When we're not in interrogation room two?'

I laughed. 'Perfect.'

Passing through the office, I overheard Gretchen inviting someone on the phone who had, according to her, 'an old set of flatware,' to stop by. An 'an old set of flatware' could mean anything from two dozen fifteen-piece sterling silver place settings from Victorian England to a set of sixteen pieces of stainless steel from the '70s.

Sasha and Fred were absorbed in a discussion about the use of a table's height to validate its age. Sasha thought height was one of many factors that should be considered, but wasn't a particularly reliable indicator.

'Not everyone in prior generations was short!' she argued.

'But all standard furniture was made as if they were,' Fred responded.

'So maybe the table was custom-made.'

'Well then, we would recognize that it was a custom piece, and consider whether the owner's height was a factor.'

'What if someone simply sawed down the table legs?' she asked.

'What if the man in the moon made the table? Don't be frivolous,' he said dismissively.

Frivolous? I repeated silently. *Sasha?* I shook my head, braced for her reaction. Not only was Sasha not frivolous – ever – but she took her work so seriously that any implication otherwise was more than an insult, it was an indictment. Tears, I figured. Or pained humiliation marked by long silences and an inability to meet Fred's eyes ever again.

Instead, she chuckled. I stared, shocked that she'd laughed. 'I wasn't being frivolous,' she said, a bubble of laughter in her voice. 'Facile, maybe. But not frivolous.'

Fred laughed, too. They were becoming friends. They shared rapport. Astonished, I shook my head. *How little I knew of people,* I mused.

'You both all set?' I asked, jumping in.

They turned to me as if they hadn't really noticed that they weren't alone.

'Yes,' Sasha said, blushing. 'We'll be going to the Grant house soon. Fred wanted to know if it was all right that he work evenings.'

'I'm kind of a night owl,' he explained.

'Sure,' I said, 'no problem. How late do you think? Eleven? Midnight? Or are we talking all-nighters?'

He shrugged. 'I don't know.' He looked uncomfortable. 'I've been known to pull all-nighters. But I don't want to guarantee it. And if it's a problem....'

'No, not at all. I'm just thinking of how we can arrange to lock up.'

'I'll be working alongside him, so I can take care of the alarm,' Sasha offered.

'Are you okay with the late hours?' I asked her.

Another blush. 'Sure. It's just for a few days, and that way, the work will get done faster.'

Satisfied that the building wouldn't ever be left unprotected, I said, 'Great. Then I'll leave it to you to coordinate schedules and hours and lock up each night. Okay?'

Sasha nodded and smiled her little smile. Gretchen hung up the phone and I turned my attention to her. 'I'm heading out. I expect to be back by, I don't know, maybe by noon.' I shrugged and smiled. 'Feel free to call if you need me.'

She looked as if she'd like to ask where I was going, but I pretended not to notice. I didn't want to tell her I was, once again, meeting the police about a murder.

★

I hugged myself, shivering, as I waited for Max. The rain had stopped, but it was still overcast and the ocean was dark and rippling with two-foot swells. Seaweed had washed ashore overnight, and the sand was pockmarked from the pounding rain. With the gray sky and sharp wind, it felt more like fall than spring.

Max made his way across the street and joined me on the dune.

'Cold today,' he remarked.

'Raw,' I agreed.

'You have the price?'

'Yeah. I had to call New York and London, but I've got it.'

'Did you tell anyone why you were asking?'

'No. I stayed vague.'

'Good.' He nodded. 'Are you ready for what Alverez is going to ask?'

'What?'

'I don't know. But the research was just part of the plan.'

I nodded, but didn't speak.

'Well,' Max said, sounding philosophical, 'we'll just have to wait and see.'

'There's one more thing,' I said.

'What?'

'I think Barney killed Mr Grant, and I think I know why,' I said, rushing to get it out.

Max turned to look at me. 'What?'

I explained about Roy's revelation, the call from the Taffy Pull, and how Barney and Paula were related.

'The Taffy Pull? What call? What are you talking about?'

I stared at Max for a stricken moment, then turned away to look out over the ocean and avoid his penetrating gaze. *How could I have forgotten that he knew nothing about the research I'd done?* In fact, he'd disapproved of conducting an outside investigation at all. Worse still, I realized I'd completely put my foot in my mouth. I couldn't reveal anything, no matter how crucial, without betraying Wes's confidence. And that was not an option.

I shrugged, trying for innocence. 'I heard about the call, that's all.'

'From whom?'

'Rumors spread, you know?' I shrugged again. 'Anyway, it doesn't matter, does it? What matters is that, apparently, no one at the store admits to making the call. And nothing would be more natural than Barney, one of the family, stopping by, and while there, using the phone. No one would think anything of it.'

After a short pause, he said, 'You're going to have to talk about how you learned about the call.'

I took a deep breath and shook my head, still looking out over the water. 'I can't.'

'Be prepared for fireworks. Alverez is going to go ballistic.'

'Maybe I shouldn't say anything about it at all.'

Max thought for a moment. 'Let me guide the conversation. I'll try to share your findings without revealing too much. But you shouldn't withhold things if they're relevant.'

'What about what you said about not volunteering information?'

'This is different. Your expertise has revealed a connection he might well have no way of knowing. We don't know its relevance, but it would be improper to withhold it.'

I swallowed, flickers of fear tingling up and down my spine, causing me to shiver. I hoped Max would think I was chilled, not weak. 'What should I do?'

'One-word answers, Josie.'

I nodded, and, resigned to my fate, went slowly across the street.

Alverez greeted us and led the way down the hall to the now-familiar interrogation room. Once we were settled, and with the recorder's red light aglow, I said, 'The highest price I found for a Matisse at auction this year was twelve million dollars, but I don't think we can count on that amount. Realistically, I think the estimate would be in the one- to three-million range.'

'Why? Why would our Matisse only go for one to three million dollars if another one sold for twelve million dollars?'

'For some reason, there's a lot of volatility in the market right now. It's true that one sold for twelve million dollars, but I think it's an aberration. It could be anything. An overly eager new collector with a lot of cash in his jeans, for instance.' I shrugged. 'The fact is that lately most of his paintings have sold for between eight hundred thousand and one million dollars.'

Alverez nodded. 'So, for a private sale....'

'Well, for a private cash sale, I should think that you have to discount a lot.' I shrugged again. 'I don't know ... I think I'd ask for two hundred fifty thousand dollars cash and hope for a hundred thousand.'

Alverez shook his head and tapped his pen on the desk. 'That doesn't seem like a lot, does it.'

'No,' I agreed.

'In making the request, would you put any restrictions on the transaction?' he asked. 'You know, like cash only?'

'Oh, yeah. For sure.' I smiled. 'Let me remind you that I have no hands-on experience with this sort of thing. But it occurs to me that maybe I could arrange to have the money electronically deposited in an offshore account somewhere if paying in cash wasn't convenient for my buyer.'

Alverez nodded and made a note. While he was writing, Max said, 'Josie had an experience that we think you need to know about.'

Alverez tilted his head and looked at me.

I detailed the picker Roy's revelation, adding, 'If Barney is broke, that changes everything, you know?'

Alverez nodded. After a moment, he said, 'Thank you for the information.'

'Were you aware of his financial situation?' I asked.

'I'm not at liberty to discuss the investigation.'

'Apparently,' Max said in a neutral tone, 'Barney is related to one of Josie's part-time employees, a young woman named Paula Turner. We don't know if that's relevant in any way, but we wanted to pass on the information. I gather that Paula's family runs a candy store called the Taffy Pull.'

Alverez snapped to attention, his eyes boring into mine. 'What do you know about the Taffy Pull?'

'Nothing,' I answered.

'Then why do you think a connection between the store and Barney is relevant?'

'I don't. I thought it might be, is all.'

'Don't quibble,' he told me.

'I don't know.'

He glared at me. 'Why?' he persisted.

I stared back, gripping the sides of the chair, afraid I would betray my weakness by crying, determined to hold my own. I reminded myself that I'd done nothing wrong. 'I've told you everything I can.'

He thumped the table. 'Now, Josie. Tell me what you know.'

I jumped, startled by his outburst and the unexpected noise, then took a deep breath. My heart was banging against my chest, and I was having trouble breathing. 'Don't yell at me,' I said in as unruffled a tone as I could marshal.

'I'm not yelling,' he shouted, agitated.

We scowled at one another.

Max cleared his throat. 'I'm not sure this line of questioning is productive,' he said.

Alverez turned on him. 'She tells me I have a leak in my department and you say it's not relevant?'

Max shrugged. 'You don't know that it's a leak. First of all, people gossip. Second of all, the police aren't the only people who knew about the connection between the Taffy Pull and a call to Mr Grant.'

'They damn well were supposed to be.'

Max shrugged again. 'Come on, Ty, what about the phone company employees?'

I'd forgotten that Alverez's name was Ty and wondered, as I had before, whether that was short for Tyrone. I also noted that using it in the midst of an angry altercation was an effective way of lowering the volume, of reminding someone that you shared a personal relationship. It reminded me of my father's instruction about handling anger. He always said that when other people are loud and shrill, you should take a deep breath, smile politely, and speak quietly and courteously. *It disarms them, kiddo*, he told me. Kill 'em with kindness. They'll follow your lead because you'll sound like a leader.

'This discussion isn't over,' Alverez said, poking his finger in my direction, but sounding less fierce.

My heart still racing, I forced myself to speak softly. 'Was there anything else or are we done here?'

I watched as Alverez, his eyes pinning me with their intensity, took several deep breaths, then, sitting up straight, he turned to Max and spoke with his usual, even tone. His rage, for the moment, at least, was reined in. 'As part of our investigation, we want to offer the Matisse for sale. Specifically, I'm hoping Josie will make a phone call, arrange a meeting, show off the painting, and negotiate a sales price.'

'With a suspect in a murder?' Max asked incredulously. 'You're asking Josie to do something illegal and put herself in harm's way?'

'She'll be in no danger.'

'How can you possibly know that? You're making a target of her! Look what happened to Mr Grant when he offered the Renoir for sale. If it's such a good idea, why don't you do it yourself? Don't you ever go undercover?'

'Nothing personal,' Alverez said to me, 'but I think it's easier to believe that an antique dealer is a crook rather than a police chief.'

'Oh, please!' I said. 'As if the news isn't full of stories about corrupt cops!'

He shrugged. 'It isn't just that. It's the likelihood of success. People who are desperate aren't looking through a wide-angle lens. Their focus is strictly on their immediate needs and nothing else. Think about it – if you approach someone, the opportunity will be seen as heaven-sent. But if I do it, my job title will signal that it might be a trap.'

I understood his point. When you're hungry, all you can think of is getting food. It's only the affluent, people who know where their next meals are coming from, who think about organic ingredients and what they're in the mood to eat.

'You don't think people would be surprised if I offered to do something illegal?' I asked.

'No insult intended.'

'Sigh,' I said, sighing loudly for effect. 'None taken.'

Alverez half smiled. 'So, what do you think?'

'I think you're crazy,' Max said, shaking his head, his tone righteous, gesturing his amazement. 'I have no idea what you're planning, but I can already hear the lawyers asking for the charges to be dismissed – entrapment.'

'I checked with Murphy. We're clear.'

'Murphy? The ADA?' Max asked.

'Yes.'

'Who's that?' I asked.

Max explained, 'The assistant district attorney.'

'So, with no worry about complaints of entrapment, may I explain?'

Max sat back, his arms crossed across his chest. 'All right,' he said, 'but it's extremely unlikely we'll agree.'

'Understood. All I want is to catch the person I think is guilty of murder committing a lesser crime. Once arrested on a felony charge, I got ya. I can process you, fingerprint you, and interrogate you.' He opened his hands, palms up. 'It's simple. That's what I want.'

Max looked at me. I thought for a moment of the courage it would take to do what I was being asked. I'd need to exude confidence and calm. I couldn't start crying if I became frightened. I swallowed, knowing that I was still vulnerable to bouts of unexpected emotionalism. Yet, despite having seen me at weak moments, Alverez felt I could be trusted with this responsibility. His faith in me gave me faith in myself. If I could help Alverez, it would represent a quantum leap on my road to rebirth. And success breeds success. Plus, I could hear my mother. *When in doubt, Josie,* she always said, *do the right thing.*

'I'll do it,' I said. I realized I was still gripping the chair as if it were my only support, and encouraged myself with my father's oft-repeated words: *Fake it 'til you make it.* I hoped that if I didn't admit to feeling fearful, the emotion would disappear, and I'd be strong and brave and resilient. I swallowed and smiled, adding, 'I'm glad to help.'

'Wait,' Max interjected. 'I'm going to draft a letter for you to sign indicating you asked for Josie's help and are appreciative of it. Just in case.'

'I'll bring in Cathy now and you can dictate it,' Alverez said. 'That way it will be on official letterhead.' He turned to me. 'It'll be easy to write, because it's one hundred percent true.'

I smiled and, embarrassed, whispered, 'Thank you.'

chapter nineteen

We spent so long going over the plan that I was almost late for my 2:00 appointment with the couple who were downsizing to a condo on the pond. Mostly Max sat still, observant, but without comment.

Alverez sent out for sandwiches around noon, and we kept working as we ate, detailing whom he suspected, what I needed to do and say, and how we'd arrange the logistics, including such important factors as telling Fred and Sasha they couldn't work late in the office tonight after all.

Keeping the warehouse empty would allow Alverez's team to set up the hidden microphones and cameras, determine where we should position the locked cabinet that the police department would provide to store the Matisse, and with any luck, execute the sting. It felt oddly natural to plan the lies I'd tell, and I felt increasingly confident that I would be able to do exactly as Alverez wanted. I began to think that I'd missed my calling. *Maybe*, I thought, *I should have been a con woman.*

At about 1:15, Alverez finished up by saying, 'That's it. If you can get those points in, we'll do the rest.'

'I can do it,' I told him.

He walked us to the parking lot and thanked me again. 'Are you okay with everything?' he asked.

'Yes,' I said, with more self-assurance than I felt. 'But it'll be good when it's over.'

By keeping my apprehension to myself, and acting as if I had no doubts that I'd succeed, both Max and Alverez seemed to gain additional buoyancy themselves. As I drove away, alone and free to release the pent-up anxiety I'd kept in check all morning, I acknowledged that their sublime confidence ratcheted up the burden on me to perform. I didn't want to let them down. I gave myself a pep talk as I drove, and mostly I believed it.

*

Walking into the big Colonial in Durham, I wondered what it would feel like to be leaving a home like this. Was this couple feeling sad? Or liberated? The house was a suburban American dream – freshly painted, beautifully landscaped – and it exuded serenity and contentment.

Taking a deep breath, I readied myself to work. I wanted to be with Max and Alverez preparing for my role, not surveying goods for sale. Still, since I couldn't be with them, I was glad for the need to focus on something besides the challenge that awaited me.

It took me an hour to list the items the owners intended to sell. It was complicated because their selections weren't uniform. They wanted to get rid of the sofa, for instance, but not the matching club chairs, all of the chests of drawers, but none of the beds, and certain knickknacks, but not most of them.

The only valuable items they were offering for sale were a collection of hand-carved wooden decoys, a nineteenth-century dollhouse, and a small Navaho rug. I offered $1,200 for the lot, and was accepted on the spot, making me wonder if I'd bid too high.

I had them initial each of the inventory pages I'd written out, and sign at the bottom that we could pick up these items first thing in the morning.

On the way back to the warehouse, I called Gretchen, and asked, 'Anything going on?'

'Just a lot of stuff. Two more callbacks about selling household goods, and an inquiry about auctioning some stamps.'

'Wow, that's great.'

'Should I come in tomorrow? We're awfully busy.'

'No. Thanks, but I want you to take your day. We'll be fine without you for a few hours.'

'Okay, but I can come in if you need me. Trust me, I prefer work to laundry and dusting, which is all I'd planned to do tomorrow.'

I laughed. 'You're a gem,' I told her, meaning it. 'Are Sasha and Fred there?'

'No, they're at the Grant house.'

'Call Sasha for me, okay, and tell them they can't work late tonight after all. Tomorrow's fine, but something came up for tonight.'

'What?'

'I'll tell you later,' I said, evading her question. 'Is Eric there?'

'Yes, do you want him?'

'You can tell him for me. I need him to get a twelve-footer and a helper and get over to the Durham place by nine o'clock tomorrow morning.'

'Whew!' she exclaimed. 'That's great! I'll get cracking setting it up.'

'I'll give him instructions when I get there today. Tell him that he should stop by the office en route in the morning to pick up the cash.'

'Okay,' she said.

Getting a truck and helper arranged so quickly wasn't as big an accomplishment as it sounded, since we were regular customers of a truck-rental firm less than a mile away, and they were always glad to subcontract one of their employees to us when Eric needed help with the heavy lifting.

Arriving back at the warehouse, Eric showed me where he'd stacked the boxes of books he'd picked up that morning from the professor, and I warned him to be certain and count the books when he packed up everything in Durham the next day. It wasn't unheard-of for a seller to show off a collection and then hold one or two favorite pieces back. Writing out the details in advance, and getting them to sign off on it, prevented a lot of headaches. But only if the person charged with the pickup actually confirmed the count.

Explaining that something had come up, without providing details, I shooed everyone out at 5:00. Alverez arrived, technicians and other police officers in tow, on schedule at 5:15, and Max drove up at 6:00, looking troubled but willing. A man of intellect, I thought, most comfortable when he had a pen in his hand and time to think. Not a man of action.

By 6:30, the stage was set and, with the automatic taping in place, Alverez listening in from the front office, and Max standing nearby, I made the call.

I panicked when Barney answered the phone, thinking, *Oh, my, you just called a murderer*, but took a breath, and willing myself to sound composed no matter how I felt, I said, 'Barney, it's Josie.' My voice cracked, as if my mouth was dry. I cleared my throat and drank a sip of water.

'Hello, Josie,' he said, sounding plainspoken, neither cordial nor irritated.

'Barney, I found something I want to show you.'

'What's that?'

'I can't explain on the phone. I know it's late, but can you stop by this evening?'

'Come to your location?'

'Yes.'

'You're making it sound rather urgent,' he said, after a pause.

'Yes, it is. It's something, well, it's a special piece that I think you'll want to buy.'

'What kind of piece?'

'It really would be better to talk in person,' I said, my words measured.

'Well, all right, you've succeeded in enticing me. I'll be glad to stop by.'

I closed my eyes. *Thank you, God*, I said to myself. First hurdle, done.

'Good,' I asked. 'What time is good for you?'

Another pause. 'I have a dinner engagement at eight. How's, say, seven-thirty?'

I glanced at my computer clock. 'About fifty minutes or so from now, right?'

'Right.'

'That'll be fine. I'll see you then.'

I hung up the phone and tears of relief that the first ordeal was over welled up. I shut my eyes for a moment and was easily able to stem the flow. As I wiped away the last moisture from my cheeks, I heard Alverez clamoring up the spiral steps.

I looked toward the door as he entered, forced myself to smile, spread my hands, and said, 'Any other little tasks you need doing?'

'Good job, Josie. That was perfect.'

'Thanks.'

'Let's just review the next phase. Where's the key to the cabinet?'

'In my jeans.'

'Show me.'

I stood up, reached into my pocket, and extracted a shiny golden key.

'I think you should put it on your key ring. It'll look more natural that way.'

I nodded and opened my purse, found my ring with its engraved Tiffany silver circle, a birthday gift from my dad, and added the gold-colored key. I slipped the ring into my pocket.

'Are you ready?' Alverez asked.

'Yes,' I said, and I almost believed it. 'I am.'

'Max and the others are moving their cars out of sight. I want everyone in place by seven o'clock. Let's go on downstairs.'

All of the cars except mine were to be parked at the truck-rental site. A police officer shuttled everyone back in an unmarked car, then left on his regular cruising detail. I followed Alverez down the spiral staircase, past the newly installed taupe-colored metal cabinet, and into the office. I sat at Gretchen's desk.

Everyone returned and moved into their preassigned positions out of sight in the warehouse or upstairs. Max, who joined a police officer upstairs, looked worried. Alverez slipped into the closet near the coffee machine where we stored office supplies, closed the door but didn't latch it, and silently we waited.

Too tense just to sit, I grabbed one of the books that Roy had sold us and began to research it. It was volume one of a twelve-volume, calf-bound, gold-tooled set of the complete works of Shakespeare, complete with hand-colored illustrations and gilt edges, published in 1804. There was minor foxing on several pages, nothing unexpected in a book more than two hundred years old. The leather needed cleaning – we mixed our own beeswax paste – but other than that, it was in near-perfect condition. I brought up a search engine and looked for comparable sets. After only about fifteen minutes, I realized we had a real find. It wasn't unique, but it was a pretty set in wonderful condition.

I decided to start stockpiling fine books and bindings. With any luck, we'd be able to devote an entire auction to them next year. I typed up the catalogue entry, stating the expected price range as $575 to $650, printed it, inserted the paper in the front of volume one, and set it aside.

As I reached for the next book, I heard a car drive up and stop. My heart began to pound, and momentarily I felt as if I might faint. I closed my eyes and breathed deeply. I heard a car door close, then faintly, footsteps. I opened my eyes as Barney walked into the room.

'Josie,' he said, smiling, his eyes impervious, his manner stiff.

I stood up. 'Thanks for coming, Barney. Especially on such short notice.'

'My pleasure.'

'Have a seat,' I invited, gesturing to the guest chair, where, not long ago, Mrs Cabot had sat while she waited to offer me the appraisal job.

'I found the Matisse,' I said, jumping in.

'What Matisse?'

'It seems that Mr Grant had three masterpieces, a Renoir, a Cézanne, and a Matisse.'

I could see the change in Barney's eyes as his demeanor transitioned from professionally attentive to guarded and wary. He said, watching me closely, 'You're kidding! Mr Grant?'

I shrugged. 'It's true. I've got the Matisse, and I'm offering it for sale. Knowing that you sometimes deal in fine art, I thought you might be interested.'

'May I see it?'

'Certainly. Come this way.'

I walked him into the area of the warehouse near the spiral staircase where we'd placed the cabinet, pulled out my key ring, and selected the right key. The unit stood about four feet tall. Two doors opened outward, revealing three deep shelves. It was empty except for the Matisse, laid flat.

Barney picked it up by the edges and looked at it. 'It's beautiful, isn't it?'

'Yes,' I agreed.

'It would need to be authenticated,' he said.

I thought of Dr Snow, the expert Alverez had brought down from Dartmouth who had, in fact, authenticated the paintings. I wondered if Barney had ever used his services. 'Of course,' I said.

'Assuming it's what it appears to be, I might be interested.' He continued to look at the painting. I had no sense of what he was thinking or feeling. 'How much are you asking?'

'A quarter of a million.'

'That much?' Barney asked, his eyebrows shooting up.

I reached for the canvas and slid it back into the cabinet, locked the door, pocketed the key ring, and gestured that Barney should precede me into the office.

'Research it yourself. You'll find that a quarter million is a bargain and a half.'

'Not on the private market.'

'Then say no.' I shrugged. 'That's my price.'

After a long pause, Barney said, 'I can hardly believe we're having this conversation, Josie.'

I nodded. 'I know.'

'What about Mrs Cabot?'

I shrugged, and, under the desk, out of sight, crossed my fingers. 'The painting has blood on it. She knows it, and doesn't care. I do. Think of me as a variation of Robin Hood.'

'How so?'

'I won't let the rich get richer from thievery.'

'And yet, here you are—'

'I'm not rich, and I don't suppose you are either.'

He snorted. 'Hardly. People think we're all rich.'

'They don't know our costs.'

'Exactly.'

'Still,' I said, smiling, 'it's a living.'

He smiled back, but as he was about to comment, the phone rang, as arranged. Hattie, one of the police officers, was calling from upstairs.

'Hello,' I answered, 'Prescott's. May I help you?'

Hattie, pretending to be Sasha, asked me if it was all right to come over and do some work.

'When?'

'In an hour.'

I looked away from Barney, the better to maintain my part of the pretence. 'Sure. That's not a problem. How long do you think you'll be here?'

Hattie faltered. 'I don't know,' she said.

'Okay,' I responded to the nonexistent answer. 'Ten or ten-thirty? That's fine. I tell you what, I'll leave the alarm off tonight, okay? Tomorrow we can get Fred set up with a key and the code to the alarm.'

'Okay,' she said.

'See you in the morning!' I said brightly, and hung up. To Barney, I said, 'Sorry about that.'

'No problem,' he said, his eyes remote and calculating. 'I was about to leave anyway. I'll call you tomorrow, all right?' He stood up, and headed for the door.

'By noon, okay?'

'What happens at noon?' he asked.

'I find another buyer.'

He looked at me, maybe to assess my veracity. I perceived agitation and anxiety in his demeanor, and it frightened me. I struggled to control an urge to back away from him, shifting my focus instead to watching as he evaluated his options and framed his response.

'Well, then,' he said, 'I'll do my best to get back to you by then.'

We shook hands, and I watched as he drove away.

Alverez's plan had worked exactly as he'd expected. My work was done, and I felt the pressure subside.

I'd helped, it had been easy and straightforward, and it was over, so now I could relax.

I sensed, more than heard, Alverez approach. When I turned I saw that he was grinning. He reached out and squeezed my shoulder.

'Way to go, Josie,' he said.

I smiled back. 'It was pretty easy,' I said.

Max came in, the worry lines gone. 'How did it go?' he asked.

'Perfect,' Alverez said. 'Now, git. Both of you. Out of here.'

It was a weird feeling to leave my warehouse in the hands of the police. I didn't know what Alverez expected would happen. He wouldn't say.

But assuming that Barney would break in and try to steal the painting, well, it was frightening to think about, and while I was glad I wouldn't be there on-site, I knew that I'd be spending an anxious and sleepless night.

Max and I said our good-byes as I drove him to his car.

'I confess that I'm relieved our part is over,' he said. 'I don't think I'd make a very good spy.'

I laughed. 'But you'd do a great job planning what the actual spies should do.'

He smiled, and sighed deeply. 'I guess,' he acknowledged, stretching as best he could in the confined space. 'But you, I think you might have to change careers.'

'Thanks,' I said, pleased at the compliment. 'I admit it – I think I have a knack for deception.'

Max chuckled. 'It doesn't sound good when you put it that way, does it?'

'No, not at all. Luckily, I'm my mother's daughter. Honest to the core.'

He patted my shoulder as I pulled up behind his car. 'Good. Talent or no talent, stay that way.'

I nodded and tucked my hair behind my ears. 'I promise.' He opened the door and started to slide out. 'Max?' I asked. He turned toward me. 'What now? What do you think will happen?'

He paused, his hand gripping the doorframe. 'I think Alverez will get him. What do you think?'

I shook my head. 'I don't know. But I'm a little scared.' I shivered. 'To tell you the truth, I thought Barney looked a little bit like a cornered rat.'

chapter twenty

As expected, I spent a restless night.

I slept some, I guessed, but the hours I stayed in bed were filled with upsetting and confusing dreams, and I awoke jittery and tense. Lying there, tired but unable to sleep, I thought about Alverez and wondered if his plan had worked, and if so, whether he was still questioning his suspect or whether he'd called it a night. I could picture him sitting in interrogation room two, struggling to stay awake, but I could also imagine that he was home, asleep, and it got me wondering what his home was like. *Was it a rental, like mine? Was it furnished with heavy, masculine pieces, like an Adirondack lodge?*

One thought led to another and at about 4:30 in the morning, I gave up trying to sleep, and went downstairs. Wrapped in my soft pink robe, I made coffee, and with a cup in hand, I curled up in the window seat in my kitchen and looked out over the meadow. I saw nothing. Thick clouds completely obscured the sky, and the darkness seemed absolute.

Determined to shift my focus from thinking to doing, I scrambled eggs, had a second cup of coffee, and just before 6:00, decided to go to work. Wearing black jeans and a cherry red sweater, I stepped outside in the dim light of another cloudy spring morning, took a deep breath of wintry-cold dawn air, and started the car. I shivered, chilled, as I used the small plastic scraper to rid the windshield and side windows of hoarfrost.

Three miles down the road I glanced at my cell phone and realized that I'd missed a call. Punching buttons, I saw that it had come from Alverez while I was in the shower. 'Damn,' I said aloud.

I pulled over to the side of the road and listened to the cryptic message. 'Josie,' Alverez said, sounding energized, 'I'm sorry to call so early, but I'm going back into the interrogation room after grabbing a little sleep, and I don't know when I'll be able to talk next. I just wanted to thank you again, and to let you know that the plan worked. We got her.'

I dialed back, but got his voice mail. 'Damn,' I said again. I didn't want to leave a message. I wanted to talk to him.

I called the station house. Whoever answered the phone said that Alverez wasn't available and couldn't venture a guess as to when he might be able to call me back. I hung up and tapped the steering wheel, frustrated and impatient for news. Impulsively, I called Max, and, after apologizing for disturbing him so early, I recapped Alverez's message and my failure to reach him.

' "Her"?' Max asked. 'Are you certain he said "her"?'

'Yes, absolutely. It sounds like he's arrested someone, doesn't it?' I asked.

'Or, at least, that he's got a suspect in custody,' Max agreed. 'Who do you think it is?'

'I haven't got a clue,' I said. 'I was a hundred percent sure it was Barney.'

After a short pause, Max asked, 'Didn't Barney tell you that Andi had hired him?'

'Andi!' I exclaimed. 'That's right, he did tell me that. Wow! And Barney could have called Andi to tell her about the Matisse. But wait a second, Max. Even if he did so, and even if she decided to come steal it, there's no way she could have gotten here that quickly.'

'What do you mean? It's only a ten-minute drive from the Sheraton. Isn't that where she and her mother are staying?'

'Mrs Cabot told me she was going back to Chestnut Hill yesterday, and I assumed that Andi would go home to New York at the same time … but you're right, it's strictly an assumption on my part. Maybe Andi did stay longer, to work with Barney, or to start the lawsuit to try and break her grandfather's will.'

'If it was Andi that Alverez caught in your warehouse, think about what that means. It implies that she stole the Renoir and that she killed her grandfather. Stealing the Renoir, maybe. But killing her grandfather? That stretches credibility!'

'Not if she was all drugged up.'

'True,' he acknowledged, sounding sad.

Responding to his tone, I said, 'It's so horrible to think about, isn't it?'

'More than horrible. Unnecessary, too, since she's due to inherit half of his estate.'

'But I wonder if she knew it at the time? She wasn't close to her grandfather, that's for sure,' I said.

'True. But still.'

'Yeah. She's pretty volatile.'

'Maybe she's mentally ill, you know, bipolar or split personality or something,' Max suggested.

I recalled her constant surliness, her occasional explosive temper, and the rapid mood swing I'd witnessed on Mr Grant's porch. One minute she'd been a shrew, the next, cajoling and plaintive.

'Maybe,' I acknowledged. A squirrel caught my eye as he dashed across the road and disappeared into the underbrush. I shrugged. 'We have no way of knowing. You know what I mean … from everything you hear, drugs make some people act like they're nuts whether they are or not.'

'I guess you're right. And I guess it doesn't matter, does it, whether she is actually mentally ill or not?'

'Not to us, maybe. But I bet Mrs Cabot cares.'

I heard Max sigh. 'Yeah.' After a pause, he asked, 'Josie, does it make sense that Andi would sneak into your place and leave the Renoir? After killing her own grandfather to get it either because she's insane or because she was high on drugs, wouldn't she have kept it?'

'You'd think so, wouldn't you? But if she'd learned about the Matisse and the Cézanne, and if she knew that I had been to the house the same morning and was considered to be a suspect, maybe she was willing to sacrifice the Renoir in an attempt to frame me. She'd still get millions from the other two paintings if she could get her hands on them, and if she did a good enough job with the setup, I'd be arrested and maybe even convicted, and she'd be completely off the hook.'

'Yeah,' he mused, 'plus, once the investigation was over, and probate granted, the Cabots would get the painting back. It was a gambit … like in chess … you know?'

'Well, actually, no. I don't know how to play chess.'

'A gambit,' Max explained, his voice animated, 'is an opening move in which a player sacrifices a piece in order to secure a desirable position.'

'Wow. I see what you mean. You're right. That's exactly what she did. She sacrificed the Renoir – temporarily, at least – as a way of shifting suspicion on to me, which, to her, was a favorable position.' I looked out at the barren street, the leafless trees, and the empty, overgrown side-walks. 'Wait. Let's not forget … ultimately, it didn't work.'

'No, but she tried. As a strategy, I've heard worse.'

'Yeah.' I shivered again, chilled at the thought that a malevolent spirit strategized how to get me. I'd done nothing to deserve her antipathy, yet I was her chosen target. I felt tears begin to form, and my heart started to thump. I swallowed, trying to regain my composure. 'Max,' I asked, as calmly as I could, 'is it truly possible that someone would do something so … so … *fiendish?*'

'Yes,' he answered softly. 'Yes, I think it is.'

'Do you think that Mrs Cabot knows what Andi did?' I asked, glad to shift the conversation to less personal ground.

'I don't know. I just don't know, Josie. Actually, we don't know that Andi did anything. We're just speculating.'

'I suppose so. Regardless, I'd like to tell Mrs Cabot that I found the paintings, but I don't want to burden her if she's, you know, overwhelmed because of Andi.'

Max paused. 'I was just thinking about whether it's prudent to reveal that they've been found. Let me put in a call to Alverez and ask him. Then, once we have an okay, why don't you get in touch with her and see how she sounds? Use your judgment. You can always just tell her the bare facts, and, if she's not in any shape to talk to you, discuss the details later.'

'That makes sense.'

'Just remember, stick to the facts. Don't hypothesize. And don't editorialize.'

I nodded and took a deep breath. 'Yes, I can do that.'

'Are you kidding?' Max said. 'I saw you in action last night. You can do anything.'

I smiled, surprised and pleased at the compliment.

I pulled into my parking lot and saw that Griff was on duty, guarding I don't know what. He told me that I could go in, no problem, and that he'd be leaving in a minute. 'We'll be coming by pretty often,' he said.

'Why?' I asked.

'Just to check.'

'Check on what?'

'A regular patrol, is all. You don't need to worry.'

I got it. I wasn't going to learn anything from him, even if he knew anything in the first place, which wasn't by any means a given, so I thanked him, and went inside.

It was eerie. I walked through every area of the warehouse and couldn't see a thing out of order, and yet, apparently, Alverez had caught a murderer within my walls only hours earlier. The cameras, microphones, and metal cabinet were gone. I felt unsettled. Ignoring the amorphous disquiet, I climbed the steps to my office, and began to work.

I drafted an e-mail to Gretchen explaining my idea for Prescott's Instant Appraisals, and asked her to contact Keith, the graphic designer we used on an as-needed basis to create a themed campaign for the booth itself, newspaper ads, and flyers that we could tuck into bags when we packed up items. It had occurred to me that if Barney was more or less broke, he wasn't much of a competitive threat, but I decided to proceed with the instant appraisal idea anyway. As a strategy to get a leg up on good inventory and build traffic, I didn't see how it could be beat. Plus, it sounded like fun.

I stretched and glanced at the computer clock. It wasn't even 7:30 yet. I wondered where Alverez was, and what he was doing. I stood up and paced, sat down, and then, a minute later, stood up and paced again, this time in a different direction.

I sat down, determined to focus on tasks at hand. I turned to the computer. I'd told Sasha that I'd take care of researching the leather trunk, and I hoped that doing so might stop me from wasting time and energy on other, pointless thoughts.

It didn't take long to find the information I needed. There were loads of comps. The trunk's silky-soft leather was a sign of the quality of its construction, and its unusually large size and remarkable condition set it apart from similar pieces. I estimated that it would sell for between $1,750 and $2,000.

Eric arrived just as I was finishing writing it up. He called out a general hello, and I shouted back that I'd be right down.

'Hey, Eric,' I said as I hurried down the steps, 'I feel like I haven't seen you in a coon's age.'

'Yeah, if we stay this busy you're going to have to schedule staff meetings so we see each other.'

'From your mouth to God's ears!' I said, laughing. 'Are you ready?'

'Yup. I just got to pick up the money and the paperwork.'

'I'll get you the money. Just give me a minute.'

I went to the safe and counted out a dozen hundred-dollar bills. We'd need to replenish our cash reserves soon. Returning to the office, I handed the money to him. He was swift to insert the bills in the envelope containing the inventory and a receipt that Gretchen had prepared, but I stopped him.

'Count it, Eric.'

'Ah, Josie, I know you're not going to screw me over.'

'Right. But everybody makes mistakes. Even me.'

'Nah. Don't believe it.'

'I'm flattered, but indulge me. Always count money, Eric. And always read papers before you sign them. I shouldn't have to tell you this over and over again. When you accept money, you're responsible. Take it seriously.'

'I do,' he said, almost, but not quite, whining.

'I know you do, theoretically. But I'm focused on practicality. Remember the old saying, "Trust, but verify"? Well, do that every time. Always ... even with me, Eric. Trust, but verify.'

'Okay, okay,' he said, not quite casting his eyes heavenward, but acting as if he wanted to. He counted the bills, grinned, and said, 'See, I knew it would be right.'

'This time.'

'Yeah, yeah, I got it.'

'Go,' I told him, shaking my head and smiling, 'I'll see you later. And don't forget to count the damn books!'

Since all I wanted to do was talk to Alverez, everything I did felt like busy-work. I wanted an update. I wanted to know the details about what was happening. Instead, I was in limbo, waiting and wondering. Curiosity and anxiety consumed me, and, as a result, I had trouble focusing.

Fred arrived as I was considering my options. Wearing a gray sweater, vest and black jeans, he looked ready for whatever came his way, office work or rolling on the floor examining the bottoms of furniture.

'Is Sasha here?' he asked.

'Not yet. I'm sure she'll be here any minute.'

He got settled at the spare desk, and I decided to go to the Grant house and do some appraisal work. Sasha would, I was certain, arrive soon to cover the office, and if not, well, we had voice mail. I told Fred not to worry about the phone, gave him my cell phone number, just in case, and asked him which room I should work on at the Grant house.

He consulted his notes, thought about it, and finally suggested that I start on a small room on the top floor that had been used, apparently, as a sewing room. I grabbed a notebook and my purse, and left.

Max called as I drove. 'When I called before, I left a message for Alverez,' he explained, 'asking whether it was all right for you to tell Mrs Cabot that the paintings had been found. I just got a call back with his answer – yes. That's it. No other information or news.'

'Thanks, Max,' I said. We ended the call by agreeing that our curiosity about what Alverez was doing – and with whom – was white hot and growing.

When I arrived at the Grant house, I saw that O'Hara, the police officer who'd kept an infuriated Andi at bay while Alverez entered the house with me, was sitting on the porch steps smoking a cigarette. He stood as I approached and we exchanged greetings.

Ten minutes after I entered the sewing room, while rummaging through loose photos stuffed in the bottom drawer of a tallboy, I found a picture labeled on the back, 'Us and Arnie Zeck, Paris, 1945.' Mrs Grant's ledger had stated that the Renoir, the Cézanne, and the Matisse had all been purchased from someone or something called A.Z. It wasn't much of a stretch to conclude that I was looking at the man who'd sold the Grants paintings that had been stolen from Jewish families.

I sat back on my heels and studied it. The grainy black-and-white image showed three people, two men and a woman, sitting at a table near a grass tennis court, drinks in hand, laughing. All three appeared healthy, happy, and carefree. Neither of the men looked familiar, and I wondered whether one of them was Mr Grant, and if so, which one.

I sorted through the rest of the photographs. They were a jumble, and I doubted that they had any market value. I put them aside to send to Mrs Cabot.

I turned my attention to the Chippendale-style walnut tallboy. It was beautifully built. Lying on my side to better examine the lower portion of the piece in detail, I noted restoration to the ogee feet. I'd already noticed that several spots along the fluted, canted corners were slightly nicked. Still, it was a bold and desirable piece, dating from the 1770s, and I expected that it would sell for more than $3,000. If it hadn't been restored, it might have been worth twice that.

I finished jotting down the imperfections and thought about calling Mrs Cabot. According to my cell phone, it was 9:30, a reasonable time to call. I stood up, stretched, and walked across the room to stand at the window and look out at an unobstructed view of the ocean.

I found her number where I'd written it in my calendar, and thought about what I wanted to say. After a moment of indecision, I realized I was in deep avoidance mode. I didn't want to make the call. I didn't want to deliver more pain to that nice, stoic woman. When I'd faced the fact that my father was dead, I'd been in shock, ragged with emotion, unable to focus on anything except my incalculable loss. If she was like me, she wouldn't even register that the paintings had been located, and if she did, she wouldn't care.

I wondered if she knew about Andi. With her father just dead, murdered, she was, no doubt, overwhelmed with grief. How could she bear knowing that her daughter was the killer? I shook my head, weighed down at the thought of the anguish she must be enduring.

Still, she had to be told that I'd found the paintings. The stolen art had to be returned. *Do it*, I told myself. *Talk to her, and, as Max suggested, follow her lead.* If she didn't want to know the details, I wouldn't force them on her.

I dialed, and after six rings, I got an answering machine. I made a fist and soft-punched the window frame. Having girded myself to speak to her, it was a real disappointment to get a machine. I closed my eyes again, and focused on the message.

'Mrs Cabot,' I told the machine, 'this is Josie Prescott. I found both the Cézanne and the Matisse, and I have important news about them. I look forward to filling you in. You can reach me on my cell phone anytime.' And I gave my number.

I felt satisfied with my message, and it was only when I noticed that my hands were trembling that I realized how hard that call had been to make. I hated disappointing people that I cared about. And, it seemed, I'd come to care about Mrs Cabot.

I turned my attention to a small sampler hanging on the back wall, but before I reached it, Mrs Cabot called me back.

'I'm sorry I missed your call,' she said. 'I stepped outside for a moment.' She sounded the same as always, polite and pleasant.

'No problem. Thanks for calling back so quickly.'

'Chief Alverez called as well, but he wasn't available when I tried to reach him back. By any chance … do you know if he has news?' she asked.

My throat constricted and my heart began to race. I swallowed twice, panicked, uncertain what to say. Max's standing instructions came to me. Tell the truth and give short answers. And the truth was that I didn't know anything. Speculation wasn't fact.

'No, I don't know anything.' I gripped the phone, hoping she wouldn't ask additional questions. Poor Mrs Cabot.

'He's very good about staying in touch,' she remarked. 'I'll try him again when we're done talking.'

'How are you holding up?' I asked.

There was a long pause. 'All right. This is a difficult time.'

'Yes,' I agreed. I didn't know what to say. I wanted her to know how much I'd liked her father, and that he'd been laughing and seeming to enjoy life in the days before his death. I determined to write her a note. The sympathy cards people had sent me had provided great comfort, more so than spoken words. When they'd talked to me, I'd had to respond, to hold up my end of the conversation, and during those first weeks, that had proven impossible. Reading meaningful recollections, though, had consoled me.

'I'm so sorry, Mrs Cabot,' I said, finally.

After a pause, she said, 'Thank you.' She cleared her throat. 'Yes, well … you said in your message that you found the two paintings?' she asked.

'Yes. They were hidden here in the house, quite cleverly.'

'Where are they now?'

I swallowed. 'The police have them.'

'For safekeeping?'

'Well, not exactly,' I said, hating that I had to be the one to tell her.

'What do you mean?'

'It seems that there's no clear proof of ownership, I'm afraid. In fact, I have to tell you that I have reason to believe they're stolen.'

'I see,' she said in a tone so low I could barely hear her. She cleared her throat and I could picture her troubled eyes. 'I thought as much.'

'I'm sorry to be the bearer of bad news.'

'No, no, don't be. I've been troubled by the thought for more than forty years. Certainty is always better than speculation. From whom were they stolen?'

I wondered if her suspicions about the paintings had led to the argument with her parents forty years ago, but I didn't want to ask. Instead of trying to find out what might have happened when she was a girl, I answered her question directly. 'My research suggests that they were taken from three different Jewish families before or during World War Two. Probably by the Nazis.'

I heard her inhale. 'How awful.'

'Yes. They were all sold, apparently, by a man named Arnie Zeck.'

'Arnie Zeck. He was a friend of my parents. They knew him in Europe. I've seen photos.'

'Yes, there's one mixed in with a bunch of others in a drawer of the tallboy in the sewing room.'

'I never knew....' she started, her voice trailing off.

'I'm sorry.'

'Don't be. I should have investigated those paintings' histories myself. Instead I kept quiet. More shame on me. Robert Louis Stevenson wrote, "The cruelest lies are often told in silence." I've kept many secrets in my life out of misplaced loyalty.' She laughed derisively.

I didn't know what to say. Mrs Cabot continued speaking before I had to decide how to respond. 'No more,' she said. 'I decided not to enable my daughter in her drug abuse either.'

'What do you mean?'

'I arranged an intervention last night.' Her voice cracked with emotion, but I also heard pride of accomplishment. It was a long moment before she continued. 'I convinced Andi to drive down with me yesterday. When we got home, I surprised her with the intervention.'

My mouth fell open. I was astonished. More than astonished, I was shocked.

I'd persuaded myself that Andi was guilty of murder – of killing her own grandfather. To learn otherwise was staggering, and I had trouble focusing on the conversation with Mrs Cabot. Alverez's message was clear – he'd referred to the suspect as 'her.' If it wasn't Andi he had in custody, who was it? I was speechless, yet I needed to react. What had Mrs Cabot said? An intervention? She'd arranged an intervention? I shut my eyes, leaned against the window frame, and forced myself to concentrate. With my mind still reeling, I asked, 'What was it like?'

'It was extremely emotional. The professionals from the rehabilitation facility coordinated everything. We invited several of her friends from New York, and we all told her the truth.'

'What was her reaction?' I asked, unable to imagine anything less than a calamitous explosion.

'She was upset,' Mrs Cabot said, in what I assumed was yet another example of understatement.

'What happened?'

'She decided to try and get over her addiction.' Her voice cracked again. 'You know, perhaps, that the goal of an intervention is that the addict immediately admits herself to the program. Thank God, she agreed.' I could sense the fear behind her words, and my heart went out to her.

'You must be so relieved,' I said.

'I am.' She stopped, her wrenching emotion palpable. She cleared her throat and when she spoke again, it was in the calm, pleasant voice I'd come to expect. 'It's only the first step, of course, in what will be, no doubt, a very difficult process. But at least it's a step in the right direction.'

I shook my head. Having seen Andi in action, I was a non-believer, yet I needed to say something positive. I gazed out the window toward the ocean. Under the cement-colored sky, the ocean looked bleak, seaweed dark, a green deeper than bottle green, and endless.

Nothing positive came to mind. I wondered whether Andi had any sense of the anguish her actions caused others. Finally, I said, 'It must have been very hard for you.'

She paused. 'Yes, well, I suppose so. But I am confident that I won't be in this position again. If nothing else, my recent liberation from the conspiracy of silence precludes it.'

We agreed to talk in a day or two about the appraisal.

Hanging up the phone, I stayed at the window for a long moment, watching the forbidding-looking ocean, trying to make sense of what I'd learned.

Since last evening, Andi was in rehab somewhere in the Boston area. I shook my head. If she was in a secure location, who then, did Alverez have in custody? I felt the icy chill of uncertainty wash over me again.

chapter twenty-one

I felt jump-out-of-my-skin on edge. Nothing made sense, and I began considering a desperate move to get more information – calling Wes. I was telling myself what a stupid idea that was when Max reached me on my cell phone.

'Cathy from the Rocky Point police just called to ask us to come on down and meet with Alverez and Murphy, the ADA.'

'Wow. When?'

'Now.'

'What do they want, do you think?'

'To review evidence, I'm guessing.'

'Do we go?'

'Yes.'

'Okay, then.'

'This probably means they've made an arrest,' he said.

'Who do you think it might be?'

'I don't know.'

'It isn't Andi,' I said, and filled him in.

'Good luck to her in getting off drugs,' Max said.

'Yeah. It's so sad. About this arrest ... what do you think the charge might be?'

'No idea. We'll know soon enough, I guess.'

As I hurried down two flights of stairs, I was flooded with relief that the waiting was over.

I called my office en route, but got voice mail. I was surprised and glanced at the dashboard clock. Ten. I was puzzled. It was unlike Sasha to be late, especially since she'd know that Fred would be waiting for her.

I called her home number and got a machine. Her cell phone went to voice mail. I didn't know what to do.

A stab of fear assailed me, and for a chilled moment, I wondered if something had happened to her. Using my pin number, I checked for messages at work. Nothing.

I couldn't imagine why I couldn't reach her, and as I pulled into the police station parking lot, I began to feel more than mildly concerned. I sat in my car and tried all three numbers again. No luck. I left messages at Sasha's home and on her cell phone, asking her to call me on my cell as soon as she got the message. Kicking myself for telling Fred not to answer the phone without getting his cell phone number, I decided to wait until noon, and then, if I hadn't connected with Sasha, to go back to my office, and talk to him to learn what he might know.

I pushed open the door and saw Max. He was standing near the front, reading notices on a bulletin board. He smiled at me, and said hello, then turned and got Cathy's attention. She led us into a big corner room, nicely furnished in blond wood. It looked more like a CEO's office than a police chief's. She invited us to sit, and we chose chairs around a circular table near a window.

'The chief will be right in,' she said, and left.

I looked around. A big desk was angled to maximize the ocean view through two sets of windows, and a wall of built-in bookcases was crammed with binders, directories, files, and matching wicker storage boxes.

'I'm so curious, I could bust,' I said.

Max smiled. 'We'll know more soon.'

'Whatever we learn is going to be a shock to me,' I said. 'Remember, I was certain it was Barney.'

Alverez walked in on my words. He looked tired, but he didn't act it. He smiled and conveyed the same level of power and confidence as always.

'Thanks for coming in on such short notice,' he said. 'Murphy just called. He got stuck in a meeting, but should be here in about fifteen minutes.'

Max nodded. 'No problem.'

'In the meantime, I can fill you in.' He sat down at the table. 'Did I hear you right?' he asked me. 'You thought it was Barney?'

'Yeah, I did. Didn't you?'

He shook his head. 'Nah, his alibi was tight. Plus, I thought it was a woman. Remember the footprint we found by the Renoir?'

I nodded and glanced at Max. 'Yeah. I remember. I don't know, I thought maybe it was unrelated or something. This morning, when you left the message saying you caught "her," well, then Max and I thought it might be Andi.'

'Andi.' He pulled his ear, thoughtfully. 'Maybe. I never liked her for it myself. All huff and puff and no action. Did you see how she ran away from me at the Grant place that day?'

'Yeah, but I thought maybe she was on drugs when she killed him.'

'Yeah, that'd be the only way she'd actually be able to do it.'

'But it isn't her.'

'No. How'd you know?'

'I spoke to Mrs Cabot just now. She had an intervention yesterday, and Andi entered rehab last night.'

He nodded. 'And now? Who do you think now?'

I shrugged and glanced at Max.

'No idea,' Max said.

An image of Sasha came into my mind. Sasha, so shy and unassuming, so quiet, so self-contained. *Still waters run deep*, I thought. *It couldn't be*, I told myself, my eyes growing wide with dismay. I felt myself choke, as if I'd swallowed too big a bite of food. I remembered suddenly that she wore size nine shoes. I closed my eyes, unable to restrain the tears that threatened me. I felt as if I might faint.

'Don't overlook the obvious,' I heard Alverez say.

I opened my eyes, stricken, but braced for the worst.

Alverez looked mildly amused, as if he thought it was a pretty good joke that what was self-evident to him wasn't apparent to us. If it was Sasha, I thought, surely he wouldn't be amused.

'So ...' Alverez began. As he spoke, I heard a rustling sound behind me and turned toward the open door. Martha, her chin raised defiantly, her hands handcuffed behind her, her head turned as if to shield her face from view, passed by, followed by a uniformed officer. I shivered and looked away.

'Martha,' I whispered.

'Of course,' Alverez said, nodding. 'It was obvious from the start.'

'Not to me,' Max protested. 'Martha Troudeaux?' He looked appalled.

Sasha had nothing to do with it, I thought, relief tinged with guilt that I could have suspected her at all. I realized how much I cared about her, and how grateful I was to learn that she had nothing to do with it. 'Martha,' I repeated softly, still shocked.

'Yup,' he said, watching me react.

'Where are they taking her?' I asked, not quite whispering.

'To a cell,' Alverez answered.

'She killed Mr Grant?'

'Yes.'

'For the painting?'

He nodded. 'For money, yes.'

'And then she tried to ruin me? It's unbelievable. She and Barney couldn't compete so she set out to ruin me?'

'Yeah,' Alverez agreed, 'no question about it. She tried to destroy you.'

'It's outrageous!'

Max reached over and patted my shoulder. 'But it's over.'

'I can't believe it!' I repeated. I shook my head, astounded that someone would plot against me. Worse, that someone I knew and had worked with would deliberately set out to wreck my life. 'How could anyone have done such a thing?' I exclaimed. 'It's disgusting! It's unbelievable! It's outrageous!'

'Calm down, Josie,' Max said.

I forced myself to breathe deeply. 'I'm okay,' I said, trying to regain control. 'I'm okay,' I repeated. I shook my head and smiled a little. 'It's just such a shock, you know?'

'I can only begin to imagine,' Alverez said.

'So,' I said, trying to focus on the facts, 'when you say it was obvious from the start, did you mean because she's known for doing Barney's dirty work?'

'That's right.' Alverez shook his head. 'And Barney counted on it.'

'I always wondered how he could stand to be with her,' I said, feeling calmer. As I waited for Alverez's response, I wondered where Sasha was and hoped that she was all right.

'Barney got a lot out of the relationship,' Alverez said, matter-of-factly. 'Her definition of caretaking was broader than most wives', and her passion was unassailable. But as far as I can tell, she has no moral core. I've never seen anything like it.'

'Like what?' Max asked.

Alverez shifted in his chair. 'She felt no guilt about any of it. Not the murder. Not trying to frame Josie. Not stealing the Renoir. Nothing.' He shook his head. 'From her perspective, she did what was necessary to protect her Barney, and if she had to, she'd do it again.'

I shivered and closed my eyes as a memory rushed into my mind. I could see her mean little pig eyes challenging me to defend my pricing of the bamboo stool at the tag sale. I could hear her sarcastic, mean-spirited tirade. I could easily imagine her murdering someone. And once the initial shock wore off, I could, in fact, believe that she'd set out to frame me. She was evil.

She chose to frame me not because she hated me but because I was an easy and desirable mark. From her perspective, if I were arrested for Mr Grant's murder, no one would suspect her or Barney, and, as an added bonus, she'd eliminate a tough competitor.

While it was natural to picture her lashing out, doing what she'd always done, protecting her beloved husband, it was appalling to think that she'd kill and then try to destroy me in the process. I shivered, horrified to realize that she had murdered an old man and set out to ruin my life.

Martha, the bitch-queen, that's how I'd always thought of her. I shook my head, aghast to realize how right I'd been.

My phone began to vibrate, and I recognized Sasha's cell phone number on the caller ID display.

'Excuse me,' I said to Alverez and Max, stood up and moved away, standing by the window with my back to the room, and answered. 'Sasha?'

'Oh, Josie, I'm so sorry.'

'Are you all right?'

'Yes, I'm fine. I'm afraid I overslept.'

'What? Overslept? You!'

'Yes, and then I was rushing to get in. Still, I should have called you sooner.'

'That's okay. It's just pretty unlike you.'

'Well, I was up pretty late....'

All at once I wondered if she'd spent the night with Fred. Wow. Hot doings in the ol' town overnight.

'It doesn't matter,' I said. 'All that counts is that you're okay.'

I turned off the phone, and stood up, a few tears of relief sliding down my cheeks. I swallowed twice, and in a moment, felt able to turn around.

'Is everything all right?' Alverez asked, standing up.

I nodded. 'Absolutely.' I waved it aside. 'All's well.' I smiled, and rejoined the table.

The meeting with Murphy was brief. He was a small, chunky fellow in his late forties, very precise and pedantic. He wanted, he said, to meet us to explain the process, which he did in a monotone. I had trouble listening and, after a few minutes, didn't bother to try. I knew Max would fill me in.

When he gathered his papers together and left, I asked Alverez, 'Is he better in court than he is in a meeting?'

Alverez smiled. 'Yeah, it's amazing, actually. He's a good prosecutor.'

I shook my head, and smiled back. 'You'd never know it.'

'What kind of case do you have?' Max asked.

Alverez shrugged. 'Mostly, it's circumstantial, but it's strong.'

'You have the footprint and what else?'

'We'll be holding a news conference later today. Nothing I say should be discussed before then. I'm not saying there's anything confidential. There's not. Everything I'm telling you has already been turned over to the defense. Still, it's important that it not be talked about idly. Agreed?'

Both Max and I nodded. 'Sure,' I said. 'Until when?'

'Until after our news conference.'

'Which is when?'

'Four. Why? Who are you planning on talking to?'

'You never know.' I smiled. 'So ... what else?'

After a pause, he said, 'I accept your assurance that you won't say anything to anyone until after we issue our official statement. That said, to answer your question, there was one set of prints at the Grant house that had been unidentified. We now know that they belong to Martha.'

The unidentified prints Wes had told me about. 'Didn't you compare them to her prints during the investigation?' I asked, surprised.

'No. Why would we? Barney was the dealer, not Martha. Until I started hearing about her personality from you and others, I never even thought of her.'

'That makes sense,' I acknowledged.

'Something that we kept quiet were two prints that we found on the tube the Renoir was stashed in. We knew that they matched the unidentified ones in the Grant house. Now we know they're Martha's.'

'That's impressive,' Max said, nodding.

'Yeah. And there's more. We've got the call from the Taffy Pull to Mr Grant. And that call was followed by another one immediately afterwards to Barney's cell phone. A clerk that was working at the store that day remembers Martha being on the phone. We've also got Josie's testimony that Mr Grant used a pencil to write appointments specifically so he could erase them if something changed, and that he made those corrections immediately. And Barney told Josie that Martha was their point person in their dealings with Mr Grant. Put it all together, what it means is that, in fact, they didn't change the nine o'clock appointment that had been scheduled for the day of the murder, and further, because of Barney's alibi, we know that it was Martha who kept it. Barney lied. He said it had been changed to cover for her.'

'Did Barney admit the cover-up?' Max asked, sounding surprised.

Alverez's lip curled, a look of contempt. 'Barney folded like a cheap tent in a light breeze. He told us everything.'

'I can't imagine it!' I said, shaking my head. 'He implicated Martha? I thought he was devoted to her.'

Alverez shook his head. 'As near as I can figure it, she was devoted to him, and he reaped the benefits.'

'That's awful.' I shuddered.

Alverez shrugged. 'People stay in relationships for lots of reasons having nothing to do with love. No one but them knows the truth of what they each got out of their marriage.'

'Still, it seems as if you have a lot of evidence,' I said.

'Yeah, but there are spousal-privilege issues relating to everything Barney told us.'

Max asked what Murphy, the person tasked with bringing the case to trial, thought of it.

Alverez shrugged. 'He thinks it's medium strong.'

'Do you know why she killed Mr Grant?' I asked.

'Only she knows why. But I'll tell you our theory of the case. Mr Grant told Martha that he was going to hire you, and she killed him to get her hands on the Renoir. Plain and simple, they did it for the money. They're in pretty bad financial shape, and they needed a big chunk of cash quickly.'

I nodded. 'Do you know why they're broke?'

'Barney, it seems, likes to place a bet or two.'

'Ah,' I exclaimed, nodding. 'That would explain the money trouble. But I still don't understand why, having killed to get the painting, Martha would sneak it into my place.'

'To frame you. She couldn't understand why you hadn't been arrested for the murder already, and she was savvy enough to know that without an arrest, eventually we might hit on her as a suspect.'

'She really wanted to frame me?' I was shocked, and turned to Max. 'That's what you thought.' To Alverez, I added, 'Max thought it was a gambit. You know, a tactic where you give up something in order to achieve a good position, but that just seems so horrible, I can't believe anyone would do such a thing.'

'Yeah. It's pretty logical, though, when you look at it from her point of view. Efficient. You know, businesslike. She had a business problem and, to her, you were part of the solution.'

'Jeez!' I exclaimed. 'Framing me was part of her business plan? That's completely diabolical!'

'Wait a minute,' Max protested. 'What about the Renoir? Didn't sacrificing it defeat their purpose? If they'd succeeded in framing Josie, then what?'

'They hoped that Grant's lawyer, Epps, would hire them to dispose of the estate. Since Epps knew only about the Renoir, and not about the Cézanne and the Matisse, they figured that if they could win the assignment, they'd be able to locate them, sell them privately, and with any luck, no one would even know the paintings had ever been in Mr Grant's possession.'

'But how did they know about the Cézanne and the Matisse?' I asked.

'Mr Grant showed them his wife's ledger. Barney told me so in one of my first interviews with him. He didn't realize what he was revealing. He thought he was just describing their first meeting with Mr Grant.'

'I wonder why Mr Grant never showed the ledger to me?'

'Maybe he knew you were honest.'

I smiled. 'Not with Epps calling me a shark.'

'It turns out that Epps didn't call you anything at all until after Mr Grant was killed. I gather it was Martha herself who planted the seeds of that slander. She was determined, it seems, to get rid of the competition – you – by hook or by crook.'

I shivered. 'It's pretty scary to think about.'

'Yeah,' Alverez said. 'But she didn't succeed.'

'No, thank goodness. Still, I hope I get the chance to convince Epps that I'm not a crook.'

'From what he told me this morning, he'll be calling you to apologize.'

'Well, well, well,' I said, leaning back in my chair. 'Maybe I'll finally get that appointment and be able to pitch my business.'

Alverez smiled. 'I think that's very likely.'

Max added, 'I'll be glad to call him for you, Josie, if you need me to.'

'Thanks, Max,' I said, touched by the beyond-the-call-of-duty tone of his offer. 'I'll let you know.'

Alverez walked us to the parking lot. The sun was trying to poke through, and I thought it might make it by the end of the day.

'You look tired,' I said as we walked slowly toward our cars.

'Yeah, I am. It was a long night.'

'Martha just walked into my place?'

'Yeah, wearing dark clothes and latex gloves. She made a beeline to the storage cabinet and pried it open with a crowbar. Our plan worked like a champ.'

He shook our hands and turned to head back inside. Max and I watched as he walked away.

Max turned to me, pulled an envelope out of an inner pocket, and said, 'Here.'

'What's this?' I asked.

'An application for a gun permit,' he said. 'Fill it out.'

I smiled and accepted the papers. 'Thanks, Max. For everything.'

Wes called me as I was driving back to the office. 'I hear they've made an arrest,' he said.

'I heard something about that, too.'

'What?'

'Just that. Do you know anything?'

'Ha. What a question. Of course I know things.'

'Forgive me. I forgot myself. Of course you do.'

'So, give it up. What do you know?' he asked, his tone urgent.

'I know enough so that we can schedule your exclusive. I'm ready to honor my commitment.'

'Where are you?'

'In my car, why?'

'Where?'

'Why?'

'So we can pick a place to meet.'

'Not now. Later.'

'No way. The story's hot now, not later.'

Alverez had said they were holding their news conference at four, so I said, 'Anytime after six.'

'Come on, Josie,' Wes whined. 'Don't do this to me. We made a deal.'

'Wes, you're making me crazy. I'm keeping my end of the deal. Jeez. Six tonight at the Blue Dolphin, okay?'

'You're buying.'

I laughed. 'You drive a hard bargain, Wes. Okay.'

Talking to Wes was exhausting. He poked and prodded and seemed insatiable. The only thing that helped me endure his picayune questioning were the ice cold martinis.

At 9:00, we walked together to the parking lot. As I stood beside his car saying good-bye, I spotted a familiar object amidst the tangle of papers and discarded fast-food containers that littered the back floor – Alverez's card.

I tilted my head, and thought for a moment. *Hmmm*, I said to myself, *I wonder if I've just identified Alverez's leak*. I pictured him yelling at me, his righteous indignation seemingly sincere. Yet maybe, I thought, he used anger to camouflage a clever strategy. What better way to control the flow of information to the press than to be the one to talk? *Alverez*, I said to myself, *you're a sly dog.*

I spent the evening puttering and thinking. I cleaned the bathroom, changed the linen, and made a huge salad. I thought about the love Martha had for Barney, and wondered if I'd ever feel that level of devotion. Not a love that led to murder, obviously, but a passion so complete, so compelling, that striving to satisfy my lover's needs transcended effort and became a source of contentment and a way of life. *Could I find such a love without losing my sense of self or changing my values?* For the first time in eons, I felt hopeful that I would.

My outrage and anxiety had passed, and was replaced, it seemed, by exhilaration. I was excited about the future. I had plans for expanding my company with Prescott's Instant Appraisals and by finally connecting with Britt Epps, an important player in the greater Portsmouth area, a potentially powerful ally in winning new business. I smiled, allowing myself a private 'atta girl.'

When I arrived at work the next morning, Alverez was waiting for me, leaning against his SUV. It was a bright, sunny day, warmer by twenty degrees from the day before. I was wearing a blue sleeveless tank top with an oversized denim shirt and jeans.

'Hey,' he said.

He looked more rested than he had yesterday.

I smiled. 'It looks like you got some sleep.'

'Like someone shot me.'

'How you doing?'

'Good. You?'

'Good.'

'So, I want to change my answer.'

'To what?'

'You remember when I drove you home? You asked me in. I said no.'

I looked at him. He wore a gray-gold tweed jacket, a tan shirt and brown tie, and khakis. He looked great. His eyes were on me, watchful and kind. He was tall and strong-looking and competent. I'd always found competence sexy.

'I remember. I asked you in during a weak moment. The moment has passed. It was a onetime offer.'

'Too bad. I'm changing my answer to yes, anyway.'

'Just like that?'

'Well, I was planning on buying you dinner first.'

I started laughing, and I couldn't stop. For whatever reason, his comment, delivered with such seeming sincerity, tickled my funny bone, and sent me into paroxysms of delight. Finally, I wound down, and when I could speak, I said, 'Don't look at me that way, or you'll set me off again.'

'So, is that a yes?' he asked earnestly.

I paused and looked at him. I memorized the moment, filing it away in my head for review whenever I wanted. And I was willing to bet that I'd want to remember this event often. I smiled, and told him, 'Hell, yes.'